"INTRIGUING ... A DEADLY MEDICAL GAME!"
—*Cleveland Plain Dealer*

Peter McKusick was wakened by three-year-old Kitty in the middle of the night. He could tell that something was wrong—unspeakably wrong—with the child he treasured more than his own life. The science to which he had dedicated his life was now threatening his baby—unless he found and unmasked the truth he feared to face. . . .

SPIRALS

"Spellbinding . . . a uniquely good thriller."
—*Roanoke Times*

"Quick-paced, enjoyable reading."—*Library Journal*

"A dizzying good read . . . intriguing, suspenseful."
—*Santa Cruz Sentinel*

"Stunning, riveting, frightening."
—Whitley Streiber,
author of *The Wolfen*

"Gripping!"—*Boston Globe*

Medical Thrillers from SIGNET

(0451)

- [ ] **GODPLAYER** by Robin Cook. (129504—$4.50)*
- [ ] **FEVER** by Robin Cook. (119932—$3.95)*
- [ ] **BRAIN** by Robin Cook. (112601—$3.95)*
- [ ] **COMA** by Robin Cook. (132963—$3.95)*
- [ ] **DOUBLE-BLINDED** by Leslie Alan Horvitz and H. Harris Gerhard, M.D. (131541—$3.95)*
- [ ] **THE DONORS** by Leslie Alan Horvitz and H. Harris Gerhard, M.D. (113381—$2.95)*
- [ ] **NOT A STRANGER** by John Feegel. (129008—$3.50)*
- [ ] **MALPRACTICE** by John Feegel. (118219—$3.50)*
- [ ] **THE EXPERIMENT** by Michael Carson. (128052—$2.50)*
- [ ] **TRAUMA** by Robert Craig. (127587—$2.95)*

*Prices slightly higher in Canada

Buy them at your local bookstore or use this convenient coupon for ordering.

NEW AMERICAN LIBRARY,
P.O. Box 999, Bergenfield, New Jersey 07621

Please send me the books I have checked above. I am enclosing $_____
(please add $1.00 to this order to cover postage and handling). Send check
or money order—no cash or C.O.D.'s. Prices and numbers are subject to change
without notice.

Name _____

Address _____

City _____ State _____ Zip Code _____

Allow 4-6 weeks for delivery.
This offer is subject to withdrawal without notice.

SPIRALS

WILLIAM PATRICK

A SIGNET BOOK

NEW AMERICAN LIBRARY

NAL BOOKS ARE AVAILABLE AT QUANTITY DISCOUNTS WHEN USED TO PROMOTE PRODUCTS OR SERVICES. FOR INFORMATION PLEASE WRITE TO PREMIUM MARKETING DIVISION, NEW AMERICAN LIBRARY, 1633 BROADWAY, NEW YORK, NEW YORK 10019.

Copyright © 1983 by William Patrick

This is an authorized reprint of a hardcover edition published by Houghton Mifflin Company.

SIGNET TRADEMARK REG. U.S. PAT. OFF. AND FOREIGN COUNTRIES
REGISTERED TRADEMARK—MARCA REGISTRADA
HECHO EN CHICAGO, U.S.A.

SIGNET, SIGNET CLASSIC, MENTOR, PLUME, MERIDIAN AND NAL BOOKS are published by New American Library, 1633 Broadway, New York, New York 10019

First Signet Printing, November, 1984

1 2 3 4 5 6 7 8 9

PRINTED IN THE UNITED STATES OF AMERICA

For Kathleen

The possibilities of existence run so deeply into the extravagant that there is scarcely any conception too extraordinary for Nature to realize.

—LOUIS AGASSIZ

Author's Note

I wish to thank Sarah Blaffer Hrdy for the freedom to draw upon her research as source material for much of what Kathleen Albriton observes in the jungles of Colombia.

THE VIRUS WAS AIR-FREIGHTED from London in a vial packed in liquid nitrogen. It was Ujiji forest, and Watson would not even unwrap it until he was safely within the P4 maximum biological containment facility.

Above his head the negative-pressure fans hummed reassuringly as they drew the air away from his face and up into the filtration system. The air was cold, circulating at an average temperature of 22 degrees Celsius, which was continually registered on a digital meter in the hallway outside the lab.

Before him on the bench, behind the glass shield, were three agar plates on which he was culturing the common intestinal bacterium *E. coli*. But Watson's bug was now anything but common. In fact, it was no longer *E. coli* in any strict sense. He had transformed it into a totally new organism, unknown to nature, by inserting selected genes from his exotic virus. He had used restriction enzymes to chop up the viral DNA, plugged the pieces into free-floating loops called plasmids, then inserted those plasmids back into the bacteria. Now it was a simple matter of scaling up—with the help of *E. coli*'s knack for rapid reproduction—before the real trick of getting those alien genes to switch on and transmit their coded instructions to the next generation.

Watson had signed up months in advance for permission to use this lab. Modeled after the army's biological warfare installation at Fort Detrick, Maryland, it was designed to be an absolute barrier against the microbial world. It was sealed with double doors separated by an air lock bathed in ultraviolet light. Its drains did not lead to sewer pipes but to special holding tanks for analysis and decontamination. Even linen and glassware could not leave this bomb shelter of a room without first passing through an interlocking chamber with autoclaves whose sterilizing temperatures reached 100 degrees Celsius.

Watson was under tremendous pressure to get results. The National Cancer Institute was supporting his work, and the grant was coming up for review. But he also had tremendous respect for his lethal study subject, and for the guidelines established to regulate experimentation with it. This was no place for a casual attitude about biohazards. He had enough virus in front of him to re-create scenes from some medieval pestilence, and every minute the *E. coli* were adding more of it to the pool. But Watson's laboratory technique was impeccable.

He had a wife and child of his own in Cambridge, as well as a healthy self-regard. Absolutely no contaminants would enter or leave this cloistered space because of him. Watson played it by the book.

With his eyes on his ever-increasing supply of recombinant bacteria, Watson reached for his pencil to make the next entry in his laboratory notebook. Something on the periphery of his field of vision attracted his attention. He shifted his head slightly as he brought his hand up in front of his nose. Then for a moment he focused on the two small antennae wiggling back at him.

Balanced like a circus performer, a small black ant rode on the upturned eraser tip of his Eagle Mirado #2 pencil. Watson stared in disbelief. This was impossible. This was unthinkable. This was against the rules.

Kitty

1

"ONE BODY WAS CREMATED immediately," the Englishman said. He was munching a stuffed mushroom as he spoke, oblivious to the crumbs raining down on the Persian rug. "The other was sealed in a coffin that had been packed with sawdust soaked in disinfectant. The gravediggers were all freshly inoculated, of course. That portion of the cemetery had to be cordoned off for months. And all of it was owing to broken glassware and a borrowed copy of an Irish newspaper."

The other guests, drawn into his circle, nodded in agreement. Drinks were sipped, and then the Englishman added, "But that was smallpox virus, of course. Quite a different matter. Quite a different matter indeed."

Outside the gracious Georgian home where they were meeting, dusk was beginning to settle over the brick walks of Cambridge, hidden now by a layer of dead leaves.

"You remember the Marburg virus?" An in-

tense woman with a short, blunt haircut began
to speak. "I was a student there when the Afri-
can green monkeys were brought into the lab.
Monkey handlers, doctors, nurses, a morgue
attendant—everyone was infected. One survivor's
wife contracted the disease three months later
through her husband's semen."

A ripple of discomfort passed in widening
rings through the cluster of senior faculty. A
distinguished biochemist mumbled, "These things
are very difficult to contain," and Peter McKusick
shared a glance with the waitress from Radcliffe
who was offering him yet another piece of quiche.

Bayard Kluer had asked McKusick to be there
early to spare anyone else the awkwardness of
arriving first. From 5:30 when the waiters from
Harvard Student Agencies began circulating, to
about 6:00 when the rooms began to fill, McKusick
had been up to his elbows in pastry shells and
pâté. The contracts people from the Cancer
Institute made their appearance at 6:15, and
the Eastern Shuttle delivered the Wall Street
crowd no more than an hour late.

"It's the slow viruses that are the most per-
nicious," a youthful voice pronounced. This was
Watson, a new post-doc who had not yet internal-
ized the pecking order. "Like kuru. You can
have it for months or maybe decades before it
takes over the nervous system. The cannibals in
New Guinea keep passing it on by eating each
other's brain tissue."

Watson looked around brightly, but no one
responded. They were each gazing downward,
waiting a beat or two before resuming the
conversation.

McKusick rattled his ice cubes and slipped out of the study, back into the entry hall where a bar was set up at the foot of the stairway. He made a casual glance into the dining room, and on a rough count came up with three Nobel laureates, the dean of the Medical School, the dean of the College of Arts and Sciences, the president of Harvard University, and the junior senator from Massachusetts. It was not a bad night; a testament to the drawing power of money. The scientists in these rooms were being pursued by money. They had gone one better on the alchemists' age-old dream of turning base metal into gold: They could turn lowly bacteria into whatever they chose. By tapping into the genetic program, they could create a new life form to gobble up oil spills. They could take the human gene for insulin, plug it into a bacterium, and then produce gallons of the stuff as the genetically altered microorganism reproduced. The possibilities were limitless—bacteria to produce fertilizers, medicines, antifreeze, cosmetics, food, fuels. But all this talk about biohazards was really beside the point. Of course there would be risks. There would always be risks.

Mac handed his glass to the bartender and nodded as the boy reached for the Jack Daniel's. Good memory, Mac thought. Smart kid. "So what are you studying?"

McKusick scanned the room as the boy began his prepared statement on youthful ambition.

Mac had a real knack for invisibility at these affairs. He invariably wound up talking to the help, or, left alone, confiding in his drink.

After a moment he found what he was look-

ing for. She was standing beneath the Water-
ford chandelier, holding a glass of white wine
she had yet to taste. She was nodding eagerly as
she listened to a small, impeccably dressed Swiss,
one of the executives of Biota, A.G. Mac knew
the routine—the toying with a button, the hand
thrust back dramatically through her dark hair.
She was playing on the sexual edge she had no
way of avoiding if she tried. Liz Altmann lived
in New England now, but she still had the year-
round tan setting off the gold jewelry, the same
Beverly Hills flair amid the dowdiness of Cambridge. She had mastered her role as Cambridge
hostess, as Bayard Kluer's wife, but she never
lost herself in the part.

"So you are the mysterious Dr. McKusick."

Mac turned and found himself pressed against
the substantial bosom of the German woman
from Marburg. She seemed incredibly close, looking up at him with a silly smile.

"My name is Ute Mayr," she said. "I am Liz's
friend, confidante, and gynecologist. She has no
secrets from me of any sort."

She extended her hand, and Mac managed
an uncertain hello.

"She tells me you are a master of technique."
For a moment her face simply hung there in
front of him. How could she have gotten so
drunk so quickly? Mac was thinking.

"I mean she is the theoretician and you are
the experimentalist. And now there is Kluer—
presiding genius and entrepreneur—setting up
his little corporations. It sounds unstoppable, in
a way, and then so ridiculous."

"Afraid I don't follow you."

"Don't be silly. You give yourself away with those puppy-dog looks at her, like just a moment ago."

Mac touched his bourbon to his lips. She was right. There was no point in dragging it all out again. "You work on infertility, right? I've read some of your papers."

"Is that so? I'm flattered, but whatever for? You're going to cure cancer, aren't you? My work couldn't be further removed from your little interferon factory."

"I took a detour for a while."

"To Darkest Africa or some such. I know. And you fell in with Stasson. Did you actually work with him? When he left Oxford, everyone said he had lost control. A mad scientist, right out of the penny dreadfuls."

"No. He's sane enough. Working on contraception."

"Aren't we all," she giggled, and Mac felt sorry for her. It was the ascetic types who could not handle relaxation. They worked eighty-hour weeks, and then twice a year made fools of themselves.

"So what about your method?" she asked. "Is it safe?"

"I'm sorry?"

"Your technique for making interferon."

Mac took a long drink. "Look. Sure. You can get Q-fever from guinea-pig carcasses. You can get anything you want by walking into the wrong lab with a cut on your finger. Plague, anthrax, cholera, Yaba virus, Lassa fever. It's all in a glass jar in somebody's lab. Risk is risk. Genetic manipulation really has nothing to do with it."

Ute Mayr stared at him with an intensity he could not quite interpret. Maybe she had simply passed out and not yet fallen down. Then in a tone borrowed from some old Garbo movie, she said, "I want to discuss this with you further," and Mac knew it was time to head home.

The baby sitter met him at the door with a knowing look and a nod toward Kitty's bedroom. "Still awake," she said.

Mac smiled and stepped into the apartment. He could hear Kitty singing to herself from behind the closed door. He would muster up some stern, fatherly expression, but secretly he was delighted that she was still up.

"Incredible will power for a kid." The sitter's name was Peggy, and she was fourteen going on forty. "I mean bleary-eyed . . . but she just won't go down."

"A tough character," Mac said. "How much do I owe you?"

She shrugged it off. "Four-fifty." She didn't need the money. Her father taught at Harvard and her mother worked for WGBH. She didn't need anything.

"Here." Mac handed her five limp singles. "Thanks a lot."

"Anytime," she said, and she was out the door and down the stairs.

The apartment Mac and Kitty shared was cramped but comfortable enough. Yard-sale furniture picked up here and there, some plants inherited from a neighbor who had left for New York. There were books lining the living room wall, creating a kind of alcove over the worn corduroy couch. They had been kept in storage while he was gone—grim, weighty books from medical school. But now there were puppets and costume dolls draped over *The Molecular Biology of the Gene* and Harrison's *Principles and Practice of Internal Medicine*. The only furniture that was entirely new was Kitty's bed and mattress, with which he had christened a charge account at Jordan Marsh. Mac's own bed had been left behind by the former tenant. He had been meaning to replace it, but to date there had been no one's sensibilities to consider in the matter but his own.

Mac gave a light tap through the Bilbo Baggins poster and then a gentle push. All he could see in the light from the hall was the trap door of her yellow pajamas and two feet sticking up into the air.

"Hey! It's bedtime. What's going on here?"

She flipped upright. "Daddy!" she hollered, and bounded to her feet, bouncing in a circle and clapping her hands.

He came over laughing and caught her in mid-bounce. She scampered around him like a monkey, clinging with hands and feet.

"Where have you been?" she demanded. Her head was in a cloud of wispy blonde hair.

"A silly old party."

"With candles and a cake?"

"No, no. Just a grown-up party. It wasn't even any fun."

"But did you get lots of presents?"

"No, sugar. It wasn't a birthday party." He sat down with her in his lap, a warm bundle.

"But it's your birthday."

"Tomorrow's my birthday. And that's just for you and me."

She gave a conspiratorial giggle, her blue eyes sparkling in the half-light. "Peggy took me to the store today. And tomorrow I'm gonna cook you a cake with lots of candles, 'cause you're very, very old."

"That's for sure."

"I bet we need this many candles." She stretched out her arms as wide as they would go.

"We'll see," he said.

Mac kicked off his shoes and nuzzled down beside her in the bed. "Now you need to get to sleep, my love."

"Tell me a story."

"Okay. But just one."

"Tell me Three Pigs."

"Naw, honey. If I have to tell that one more time I think I'll throw up."

"How about the Wizard and the Scarecrow and the Lion?"

"Okay. But just a little bit." And they were not very far at all down the yellow brick road before she was sleeping soundly.

Mac listened for a moment to make sure all was well. He placed a kiss on her forehead, filling his lungs with her scent. Then he got up and tried to make some use of what was left of the evening. He went into the kitchen and ate a few bites of the hamburger he had picked up on the way home. Then he settled down on the couch with a beer and the stack of journals that never seemed to diminish despite his steady plugging. It was always an open question whether this attempt to be both hotshot scientist and bachelor father was going to work. This was the week the government would decide whether or not to invest three million dollars in his work; this was also his week to feed the gerbils at Kitty's nursery school. And while Kluer was orchestrating federal contracts and venture capital, Mac was fending off the bake-sale gestapo, dodging threatening phone calls demanding three batches of cookies, no donations, no bakery goods.

He tried to read, but his mind kept losing focus. It was the party, he knew, the feeling of total-body discomfort from trying to socialize with the ivy-covered types, the businessmen, the bureaucrats. He always felt that he inhabited some different part of the galaxy. He was, after all, from California—the Other Coast. For all he had in common with these people he might have been from Mars. He had never even heard of Harvard until he was at UCLA. Still, the light-years he felt separating him from Liz were the real cause of his uneasiness. He was amazed by his failure to find some way of dealing with her that did not hurt. The pain was déjà vu from his first stint in Cambridge, just like all this talk about biohazards. In his mind, that very public issue was always going to be associated with his own very personal humiliation and frustration. Now that genetic engineering was ready for commercial development, everyone wanted to hold hearings all over again, to drag out all the old arguments, to revive the image of some tumor virus spliced into an airborne bacterium and sent wafting over the city. The whole controversy bored McKusick to tears, as did the review article propped up on his belly. Before long he gave a look into Kitty's room, walked through the apartment turning out the lights, and settled into his bed to sleep.

He was awake. Through the darkness he had heard a thud and then a cry. He bolted up off the pillow. "Kitty?"

"I bumped my head." She was padding into his room, sobbing mournfully.

"What happened?" He glanced at the luminous dial of the clock. It was almost three in the morning.

She was over to the bed now and climbing in with him. "I walked into the door."

"Aw, so sorry." He held her head and kissed it. She felt warm. "Don't you feel good?"

"No."

"What's wrong? Does your tummy hurt?"

"I wet the bed."

He felt down below. She was soaked. "God, you're a mess. Poor babe. Snuggle in and let me get you some dry pajamas."

He made his way by dead reckoning through the silent apartment, into her room and to her chest of drawers. He found the pajamas, again by touch, pulled out a pair, and headed back toward the bed.

"Here. Where are you?"

"Right here."

He reached for her and stripped her down, unsnapping the snaps, guiding the sleeper off shoulders and feet. Then he helped her into the warm, dry clothes. "There now. That feel better? Everything okay?"

"No."

"What's the matter?"

"Head hurts."

"I'm sorry, babe. It'll get better. But you gave it a pretty good bump."

"No. Before I bumped it."

"What's that?"

"That's what woke me up. I had a scary dream and then my head hurt."

He reached for the bedside lamp. He turned it away from their faces and then flipped it on. They squinted at each other. "Tell me what's the matter." He looked carefully into her eyes, her ears, her nose. He felt underneath her chin for swollen glands.

"I told you. My head hurts."

"Hurts like what, honey? Where does it hurt?"

"Back here." She worked her hand along behind her ear.

"Can you tell me what it feels like?"

"It's okay."

He looked into her immense blue eyes for some sign. "Really, honey?" It might be nothing more than a stiff neck from sleeping in a draft.

"Yeh. It's better now."

She cuddled closer. It was just the two of them. This was all either of them had ever known of a family, or ever would know. She smiled. "Do you know what I got you for your birthday, Daddy?"

"No. What?"

"A ladybug. I got it at the store."

"A ladybug?" He hugged her up against him. "Thank you, honey. That's the sweetest present I ever got. Thank you." He watched for a moment, wishing he could tap into the thought process that had produced this particular notion. But she was looking back at him with heavy-lidded eyes.

Mac flipped off the light and drew her to him again. She was already breathing in the calm, steady pattern of sleep, and McKusick wished it were as easy for him. As a doctor he could rationalize her little aches and pains; as her father he had no easy time accepting them. Her health, her survival, had been the main purpose of his life since the day she was born, since before she was born. He was doing all he could. He was stretching his limits, but he could never know what the ultimate effect would be. He remembered the technician at the tumor in-stitute—the one who had brought home a pair of laboratory mice for his child to play with. It was one of the stories he had heard at the party that night. The mice were not the healthy con-trols the technician had assumed they were. Within six weeks the child was dead.

2

SEVEN BIG MEN came thundering down the court, and in the center one short man, Michael Giacconi, dribbled the ball. It sounded like a cannon booming as it bounced off the old wooden floor of the YMCA gym in Central Square. The little man hit the top of the circle and kept coming, forcing a drive right up the middle, weaving through a net of arms and legs. He went up and came right back down, his arabesque interrupted by a beefy arm. He landed flat on his bare back and slid six feet on the coating of sweat. The other players came to a stop, milled around looking tired. It was time to quit.

"Hey! Mikey boy! Get off your butt! You can't play like that!"

Michael sat up, looked around, and saw City Councilman Vincent Giacconi standing just inside the door of the gym. The other players were grabbing towels off pegs, heading to far

corners for T-shirts cast off during the game.
As they began to file past the man in the rum-
pled suit one of them mumbled, "Hey, Your
Honor. What's happening?"

"I'll call the Celtics," the old man said. "See
what I can do for you."

Michael was coming up, slipping a sweatshirt
over his head.

"Where's your gun?" Vincent asked him. "You
just got mugged."

The young man gave a tolerant smile.

"I need to talk to you," his uncle said.

"Come by the house. Gimme fifteen minutes
and I'll meet you there, okay?"

Vincent pulled a cigar out of his pocket, and
Michael started down the steps to the locker
room.

Michael Giacconi was the youngest detective
on the Cambridge police force. He liked to think
it was because he was smart, that he was a good
cop, that he had done well in college. Vincent
Giacconi liked to think it was because Michael
was his nephew. In the elder Giacconi's world,
all human actions were linked by a tight chain of
political cause and effect. Voters did not keep
sending you back to city hall because they believed in some political philosophy. They gave
you their vote because you made a call and got
the oil company to give them a little more credit,
because you found a rent-controlled apartment
for somebody's mother. The politician was the
servant of the people, but he was also the force
that drives the wheel, the unseen hand. Vincent
Giacconi was convinced that in the celestial coun-

cil chambers, deals were being made every day to get the sun to rise.

When Michael stopped in front of the two-family house he rented on Fifth Street in East Cambridge, his uncle was standing just inside the chain-link fence, his cigar glowing dimly, now just a stub. The night air was unusually cold for October. A foretaste of the long winter to come. Michael edged a few houses down and found a space for the car.

"So what are you parking way down there for? There's room right here in the yard."

"For the landlady," Michael said, coming up the street.

"Humph. I'll talk to her."

Michael pushed open the gate, and Vincent threw his cigar stub onto the pavement. "You gotta have a better place."

They went up the steps together and, after Michael unlocked both sets of doors, stepped into the mostly dark house and began taking off their coats. The only light was coming from the kitchen. "More room. I mean you owe it to Diane and the girls, right? What you spend your money on now?"

"Food."

"No. You gotta save. Put a little . . ."

"Michael?" They heard Diane's voice from the back part of the house. They were coming through the dining room and she appeared in the kitchen, half asleep in her robe and slippers.

Michael held her and gave her a kiss. "Hi, doll."

She smiled and murmured, "Hi, Uncle Vincent." She was really very sleepy. "Let me get you something to eat. I have some raviolis on the stove. All I have to do is warm the sauce. Get some wine, Michael."

He put two glasses on the table as Vincent excused himself and headed toward the bathroom. Then, while Di drifted around the stove like a sleepwalker, Michael flipped through the mail sitting on the counter under the wall phone. New England Merchants Bank. They were over the limit again on their MasterCard. Cambridge Electric. Only thirty dollars higher than expected. An envelope without a stamp. The notice from the day-care center that tuition was due. Fantastic. And a small brown envelope from the paper boy. They owed $5.05 for September and $5.05 in advance for October.

"You know if the little bastard would deliver the damn thing so we could read it . . ." He was talking to no one in particular. "He won't even come inside the fence. He just drops it there and half of it blows away. I can read the sports section sticking out of a bush." Then to Diane, "You didn't answer the door?"

"Yeh. He just left the bill again."

"Well . . . Soon."

They heard a flush, but it was several minutes before Vincent reappeared. When he came back into the kitchen he was nodding with the sides of his mouth pulled down like Il Duce about to make a point. "Angels," he said. "Little angels, just like ours." Diane was setting the warmed food on the table. "I had to peek at the girls, Mike. Bellissime!"

Vincent sat down with his wine, and Michael helped Di bring the food to the table. A steaming bowl of raviolis, another bowl of sausages and meatballs, a bowl of salad. Di said, "You fellows will have to forgive me, but I've got to get back to bed."

"Good idea, Diane," Vincent offered.

She kissed her husband and padded out of the room, and Michael began downing the raviolis, pouring himself another glass of wine. "So what you want to talk about, Uncle Vincent?"

The older man was rearranging his food with his fork. He seemed to be looking through the lettuce leaves. After a moment he set down the fork and looked his nephew in the eye. "They're trying to kill us," he said.

The effect was so melodramatic that Michael wanted to laugh. "Who, Uncle Vincent? Who's going to kill who?"

"You know who. Harvard! The bigshots! The scientists."

"Okay. Now what's the other who? Just you and me, or . . ."

"Don't get fresh, my boy. You pray to God it isn't those little angels in there sleeping that have to pay the price."

"So what is Harvard doing now?"

"The DNA again."

Michael groaned. Fighting the scientists, threatening to turn Harvard Yard into a parking lot on the CBS Evening News, had been the high point of Vincent's career. "I thought that was all over," he said. "You went around and around with them and you won."

"No, no. This is a new game. Now they want factories pumping it out. They want to keep going till they have thousands of gallons—like a brewery. Only it's God knows what."

"You got the citizen's review board or whatever."

"But these new guys are slick. They're gonna go into these hearings this time and make it sound like they're gonna start up some nice little business, pay their taxes, make some jobs, maybe sponsor a Little League team someday. They're lulling the people to sleep. I'm awake! But I'm not the mayor anymore. There's only so much I can do."

"Uncle, if you want somebody to look through their laundry there's plenty of cheap lawyers hanging around the courthouse. I can't get into anything like that. They'd have my badge."

"I can't believe you would insult me that way."

He let his uncle go with wounded pride for a moment. Then he said, "I don't even know that I agree with you. I mean, those are pretty smart men over there."

"So were the assholes who built Three Mile Island." Giacconi put down his fork, wiped his mouth with his napkin and laid it on the table. "How many people you suppose live in each square mile of Cambridge? How many kids? We're talking about cancer genes cloned into bacteria, you know? The same kind of bacteria that live down in your gut. Once they start scrambling the rules like that, where's it gonna stop?" The melodrama was gone. The old man sounded deadly serious. "Let's say one of these doodads they create washes down the drain and gets into the sewer. Let's say something blows out a vent because the air-conditioner repairman is a jerk-off. Even if they can find some way to kill this thing, how many kids are gonna die while they're still trying to figure out what the hell it is?"

Michael tossed down the last of the wine and looked at his uncle. He was really very tired, and he wished the old man would shut up and go away. He had enough to worry about just dodging the paper boy and collaring psychopaths. What the hell were they doing now trying to throw biology at him?

"I'll tell you this," Giacconi said. "Anybody so much as sneezes over at the Bio Labs, I'm gonna know about it."

3

PETER McKUSICK WAS LEANING over a Plexiglas vat of gently swirling liquid, observing the slow spiral of a billion human cells growing on a million microscopic beads. He had shut off the supply of oxygen and was measuring its rate of consumption. He did not want these cells wasting his time, or his calf serum. They were in the vat to produce interferon, the antiviral agent that might or might not be the magic bullet in the war against cancer. He wanted to milk them for all they were worth.

It was a relatively simple-minded technique they were using, the result of an engineering problem he had solved by accident. As it turned out, his solution was useful at a time when utility in biology was very much in demand. It had been his ticket back into respectable science. It was what gave him access to Kluer's lab and Harvard's other resources for the work that he really cared about. He was using Kluer while he allowed Kluer to use him. Symbiosis. That's what they call a relationship when they can't tell who is the parasite and who is the host.

Mac heard a rumble of footsteps in the hallway. Kluer and Liz were leading their somber Wall Street guests into the lab. At least they had waited until the end of the day. The real work was over now. It was time for show and tell.

"This is Dr. McKusick, gentlemen."

Mac turned to face a sea of pinstripes and suddenly became very much aware of the running shoes and blue jeans below his lab coat.

"He and my wife can lead you through our cell-culture operation. If you'll excuse me for a moment, I have to return a call that may bear on our discussion."

Liz stood at the rear of the group looking prim in a black turtleneck and a gray skirt. In all the years Mac had known her, he had never seen her in the lab wearing anything but pants. She said, "Maybe you could give a little background on microcarriers, Mac, then run through the induction process."

McKusick nodded, avoiding her eyes, and took a deep breath. He could not help feeling like some sort of precocious flunky, but this was simply the Kluer style—walking off and leaving the details to someone else.

"Okay, gentlemen." But no sooner had Mac begun than the phone started a loud, insistent ringing just behind his head. "Here we have a fifty-liter fermenter in which we're culturing a line of F4 fibroblast cells derived from human foreskins. We inject a synthetic double-stranded RNA—"

"Foreskins?"

Mac glanced at the heavyset young banker with the puzzled face, then over at Liz. He saw a sparkle in her eye, the slight arching of one brow. He wished Sandy would answer the damn telephone! He needed all the help he could get.

Maybe we should skip the science and just talk about the money, he was thinking. The money was all that really counted around here, wasn't it?

"We use foreskins," Mac continued, "because they're a cheap and readily available source of human cells. They're also from newborns, which means a longer life for the cell line. Every nontransformed cell line dies out after a certain number of doublings. It's predetermined. It's in the DNA."

The ringing had stopped. But then Sandy was leaning around the corner, holding out the phone. She said, "I think you better take it, Mac." The forced calm in her voice was unsettling.

McKusick excused himself and made his way toward the adjoining room and the waiting phone.

"Dr. McKusick? This is Yvonne ... from Day Care."

There's a problem, Stasson said ...

"What's happened?"

"No, no. Kitty's okay."

"Where are you?"

"City Hospital. The emergency room. I don't think it's serious, really, but we had to bring her over. She sort of passed out, really, is all, but—"

"I'll be right there."

For McKusick, the group of people waiting in the other room no longer existed. He left the lab through a side door, ran down three flights of stairs, then burst through an emergency exit with an alarm on it. The hospital was only a few blocks away. He could get there most quickly on foot. He rounded a corner deep in leaves, sucked in the brittle October air, and began to pick up speed. He raced past the huge stone houses on Francis Avenue, crossed Kirkland Street, then ran down a block of three-deckers leading to the hospital. His mind was flooded with images. He could see the jeep rolling over and over. He could hear Kath's screams. He was running back up the hill toward Stasson's. He was trying to coax her into staying alive.

He hit the emergency entrance and burst through the doors looking wild-eyed in his lab coat, like some mental patient playing quarterback. He sidestepped a technician with a specimen cart, glanced around madly, and then spotted Kitty sitting on Yvonne's lap in the waiting room, unbraiding the teacher's hair. His adrenaline suddenly seemed out of place. She was okay. He tried to take his time, to calm down. But when he suddenly appeared, huffing and puffing, Kitty was startled all the same. The anxiety on his face brought back her own fears. She broke into tears.

He knelt down and took her in his arms. "Poor angel," he whispered. She was wearing her spare clothes—a red jumper, a yellow pullover—not what he had dressed her in that morning. As he held her, comforted her, he felt her neck glands, he studied the pupils of her eyes.

"What's the trouble, little one?" She was so small, and he was all she had.

Kitty gasped for breath. "Where were you, Daddy?"

He squeezed her to his chest. You can't always be there, he told himself. You have to live with the risks. Then, after a moment, he looked at Yvonne. "What's going on?"

"She seems perfectly okay now. I really feel silly dragging you all the way over here."

There was something so marital about this that Mac found himself avoiding her eyes. She was the woman who cared for his child. In the primal ordering of things, what should be the nature of their relationship?

"Don't be ridiculous," he told her. "You did the right thing."

"The doctor said he wanted to talk to you."

"Right," he said. But a strange resentment came over him. No one other than Mac had ever taken care of Kitty. He was the only one who had ever examined her, and now he was guarded and distrustful. "What's the name?"

"Nelson."

He nodded, trying to bring his emotions down to scale. Surely there was nothing to it. Surely this was all routine. Even so, nothing could overcome the fear that Stasson had instilled.

"Can you manage another minute?"

She smiled and Mac leaned over to place Kitty back in her lap. But the little girl clung to him. "Stay with Vonnie, sugar. Just a minute. Daddy will be right back." He kissed her, then stood up and removed his sweaty white coat.

The resident was a pale boy with rimless glasses. He spoke to Mac in the out-patient corridor with people passing by in twos and threes. "Looks like nothing more than a simple fainting episode," he said.

"Did you do an EEG?"

"No."

"Did a neurologist look at her?"

"There's really no sign of anything organically wrong."

Mac was testing him, looking for a sign. "She complained of a headache last night."

"Doesn't surprise me." He closed the manila folder he had been holding in front of him. "To tell you the truth, I think she's under quite a bit of stress."

The resident gave a smile meant to be calming. He had the clear teeth and perfect skin of prep school. He had probably explored life's boundaries all the way to Yale and back.

Mac felt stunned. Despite his obsession with Kitty, was he still somehow neglecting her?

"Must be hard by yourself," the young man said, his manner wise and paternalistic, learned from a second-year course. "What kind of work do you do?"

"Research. At the Bio Labs."

"Right, right. I noticed that on the health forms. Must be an interesting place to be these days."

"Yeh. I suppose."

"But I guess it's a lot of midnight oil. A lot of pressure."

"Yeh."

"She's feeling it."

McKusick nodded solemnly, seeing an image of Kitty dancing along behind him in her pajamas as they went back to the lab after dinner. She seemed to find nothing odd about hearing her bedtime story on a cot by a laboratory bench. She liked being near her father, but obviously it was no good. It had to change.

The two men were walking back toward the reception area. With the initial jolt fading, the diagnosis was becoming more and more of a relief. He was doing it for her, of course, but fathers who pushed too hard always claimed it was for the kids.

"Huh." The resident glanced at Mac. "Perversely enough, this is the kind of thing they'd be interested in."

"What's that?" Mac was trying to rethink his schedule, trying to redistribute his time among Kluer's work, his own work, and Kitty.

"Researcher's immediate family. Uncertain diagnosis."

"I'm not following you."

"The biohazards committee. The city council." He twisted his Cross pen and injected it into his pocket. "It just shows how absurd the guidelines for recombinant DNA are, you know, but this is just the kind of thing we're supposed to report."

When Mac came back into the waiting room Kitty was sleeping in Yvonne's arms. Her tiny hand was clamped tightly on the teacher's right breast, so much so that Vonnie had to reach down and break the grip to move the child to her father. Embarrassed smiles passed between the two adults.

Yvonne said, "Is there anything I can do? Do you have food in the house? I'd be happy to come by with some groceries and cook up something."

Mac smiled and shook his head. She was amazingly young, probably just about as old as Kath was when they met. It had seemed such a difference then, and now Mac was even older. He said, "That's very sweet of you, but . . . I've got some stuff thawed. No need to put you out. Thanks, though."

"Can I give you a ride home at least?"

"Yeh. That'd be fantastic."

Kitty slept against Mac's shoulder as he followed Yvonne out to the parking lot. They made an impromptu family, heading home. The sky was turquoise; the clouds were tinged with pink. It would be dark soon. It was time for settling in for the night. He watched the young woman walking ahead of him, the graceful curve of her hips, and he gave a thought to the more natural scheme of things. Two caretakers per child, he was thinking. It's not a bad idea.

Yvonne held the door as he crouched down into the back seat of her beat-up Datsun station wagon. She came around to the driver's side, and he shifted Kitty in his arms and tried to relax. A stack of poster board was beside him on the seat. In the back, a potter's wheel. Vonnie put the car in gear and pulled out of the parking lot.

"You know, I was really scared out of my wits," she said, glancing back. They were head-

ing down Cambridge Street toward the construction tie-up near the Law School. "Kitty was very
upset—a squabble with a little boy over a truck
—and then suddenly she was going through
these contortions. I'd never seen anything like
it."

"You handled it just right," he said. "I appreciate it."

Yvonne glanced back again with a smile. "She's
such a lovely child. Really a pleasure to be with,
you know?"

"Yeh. I know."

"Her mother must have been very beautiful,"
she said. She was pressing. She watched in the
rearview mirror for his reaction, but he was
distracted, staring blankly at the traffic coming
out of Harvard Square.

"I mean, she's such a gorgeous child." She
glanced back again. "Not that ... That didn't
come out right. I just mean she's very fair, and
very petite. You're darker and ..."

"She does look like her mother," he said.

Yvonne turned left onto Langdon Street,
edged her way through the cars that lined the
curbs, and, at Mac's direction, stopped in front
of the three-story stucco apartment building.
Kitty began to stir as he opened the door and
shifted his weight.

"You sure you'll be okay?" Yvonne turned
around with her arm extended to the passenger
seat, the angle outlining the shape of her breast.
"I'd love to help."

Mac smiled. The responses were there. He
felt the tug, but it was all deep within, buried
under the layers and the years.

"Really, we'll be fine." He swung his feet out and tried to stand without jostling Kitty. He looked in the window at Yvonne leaning across toward him. "Thanks for the lift," he said.

She waved hesitantly and pulled away.

With his one free arm Mac fumbled at his mailbox, then unlocked the glass inner door of the building. Kitty was quiet and still, but he sensed that she was only pretending to sleep, enjoying the ride. He was on the third flight of stairs when he heard the small voice say, "Happy birthday, Daddy."

He reached the landing. "Thank you, puppy. You're sweet to remember."

Once inside their door he set Kitty down, then tossed the unopened mail onto a bookshelf. The catnap must have done her good. It was really just stress. That's all it was.

"And now we shall have dinner," she announced. "And a cake!"

He groaned. He *knew* he was going to forget. Kitty was expecting some kind of party and he was scanning the bareboned racks of an all-but-empty refrigerator. There wasn't even any beer. He could have used several at that moment.

"Can I make the cake, Daddy?"

"Tell you what. You can help me blow out the candles."

He poured a cup of juice for Kitty, put a frying pan on the stove, and began warming a thin piece of ham. Then he opened a can of green beans and emptied them into another small pan. He watched Kitty on the floor now with her cup. She had turned her attention to the toy animals she had left scattered there that morning. She seemed fine. She was energetic. Busy. He was simply going to have to learn to cope with the uncertainty. All life is carried out at risk. All children are vulnerable. Kitty was only slightly more so than most.

She picked up a miniature Holstein with obscenely pink and swollen udders.

"I'm a cowgirl! I ride cows!"

Mac turned and smiled. "Yippi ti yea, sweetheart." He was spooning green beans onto a plastic plate embellished with pictures of the Muppets. He took a knife and sliced the ham into tiny bites. Then he set the plate on the kitchen table and reached down to lift her into the air. He gathered her up to his shoulder and squeezed her tightly, but she was wiggling free.

"Don't," she said, and pressed her fist into his neck. "I have to get your present."

She ran off to her room, and Mac went back to the refrigerator to consider the possibilities, grim as they were. He was an idiot not to have accepted Yvonne's offer. His gaze settled on the wax-paper wrapper of the half-eaten Whopper Burger. He grabbed it reluctantly, remembering the indigestion that had caused him to set it aside the night before.

Kitty came running back into the room with a tiny white paper bag. "Happy Birthday!" she yelled, thrusting it toward him.

Mac shook his head and opened the package. As promised—a ladybug, made of porcelain, red with black spots, sitting on a pin. "You did get me a ladybug! Where did you get it, honey?"

"Peggy took me to the store. Like I told you."

"This is terrific. I'll wear it on my shirt. Every day."

"What about cake?"

"Okay, sweetie. As soon as we eat, we'll go down to the Evergood and get a cake."

"With candles."

"Right. But you have to eat your dinner."

"Okay."

She settled back at the table and he joined her with the day-old hamburger. He was not going to be able to get this down without something to drink. He went back to the refrigerator for one last scan, and there, lying on its side on the bottom rack on the door, was a bottle half full of half-flat champagne left over from the party for Arnold Goldman's Nobel. He pulled it out, popped the plastic cork, and poured a limp glassful. A hot time in the old town tonight, he was thinking. They clinked their glasses because Kitty liked that, and he made a toast—to his thirty-third birthday, and to Kitty's health.

4

IN THE CELL-CULTURE LAB, Sandy O'Donnell was keeping one eye on a digital read-out and the other on her Norelco coffee maker. It had been a long night with no breakfast, and she was getting a headache waiting for the water to finish dripping through.

She had propped herself on the lab bench, half asleep, dreading the urinary-tract infection she knew she was going to get and trying not to even think about herpes. She should have known the guy was a loser the minute he started pumping her to "guess his sport." Definitely a sprinter, she decided later.

The red light of the Norelco began to glow, and she followed the smell of coffee to the table by the door and breathed deeply as she filled her mug. She was frustrated, eager to get out of this barn and into the new facility. If Kluer would only get his act together they could be rolling and scaled up to commercial production by spring. She pushed back the piece of plastic covering the sugar and the Coffee-Mate. She had forgotten to get a muffin, and she needed all the food value she could get.

"Shit!"

She thought she was going to be sick at her stomach. She grabbed the plastic and used it to shove the sugar off the table and into the trash can. The bag contained equal parts white crystals and swarming brown ants.

5

THE BIOLOGICAL LABORATORIES is a grim, red-brick building to the north of Harvard Yard, with the look of a factory in Manchester or Lowell. Peter McKusick held Kitty's hand as they walked between the two pigeon-stained rhinoceroses guarding the main entrance. They stepped into the cool, dim foyer, through doors with grillework depicting insects the size of mammals, and began making their way up the three flights of stairs leading to the lab. They had counted these steps many, many times before. Kitty usually liked to climb by herself. Today she wanted to be carried.

As Mac and Kitty stepped into the lab, Sandy glanced up and shook back her hair. "How's the kid, Mac? Didn't think you'd be coming in." She was sipping her coffee—black—looking like a relaxed volleyball coach in her golf shirt and sneakers.

"Running on all eight," Mac said, setting Kitty down.

"Just had another attack of pharaoh's revenge," Sandy went on. "We're going to have to start keeping the sugar in the vault."

Mac stepped closer and glanced at a clipboard listing rates of O_2 consumption.

Sandy gripped her cup with both hands, warming herself. "I heard in Cohen's lab they broke into some radioactive sucrose he was going to use as a tracer. The grad students spent the day with Geiger counters tracking the ants through the walls!"

"This is Princess Leia," Kitty said, holding up a small plastic figure. It was a character from a film she had never seen but that provided the central mythology for the kids at Garden Nursery.

Sandy gave a half-hearted smile.

"I've gotta talk to Liz," Mac said. "Is she here?"

"In her office."

"Keep an eye on Kitty for a minute, okay?" Then he slipped back into the hallway before Kitty could protest.

The corridor gave the feeling of a well-ventilated mine shaft, narrowed at the moment by a huge cardboard box with stenciled letters saying, LIVE REPTILES. KEEP WARM. The building was simply too old. The pipes burst in the winter and flooded the place. The roaches fought it out with the ants. Electrical fires had broken out on the second floor twice since the summer.

Mac looked across the way and saw light coming from behind the rippled glass in Liz's office door. Knocking once, he stuck his head inside.

"Got a minute?" he said.

Liz Altmann Kluer sat behind an immaculate white metal desk, sorting a stack of 35-millimeter slides to be shown at her noon lecture. Her office, brightly lit and brightly colored, seemed to occupy a different world, or at least a different building, from the cavern surrounding it.

"Hi," she said, looking up apprehensively. "What happened to you yesterday?"

"They took Kitty to the hospital. Didn't Sandy tell you?"

"Right. I forgot."

"Nothing serious," he said. "Day-care centers tend to overreact. It's a liability thing."

"I meant to call, but . . . I . . ."

"You were busy."

"We had to get rid of the Bates, Hawthorne crowd."

"Right."

He looked into her eyes until she turned away. They were alone now, behind an office door that could be bolted from the inside. He wondered if this was really the same woman who had come up to him with a silly grin all those years ago, coyly flicking the blue foil wrapper of a Trojan prophylactic. It had been in a lab just like this in Los Angeles. The devilish look in her eye, the demure smile giving way to hysterical laughter as he began to shake his head.

"It's strictly science," she had assured him, her tone mild and beatific.

"No thanks." He was backing away from her, circling the lab bench.

"I need it for the motility study."

"Unh-uh."

"Since when are you so shy?" She was trying

to be nonchalant, but she couldn't keep from laughing.

"Standing here? Whacking off in the lab?"

"Oh no. I intend to help."

"Oh." He stopped backing away. "Really?"

"Of course." She palmed the foil packet and began tugging at his belt. "Come here."

"Say . . . Is the door locked?" he asked.

"Relax. You're in good hands. Let's go over to the couch."

He hobbled and stumbled with his pants falling down, laughing as she pulled him by the elastic of his underwear, the tip of his erection peering over the top like a curious observer.

He fell onto the couch and pulled her down on top of him. "Take your clothes off, too," he said.

She shook her head. "Strictly science, dear boy."

He reached up to stroke her neck, and she kissed his hand. She broke open the packet and unrolled the latex sheath onto his swollen penis. "Is that comfortable, Dr. McKusick?"

"Quite."

"Then we'll begin the procedure."

"You're crazy."

"Umm," she murmured as she wrapped her hand around him, gently squeezing with a downward pressure. Her touch was warm. "Don't worry about it," she said. "Just relax."

She leaned back and held the slide up to the light. She closed one eye, focusing tightly on the Kodachrome.

"You coming to the hearing tonight?" she asked him.

"I doubt it." He was filing the memory away. Their relationship had been little more than an experiment for Liz, and whenever she finished a study she froze it all down, storing it away in cryogenic suspension. "Actually, I've got to duck out for a while today. Some personal business."

"Yeh?" She placed her hand on the desk, still holding the slide in her fingertips.

"Kitty's having some problems. I need to spend some time with her today. Take her to the park or something."

Liz looked at him calmly. Behind her, a framed print of a *New Yorker* cover showed a map of Manhattan, the Hudson River, and a disproportionately small and vaguely defined North America beyond. "You've got to be kidding."

"Liz, come on. We talked about this sort of thing at the beginning."

She went ahead and inserted the slide into the carousel, tapping it into place with a brightly polished nail. "Bayard is running a circus with patent attorneys and Wall Street. I'm trying to crank out some papers because it might just be useful to have our data in the record. The whole thing could ride on what the city council does tonight, and you're taking time out for Ring Around the Rosie."

"Sandy could run this project, for Christ's sake! The lab does not need me at the moment. My kid does!"

She sat looking at him impassively, impeccably groomed and self-contained, and Mac wondered why he bothered. It was like a marriage that had gone on too long. Every response between them was complicated by layer upon layer of past history, interdependence, and resentment.

"I've saved your ass twice," she said, "and twice is enough. But right now my credibility happens to be riding on the line with you. It would be nice if you didn't screw it up."

"I am unfathomably grateful for your efforts on my behalf. How's that?"

She pushed back her chair and stood to place the carousel on the table to her right. "Fuck you," she said.

He stepped back out of the office and closed the door behind him. "You had your chance," he muttered.

When he came back into the lab, Sandy was on the phone and Kitty was standing by the sunlit row of windows, peering down listlessly. Mac looked at her, a tiny form in trainman's overalls, and he realized what a rotten job he had done with her hair. The braids were uneven, standing on her head like sprouts. He came up behind her and looked out. She was watching the children playing down below in the dirt between the labs and the old ROTC barracks in back. Contained between the two buildings and the high wire fence, they looked like tiny prisoners of war.

6

LELAND ALBRITON SAT on the edge of a freshly
made bed at the Parker House, actively resisting
the urge to turn on the television set. It was the
middle of the afternoon. The maids had come
and gone, his wife was out shopping, and he
had the sense that the newly renovated walls
were going to implode unless he did something
to ease the silence. Most people would have
flipped the switch without thinking, but for
Albriton that would have been a lapse in self-
control, a weak, petty indulgence, like hating
Peter McKusick.

Albriton was a southerner, a traditionalist, and
very much the sort of man who valued control
above all else. He almost never displayed his
emotions publicly, even when he might have
wanted to. He was a civilized man. He had
standards, and he had seen far too much self-
destruction brought on by violent anger and
vindictiveness. Even so, he and Nina had re-

sponded quite differently to the death of their daughter. She had accommodated the loss by transferring some of her parental attachment to McKusick. This young man had been Kathleen's choice. They had loved each other, and Nina looked on Peter as a part of Kathy that could be kept alive. Lee Albriton saw him as the man who had killed his daughter, accident or not.

He stalked around the room, aware that he was going to have to short-circuit the loathing he felt welling up inside him. He was going to have to make the call. Nina simply did not want to go back to Texas without seeing Peter.

He flipped through the visitor's guide, then went over to the window. By craning his neck, he gained a partial view of the harbor, and he could see the jets lifting off the runway at Logan. Maybe it was being in Boston that was stirring him up. He thought of it as Kathleen's town, the place she had always wanted to be, the place where she had come into her own and been so very much alive. But now it had an aura of unreality about it. He and Nina had spent the morning eating their way through Quincy Market along the restored waterfront. The town seemed to have been transformed into a sort of thinking-man's Disneyland, packed with tourists licking ice cream cones. The change offended him. He'd liked it the way it used to be, seedy and old and down-at-the-heel, just as it had been when they first brought Kathy there as a freshman starting college, lovely and bright, seventeen, her whole future ahead of her.

Albriton sat back down on the bed and picked

up the telephone. The only way to make a call like this was to start dialing.

The phone rang only once before there was a voice on the line, a quick, abrupt "Hello."

"Peter!" It had to be him. "This is Lee Albriton . . ."

There was the hum of silence.

". . . from Dalton."

Kitty had just gone down for her nap, and McKusick had yanked up the phone to keep from waking her. He had forgotten to take it off the hook. Now he was trying to avoid panic. He was letting it all roll over him.

"Hello!" he said, perhaps too heartily. He could tell that this was a local connection. His mind was racing for some way to handle this. "How've you been?"

"You must've not got my letter. We're just up here for a day or two. Marie's at Wellesley now, you know, and MIT's having this seminar on rock fractures. Kind of a Mickey Mouse affair, but it covers the vacation for tax purposes."

Albriton waited again, but McKusick was still dumbstruck.

"They told me you were out baby-sitting today. I thought all you mad scientists were a little more intense than that?"

McKusick did his best to respond casually, but his voice was stiffening. "Just covering for a friend," he lied. "A neighbor, really."

"We haven't caught you at a bad time, have we?"

"No. Not at all."

Albriton considered Mac's tone. He wanted to chalk it up to a naturally awkward situation, but maybe he was not as good as he thought at concealing his own hostility.

"Can we get you away for dinner tonight?"

Mac calculated. Dinner would keep them away from the apartment. He would get Peggy to baby-sit. They would spend a few hours together, get it over with, then the Albritons would be safely packed off back to Texas. "Sure," he said. "Dinner would be fine."

But McKusick knew it would not be fine. There was the matter of a daughter. There was the matter of a granddaughter.

7

MAC SAT ON THE bathroom floor while Kitty took her bath. He wanted her in bed by the time the sitter came. He did not want her to know that he was going out.

"The show begins!" she yelled. She sat up, stiffening her hands and forearms into imaginary flippers. Then she pushed herself up the slippery backside of the tub, held for a moment, and slid back down into a warm splash.

Mac was staring down at the white octagons of tile lined in grime.

"Clap, Daddy!"

He caught himself. He began to applaud, but there was simply too much on his mind right now. "Excellent, little dolphin! Great show!" Kitty flopped down onto her belly and he knelt at the edge of the tub to wash her hair. He ought to be staying home with her rather than rushing her to bed. But why had the Albritons shown up? Why now? The business crap and the city council crap were already putting him behind. This was the beginning of the slide, he was thinking. It was all going to be getting out of hand.

Kitty lay with her mouth just above the water line. As he poured on the shampoo and began lathering her hair, he noticed, almost against his will, the dark circles under her eyes. The skin was puffy, sallow.

"We've got to start getting you to bed earlier," he said. "You look like a baby raccoon, honey, with little rings around your eyes."

8

A PALE WASH of moonlight was coming in the windows of the Bio Labs. It was faint, made more diffuse at times by clouds drifting by in the night sky, but adequate for the lunar compass of the *Monomorium pharaonis* scout making her way back to the nest. The ant was marking a trail with a secretion of her Dufour's gland that would lead her colony to the food source she had just discovered. She circled back once along the gritty surface of the floor and, encountering a nest mate, headed directly for him, placed her right legs on top of the worker, and began shaking in a vertical plane.

Monomorium pharaonis, pharaoh's ant, is a tramp species always ready to move on. Native to tropical climates, where they inhabit cavities within plants, they have been transported all over the world. They live in the walls of houses as far north as Scotland. They are so prevalent in certain hospitals that patient beds must be placed in moats of mineral oil to keep the ants from climbing up and eating the flesh of open wounds.

The scout turned off from the main corridor and walked under a locked wooden door. On the door three signs were posted. One was the purple and yellow emblem warning of a radiation source. Another carried interlocking red circles and the word *Biohazard*. The third said, "In case of emergency within this lab call Peter McKusick—594-3702."

The ant made her way along the molding that lined the base of the laboratory bench. She was on a direct bearing toward a crack that had appeared in the wall six months earlier but, covered by a refrigerator, had gone unnoticed by human eyes. The scout could sense her proximity to the nest. Her receptors were being bombarded with pheromones, diverting her from her purpose. Her odor trail ended in an overload of confused signals. The entire colony was already swarming. In wave after wave the workers washed out of the crack and down the wall, carrying their larvae, eggs, and pupae in their jaws.

9

After calling up on the house phone, Mac had nothing to do but wait in the lobby. It was dark and small and subdued. A "European" atmosphere, he supposed. A little brass, a little polished wood, a few potted palms. He watched the business people in their expensive clothes, the finely groomed stewardesses pulling their suitcases on collapsible carts.

He drifted into the lobby newsstand to wait. It was a cramped, glassed-in affair, and it sold the kind of last-minute toys and gifts they sell in airport terminals. Red Sox caps, inflatable airliners, a few dolls and cars and trucks, all hanging down above the stacks of East Coast newspapers. Perhaps he should get something for Kitty. He looked at the selection of toys, but his mind was elsewhere. It had been so easy for him to forget this business of the family tie. It had been alien to him from the beginning, when Kath first took him to meet them in Texas. He had always been on his own, more or less, a displaced person. He had grown up with his mother in Venice Beach. He had experienced the Great American Cliché of the long-suffering wife dumped for the younger woman, except that he was the product of that second union. His mother was the eighteen-year-old secretary.

"There he is!" It was Albriton's voice, part greeting, part announcement.

Mac turned and saw two broadly grinning faces. He would not have recognized them on the street.

"Hello, hello!"

They stumbled awkwardly in an effort to reach each other in the cramped space of the news-stand. Mac hugged Nina and kissed her cheek while he reached around her to shake Lee's hand. They exchanged the obvious questions, and in the general confusion left them un-answered. They were blocking the cashier's counter, obstructing the commerce in cigars and evening papers.

They walked toward the restaurant, awkward as newlyweds. They were the first guests of the evening, and the maitre d' whisked them to their table as if they were making some unspeak-able social gaffe.

"So Marie's up here at Wellesley, now," Mac started in. He felt like an actor whose cues were not coming. How could he have thought that he would never see them again?

Nina nodded. "Uh-huh. She wanted to follow Kathy." But that was all the woman could say. She seemed to be on the verge of tears.

A young man sporting penny loafers and a

fake French accent arrived to take their cocktail order. Then a woman came with a "martini cart" to spray Nina's glass with vermouth from a crystal aspirator.

Mac had forgotten the almost supernatural resemblance between Kathleen and her mother. Mrs. Albriton's features were slightly thicker now, her hair speckled with gray and cropped in a short, smart-looking style. Lee was wearing gold-rimmed eyeglasses that seemed to brighten his face and make him more contemporary. For a man who ran cattle and drilled wells near Dalton, Texas, he looked as though he had just strolled over from the Union Club.

"Dean's in law school now."

"You're kidding! It's really been that long, hasn't it?"

Lee nodded.

After a moment, Nina reached for the bread basket. "Parker House rolls," she said. "I guess this must be the right place."

Amid the awkwardness, a wave of panic rose up and swept over Mac. What were these people doing here? They were supposed to be sealed off in his memory, safely confined to Christmas cards. Now they were in Boston, actually on his doorstep, and every word of small talk was a blatant lie. One simple piece of missing information was making his behavior unforgivable. He wanted the Albritons back where they belonged, not just for his own safety but for theirs as well. He liked them. He liked the way they had accepted him from the beginning. And their own way of life had such an integrity to it and had meant so much to Kathleen that Mac was depressed to see them here in this ridiculous restaurant. But the waiters came and went, struggling with the fine points of the service, and Mac tried not to think about the vast incongruity in his relationship with these people.

The conversation finally picked up when they began to talk about Mac's work. Being in the oil business, they could easily understand the boomtown mentality that had taken over molecular biology.

Mr. Albriton looked up from his veal. "Did you know that Tecumseh Drilling sold out to Texaco?"

Mac shook his head. He was exhausted from feigning interest.

"I never thought about it much along the way, but over the years we picked up a share or two. Now that our kids are grown, we find ourselves sitting on about six hundred thousand dollars. The damnedest thing, but anyway, we plan to use it to help our kids. If there's any way we can help you ... I mean, if you ever need anything, Mac, don't ever be afraid to ask. Okay?"

Mac looked up at them. He could not help remembering their final exchange when he had gone to see them in Texas. It was as he and Kath were leaving, en route to Bogotá. She was still inside, and Mac and her father were standing on the wide verandah of the stone and cedar house. "Kath's mother and I want to help you two every way we can," Albriton had said. He grasped Mac's hand to shake it, but then did not let it go. "You can always count on us if you need us, son. But where Kathy's concerned" —the grip tightened—"just don't you ever cross me. You don't ever want to have me anywhere but on your side."

10

"WHO IS THAT MAKING all the fuss?" Liz asked.

Kluer leaned toward her ear and whispered, "Vincent R. Giacconi."

"Of course," she said, nodding. "I remember now."

They were sitting in the back row of the spectators' gallery in the ornate council chambers at Cambridge City Hall. They were listening to the testimony of Fritz Weibel, the Biota financial officer who had followed her all evening at the party. The hearings had been in progress for fifteen minutes, and so far they had dealt with the spelling of Weibel's name (Giacconi wanted to be sure) and with the sound system. Mr. Weibel mumbled in an inaudible monotone, and various technicians had been called over to adjust the equipment. But the Swiss was also very short. At one point Giacconi offered him a telephone book to sit on.

Liz was relieved that Bayard would not be

testifying this time around. However much their plans might be affected by the ruling tonight, at least they were to be spared the personal indignities. She felt her husband's hand come to rest on her knee. How odd, she thought for a moment. There was a time when he had been tender, but she never kidded herself. Even when she thought she loved him, it was his mind that had fascinated her. The impeccable clarity of his intelligence, the range of his vision. Now even that had dimmed. He was no longer disturbing the universe to unravel its secrets. He was simply buying and selling. And there was certainly nothing loving in the touch she felt now. It was merely possessive. A television cameraman had been staring up her skirt ever since she sat down. The man was being so brazen about it that even Kluer was noticing.

It was ironic to be back in these chambers after four years. They had been lovers, supposedly, at the time of the first hearings. And this evening, they had played the part of an old married couple sharing a quiet dinner alone. Excruciatingly quiet. With their guests back on their planes and no new business to discuss, they made small talk like socially inept acquaintances. After two hours of awkward silences broken by embarrassed smiles, she was already exhausted. She wished she were home with a hot bath and a stiff drink. She wished she could talk to Peter and apologize for acting like such a bitch.

Weibel was droning on about the contribution his corporation would be making to the Cambridge tax base, estimating incremental growth figures for the next five years. The television people sat idly behind the council members' desks, their lights and cameras off. Even Giacconi seemed to be napping now, resting up against the ropes, waiting to come on strong in the final rounds. He had won the opener. Weibel was clearly starting on the defensive. Several times he had acknowledged that Biota could simply go to Watertown or Waltham if Cambridge did not want them. This tack merely emphasized the man's actuarial coldness, a style that might have gone over on Beacon Hill but did not make it in Central Square. These people carried lunch pails to work, and here was Fritz Weibel with his wafer-thin briefcase and exquisite tailoring telling them what was good for them.

Assembled now across the podium, the Cambridge Experimentation Review Board had been cast like a platoon in a World War II movie—a black, a Pole, a Jew, an Italian. There was one doctor, one nurse, a housewife, and a haberdasher, but after four years of wrangling with the issues of recombinant DNA, they all had a fairly sophisticated grasp of the subject.

When Weibel concluded his prepared remarks, the chairman, a professor of environmental engineering, shuffled his papers and leaned into his microphone. "Mr. Weibel, I want to thank you for your candid and most helpful statement. Now if I may, I would ask you to tell us a bit about your plans for waste disposal and water treatment."

Weibel addressed the question as best he could, and everyone but the engineer appeared to doze.

Liz was growing restless in the cramped, stuffy gallery. Then the nurse, a black woman from North Cambridge, took the floor. "Mr. Weibel, you've said that all industrial work will be carried out at the Pi level. But of course you're also going to be engaged in research. Can you tell me what specific organisms will be involved, and specifically, if there is to be any work with tumor viruses?"

This was not the stuff that a financial manager was prepared to answer. He began fumbling, stumbling over his words, and glancing about in obvious discomfort. His slick confidence was a very thin veneer, and Giacconi was starting to smile. He was straightening up in his chair, ready to get back into the fight. But then like a friendly passer-by who just happened to be in the neighborhood, Arnold Goldman pulled up the chair behind Weibel and sat down. "Perhaps I could answer that one," he said, moving into the microphone's range. The cameraman gave a short burst of light and film.

Arnold Goldman's Nobel Prize had been announced only the week before. With his broad smile, unruly hair, and bright-orange parody of a necktie, he looked like the boy genius who might save the day for Andy Hardy. Goldman started in, and smiles of comfort and confidence began to show on the faces of the panel members. Here was the great man, descended briefly from Olympus to chat with them. They were all impressed. He was obviously in command of every conceivable fact and figure, but more than that he was likable. He looked like someone you could trust. Everyone seemed to be smiling now; everyone but Vincent Giacconi.

The councilman could feel the audience being won over. He could feel the panel moving further and further out of his control. Goldman was offering firm assurances that, if anything, their commercial work would be far safer than the experimental work presently going on in the university labs. He made the whole affair—these hearings, the television coverage—seem preposterous. He made a rousing finish, summarizing the years of lab experience that had been accumulated now without a mishap. He quickly reviewed the Senate hearings and the scientific conferences that had probed into the issue of biohazards without finding any cause for alarm. When he stepped away from the microphone, even the hardened skeptics were shaken. The chairman gave a fulsome statement of thanks that forced Giacconi out of his seat to go have a smoke.

As the next witness came forward, Kluer glanced at Liz with a self-satisfied smile, but she did not notice. She was remembering the look in Peter's sad green eyes four years ago in this very room. When she considered all that he had been through, it hurt to realize how much of it could be traced back to her. She remembered those eyes the first time she saw them in her lecture hall, so sullen she half expected him to pull out a knife and start carving up the desk top. The shaggy sun-bleached hair, the blue jeans and huarache sandals, and that godawful Hawaiian shirt with palm trees. She was having a hard time with palm trees then. She had been in L.A. for about three weeks and she could not get used to them. She could never remember that the desert was *east*. Her first week in Westwood she almost caused a thirteen-Mercedes pileup just by stepping off the curb in the middle of Wilshire Boulevard. In California they stopped for pedestrians. In California . . .

There was a disturbance on the floor. Vincent Giacconi was rushing in from the anteroom waving a piece of paper over his head.

"Mr. Chairman! Mr. Chairman! I have something important here!"

The cameramen got out of their seats and turned on their lights and sound equipment.

The environmental engineer, a bit dismayed, leaned into his microphone. "The Chair recognizes Councilman Giacconi."

"This man was born for community theater," Kluer mumbled, and Liz saw a pained look coming over even Goldman's rosy face.

11

When the albritons left Mac at the Park Street station and turned back toward their hotel, Nina immediately burst into tears. Her husband put a strong hand on her shoulder and drew her to him as they walked.

"Why, Lee? Why?" They were walking in step along Tremont Street, past the high iron fence of the Granary Burial Ground. "They loved each other. They loved their work. They would have made it, Lee. A good life. Kids. All of it."

Albriton simply lowered his head against the wind sweeping down on them from Beacon Street. The only answer he could give to her question was Peter McKusick. Kathy had trusted him with her life, and he had violated that trust. Kathy was dead because Peter had been careless. But he pushed back the thought. It would only hurt Nina more.

By the time they reached their room Nina's tears were gone, but her eyes still showed the sadness. She stepped into the bathroom to wash her face, and Lee fell onto the bed. He was in no mood for self-discipline now. The news was on, and he wanted to bask in the warm glow of someone else's problems. He flipped on the set. He kicked off his shoes and threw his tie onto the chair.

Nina came into the room, drying her face. They exchanged a glance which showed that nothing needed to be said. They had been partners for too long to need words now. She took off her dress, hung it carefully in the closet, then crawled up beside her husband on the bed. He kissed her, then let his hand glide down the silken surface of her slip. For a moment, they stared together idly at the flickering screen.

". . . outside Cambridge City Hall where only a few short moments ago former mayor Vincent Giacconi made a last-ditch, grandstand play to stop the commercial development of recombinant DNA in Cambridge."

Albriton's mind was a million miles away. The frantic episode on the screen meant nothing to him. Tomorrow he would go to his lecture, then meet the girls for lunch. He was ready to file it all away. It was best to forget. To let the old wounds heal.

On the screen a stocky, gray-haired man was thrusting forward a piece of paper as if it were the latest thunderbolt from Zeus. Spittle sprayed out of his mouth as he shouted toward the camera. ". . . These gentlemen have been calmly telling us how harmless their bugs are. Well, even as they spoke, I want you to know that the first reports were coming in! I have in my hand the report from the Health and Hospitals Committee." He glanced down to read. " 'Kathleen McKusick.' That's the little girl. She's three years old. Just yesterday they took her to Cambridge City Hospital with a disease the doctors there couldn't even diagnose. Nobody knows what the hell it is! And would you like to know where little Kathleen McKusick's father works? One Dr. Peter McKusick? He works at the Biological Laboratories! Dr. Peter McKusick. He works right next door to our distinguished Dr. Goldman here!"

There was a moment's delay, and then Lee Albriton was up off the pillow. He was coming toward the television set.

Nina sat up. She had the feeling she was losing touch for a moment. She muttered, "Could there be another Peter McKusick?"

"He has a child," Albriton said.

Nina nodded dumbly. A child three years old.

They stared at each other for a moment as if to test their complicity in the same hallucination. Then Albriton said, "Her name is Kathleen."

12

CHARLIE WHARTON WAS supposed to be on his way back to Atlanta this morning. Instead, he was on the early-bird shuttle to Boston, his trip extended by a late-night call from his section head at the Center for Disease Control.

The engines whined as the jumbo jet leaned down into its final approach. Wharton's seat was upright, and his back was pressed against it as he resisted the gravitational pull.

The work at Sloan-Kettering had taken longer than expected. Male homosexuals were dying right and left down in the Village and there still weren't any answers. Kaposi's sarcoma. A cancer usually limited to elderly Mediterranean men. Only now it was hitting promiscuous gays, junkies, and, for no discernible reason, Haitian immigrants. It was a sci-fi nightmare—a communicable cancer working its way up to epidemic proportions.

Out the window he could see Boston Harbor

sparkling in the sun, and a freighter making its way out into the Atlantic. He remembered the same sort of approach along the Delaware coming into Philadelphia. They had had eighteen dead Legionnaires by the time he arrived. Malaise, aches and pains, cough, diarrhea, and patches of lung congestion on the x-rays. They were calling it Broad Street pneumonia at the beginning, and the CDC had absolutely nothing to go on. They counted the number of pigeon feathers on the tops of air conditioners. They analyzed the dust on the ceilings of the elevators. They traced the source of ice cubes from room service and checked out the insecticides sprayed on the trees lining Broad Street. Two days after tissue samples from the autopsies and specimens of survivors' blood, urine, feces, and sputum had been flown back to Atlanta, infection from all known highly hazardous exotic agents was ruled out. Within three days they had written off all the more common viral and bacterial diseases, including influenza, and still they were stumped. Before the end of the month 153 people were sick and 29 were dead.

To Wharton it seemed they had been gliding down forever, but still there was nothing but water and sky outside the window. His palms were sweaty—it never failed, no matter how many thousands of miles he flew. "Put it *down*," he whispered to himself, and the pier with the lights flashed underneath, and then the sea wall where the Delta had flipped in '73. The big plane hovered interminably with the tarmac underneath it, and then it bumped, and bumped again, and they were on the runway at Logan.

*   *   *

Wharton spent more time in the Sumner Tunnel than he had spent in the air. By the time the cab broke out into the sunlight of downtown Boston, his head was tingling from the carbon monoxide. They rode up on the expressway briefly, then came down to cross the river into Cambridge.

He hoped this was a wild-goose chase. He derived no pleasure from the "big scoop," from uncovering the major disasters that could advance his career. But he especially did not want an outbreak under these circumstances. Scientists were supposed to conquer diseases, not create new ones. The potential of recombinant DNA was tremendous, even in his own work, and he wanted to keep the nightmare scenarios in the realm of pulp fiction. Still, if this was the real thing, better to be on the case now, at the beginning.

Wharton's perspicacity and diligence had made him the CDC's lead troubleshooter. In the Legionnaires' case, all the textbook truisms said that it was not a bacterial agent, but Wharton had pressed on with his hunch. Cultures from guinea pigs inoculated with postmortem lung tissue had not produced anything infectious. The pathologists were dismissing what bacteria they found as the run-of-the-mill contaminants that always turned up in tests for rickettsiae. But Wharton had not been convinced. He took tissue samples from the deep-frozen spleens of the guinea pigs instead of from the lungs. He thawed the tissues and injected them into eggs containing chick embryos. When the embryos died a week later, they were swarming with lethal bacteria.

13

IT WAS A QUARTER after six when Kitty stumbled out of her own bed and crawled into Mac's. Her feet were like ice as she scrambled under the covers, kicking him in the groin. "Hi, sugar," he mumbled. He raised one arm to bring the sheet and blanket over her and up to her chin, then wrapped it around her and drew her close. "Let's sleep."

"Get me some juice, Daddy."

"In just a bit, sugar. Go back to sleep."

Her eyes were immense. With small fingers clutching at the border of the blanket, she looked up at the ceiling innocently and whispered, "I want some juice."

He rose up on one elbow now, his stern face meeting hers, but it was no match. He was reminded of butterflies so fragile that they threaten each other with bright colors. "How do you feel, honey?"

"Juice please, Daddy."

"Okay." He threw back the covers and rolled over her. Then, seated on the edge of the bed, he turned on the lamp. He touched her temple, the side of her mouth. Her skin was dry. It felt rough. She did not look rested. Her eyes were watery, a cloud of moisture settling over the irises. So maybe she was getting a cold, he thought. Maybe that was it.

He worked his way into the kitchen, his feet slapping cold on the bare floors. At least the Albritons were gone. He had faced one crisis and put it behind him. And Kitty was not getting sick. He simply refused to allow that to happen. He came back to the bedroom with a cup of orange juice. He helped her sit up, then held the cup while she drank. "That better now? Hmmm?" She scooted back under the covers. "Good girl. Now. Let's please let Daddy sleep just a few minutes."

He rolled under the covers and closed his eyes. Just a few minutes of relaxation before he started in. That was all he wanted. He felt a tiny hand patting him on the shoulder. He tried to ignore it. Then he heard her say, "I love you." He rolled back toward her. "That's why I petted you."

"You're a sweet puppy," he said.

"Arf, arf." Then she was giggling and wiggling under the covers, and he gave in and started tickling her, kissing, holding her upside down, smiling at the same bright blue eyes he had first seen running toward him all those years ago at Fresh Pond.

14

Liz Altmann awoke with a start. She glanced around quickly, reassured that she was in her bed in Cambridge. The familiarity was comforting, for once, at least compared to the dream.

"What is it?" Kluer muttered. His voice was muffled by the pillow.

"Nothing. Nothing. Just a fright."

"Go back to sleep," he said.

But she glanced at the red digits on the radio. It was seven o'clock. She began to hear the faint chirping of birds.

She ran her hands down her belly where her nightgown clung, damp with sweat. Her fingers came to rest on the tiny scar just below her navel, the scar that Kluer had never bothered to notice, the result of the procedure they had never bothered to discuss. The first time they had made love, calmly, competently, she had merely whispered, "It's okay." Kluer had never

inquired further. An IUD, the pill, tubal ligation—
it appeared not to matter to him.

So little about their life together really mattered to him. She looked around the room now
in the morning half-light and measured the cost.
She was growing tired of the stark Scandinavian
oak, the metallic wallpaper. The bedroom had
been her one act of domestic rebellion against
the faded drapes and balustrades, the worn
Orientals, the chipped Wedgwood, the scratched
Chippendales. Everything heavy and stuffed and
dusty. Ute called it seedy posh—so right for
Kluer. Seedy posh even now where he lay, his
head as pink and bald as a baby's. He was sleeping in his shorts and a stained T-shirt that was
developing a fist-sized hole under the arm. For
all his awesome credentials, he could have been
lining up for a shower at the Salvation Army.
Where were the silk pajamas wealthy men were
supposed to sleep in? In the drawer, of course,
just where she had folded them. And where
were the lovers to envy the wealth, to defy the
great man in his own bedroom? . . . Her mind
was whirling like the plot of some bodice-ripping
novel. The T-shirt would not find its way back
again. She would throw it away before Doreen
had a chance to wash it.

She was growing perilously close to forty. Men
still responded to her as they always had. Perhaps they were even more aggressive about it
now. It was either the times or their assumption
that she was at some "dangerous age." She was.
She knew she was. And her husband's years
were even more dangerous. He was leaving
"middle age." He was becoming merely old.

Other men noticed it and sometimes wondered. Remarks had found their way back to her. At least she was still young enough, and attractive enough, to kindle thoughts of lusty wives and wheezing cuckolds. But that was slim consolation. Even the functionalism of simple sexual necessity had faded. He made excuses about his heart—the double by-pass—but they both knew that was sham. The problem was indifference, and it was becoming insulting. Before, she had felt put upon, used. But now, what conceivable right did he have—pale and paunchy, his white feet growing dry and brittle—what right did he have to be bored with her!

". . . and now the news for this Wednesday morning, October seventeenth, edited and reported by your 'Morning Pro Musica' host, Robert J. Lurtsema."

Kluer sat up, issuing an unnecessary "Shhhhhh."

"The battle over genetic engineering in Cambridge continues. Last night at a special meeting of the Cambridge Experimentation Review Board, former mayor Vincent Giacconi took the floor to announce the first outbreak of disease associated with the new biotechnology. Councilman Giacconi promised a full investigation, but declined to give further details at this point. At issue is whether or not commercial firms will be allowed to engage in the so-called recombinant DNA work within the city."

"That's not bad," Kluer said.

"But it's irresponsible! Leaving it like that— you'd think there was an epidemic."

"He's always vague with the news. I want to

see what the papers do with this. Try McKusick again."

She picked up the phone and dialed Peter's number. It was busy, just as it had been the night before. "Still off the hook," she said.

"If we can't reach him at least no one else can. I want him in my office before he says a word to anyone. So far this has only made Giacconi look foolish. But we have to be careful."

The phone began ringing in her lap. She yanked it up, but then handed the receiver over to Kluer. "For you," she said disappointedly.

She watched, nibbling at her thumb, while Kluer listened intently. Then he groaned.

"What is it?"

"Right. Right. We'll talk at the lab."

He hung up and turned toward his wife. "Those news people last night—they were from Channel Four, weren't they? That's NBC."

"I don't know. Why?"

"They just ran it on the 'Today' show. The world must not be producing enough news. Giacconi is back on the networks."

15

THEY CAME DOWN THE polished oak stairs together hand in hand, Mac waiting each time while Kitty hopped, repositioned herself on the next step, and then hopped again. It was three flights, a major expenditure of energy for anyone but a three-year-old.

He held open the glass door to the foyer, and Kitty hopped through. He had a knapsack slung over his shoulder and, in his free hand, a plastic string bag with Kitty's lunch and a change of clothes. He glanced up and saw the black lens of a television camera facing him through the outer door. How very peculiar, he was thinking.

"Let's get out of their way, sweetheart."

"Dr. McKusick!" somebody yelled.

The day was brisk and glaring, and McKusick was suddenly confused. He led Kitty through the second door and saw the cameraman, flanked by an audio technician, backing away.

"Who are they, Daddy?"

"Shoot the kid. Tight shot on the kid!"

The cameraman bent down to close in on Kitty.

"What is this?" Mac scooped Kitty up and held her against his shoulder. "What's going on?"

A heavily made-up woman in a blazer stuck a microphone in his face. "Dr. McKusick . . . what do you make of Councilman Giacconi's allegations? What's really wrong with Kathleen?"

The child began to cry. The camera crew was blocking the walkway. "What's wrong with you? Are you nuts or something?"

"Is it related to recombinant DNA or not?"

"What the hell are you talking about? I'm trying to get to work."

"Doctor, why don't you just set our minds at ease. Is the child sick or not?"

"My daughter is not sick! But right now you're scaring the hell out of her!"

"Why was she taken to the hospital, Doctor? What was the diagnosis?"

"This is too much . . . Really. Get out of my way." McKusick put his hand on the woman's shoulder to move her aside.

"Don't push, Doctor. No need to get hostile."

"I'm not hostile! I'm just trying to get to work! Get that thing out of my face, would you!" And he shoved the camera.

"No need to do that, Doctor."

McKusick edged past, and the cameraman panned with him, the electric eye absorbing everything that transpired. Mac held Kitty tightly and tried to console her. "There, there, babe."

"Why did they yell at us, Daddy?"

"It's okay, babe. It's all over."

McKusick continued down the broken sidewalk toward Chauncy Street. He glanced back and saw the technicians clustered around the reporter, filming her summation. He shook his head to clear it, then pulled out his handkerchief to dry Kitty's tears. I never should have come back, he was thinking. Never.

The leaves whirled in front of them and Kitty rested her head on his shoulder. They passed a light-blue Mercury parked at the curb. Inside the car, a man was leaning over making an intensive search of an empty glove compartment. It was Lee Albriton.

Albriton had not slept well the night before. Nina drifted off fairly soon, but after an hour or so he gave up, wrapped himself in a blanket, and moved over to the chair near the window. He pulled the drapes and stared out at the dark office buildings and the empty streets below. What possible reason was there for Peter to hide Kath's child from them? And what did this mean about her death? He and Nina had simply accepted the story of the accident at face value. What if there was more to it? Did she die in childbirth? But why would Peter conceal that from them? It was unspeakable. And then conceal a grandchild? Incomprehensible.

Albriton was up at five, too impatient to shave. He took a cab to the airport, rented a car, then drove it back to Cambridge. In Central Square he stopped for two containers of black coffee. Then, following along Mass. Avenue, he kept asking passers-by until he got plausible directions to Langdon Street. He was sitting at the curb, two empty Styrofoam cups at his feet, when the film crew arrived.

Albriton sat up behind the wheel and adjusted the mirror. His heart was pounding as he watched Mac and the little girl. She was tiny and blonde. He only caught a glimpse of her, but the image was like a memory of Kathleen. This was her child. It had to be.

When Mac and Kitty had rounded the corner at Chauncy, Albriton started the engine. He pulled up to the driveway just ahead and turned around. He came back to the same corner and only then realized that the street was one-way. He killed the engine, grabbed the keys, and stumbled out.

Mac and Kitty were a block ahead of him following the uneven bricks, walking in the shadows of tall trees and red-brick apartment buildings. He had to resist the impulse to race after them. He felt awkward and conspicuous stalking them like some sort of criminal. He was a large man in a strange town, in a very disordered state of mind. His agitation worried him. They stopped for an instant and he panicked. But Mac was simply stooping to let her down. That was all there was to it. Albriton knew he had to maintain control. Her steps were so small, springy. The bouncing of blonde hair. He wanted to be closer. To see her face. As he walked along he realized that all the conflicting and angry thoughts he had harbored for the last ten hours were fading. All he felt now was excitement—joy that this child existed. Kathleen's child.

Mac and Kitty reached Garden Street and

turned left. The moment Albriton lost sight of them he raced ahead to the corner. This was a wider and busier thoroughfare, and in the bright sunlight he felt less conspicuous. Up ahead Mac stopped at the curb and started looking back and forth, waiting for the moment to cross. Albriton slowed his pace but did nothing to avoid being seen. He was far enough away. There was a lull in the traffic, and Mac stepped off the curb. Albriton followed, but the street was wider where he was, one street crossing and two merging, and he ran to dodge a Volvo racing across from Concord Avenue.

They followed the curving border of Radcliffe Yard, then reached the gray wooden church looming over the burial ground across from the Common. Johnson Gate and the red and white colonial buildings of Harvard were just beyond. Mac turned in at the corner of the iron fence and disappeared from Albriton's view. Albriton hurried again, up to the church and the fence, and saw their destination—another gray wooden building behind the church, just beyond the deepest corner of the burial ground. It was like a cottage. He could see the bright colors of construction-paper decorations in the windows. Orange pumpkins. Yellow Indian corn. Peter would not be staying long. He might be coming out at any moment.

The vestibule of the church was unlocked, and Albriton stepped inside to watch and wait. Through the open door he could see mothers leading their toddlers along the path, mothers with lunch boxes for the children and briefcases for themselves. And then he saw Peter coming back down the walk. He was moving briskly, turning sideways against the iron fence to let a mother and her children pass. Then he reached the end of the path and turned right onto Garden Street, heading toward Harvard Yard. The sunlight hit the white spires and cupolas, and the brass weather vanes gleamed.

Albriton started down the path. He simply wanted a moment with the child. He wanted to see her; he wanted to be sure. He closed the gate behind him and went up the steps to the bright red door. He stepped inside and felt very much an intruder. To his left was a room lined with wooden cubbyholes in bright yellow, each holding a child's jacket on a peg, a child's lunch in a bag or lunch kit. A young woman was trying to coax a small boy out of a heavy pullover sweater, while her younger offspring napped in a collapsible stroller. Ahead of Albriton a door led out into the yard. He stepped toward it, looked to his right, and saw a larger room filled with wooden toys, a piano, an enormous doll house. And at a very low table sat two little girls in even lower chairs. They were working with a puzzle board, trying to fit variously colored pegs onto it. One of them was Kathleen McKusick. Her back was to him, her blonde hair in a ponytail reaching down to her frail shoulders. She was wearing a green turtleneck and red corduroy pants. Her feet, in sneakers, dangled even from this miniature chair. She was tiny. Amazingly small. Across the room, in the far corner that served as a kitchen, another young woman was mixing up bowls of paints for the children.

He pulled out one of the chairs across from her and sat down. Her doll's hands were busy with the pegs. She was working hard to fill the spaces of the puzzle. And as he watched her, fascinated, tears began to form in his eyes. This was his grandchild, there was no doubt in his mind. Her face was totally Kathleen's. Her eyes, her hair, the way the hairline itself framed her face with a distinctive widow's peak. How could he not know her? How had three years gone by with this child hidden from him?

"Hi, Kathy," he whispered.

She glanced up with her watery blue eyes. He was afraid she might shy away from him. He was a stranger to her. But she simply said "Hi," and went back to her work.

"How are you?" he whispered again.

Without looking up, she mumbled "Pretty good," but he did not believe it. He could see the same traces—the shadows beneath her eyes, the weathered-looking skin—that Mac had seen, but without Mac's impulse to deny it.

He heard footsteps, then a woman's voice. "Can I help you?" she insisted. Her tone was resolute—civil words with hostile intonation. She was young and pretty, in blue jeans and a sweater. Albriton knew how peculiar he must look, sitting in this tiny chair, staring at the child.

"This little girl is not well," he said.

Yvonne shook her head impatiently. "You're going to have to leave. You people really have a lot of gall."

"Oh . . . Oh, I'm not . . ."

"I was with her the whole time. The child

fainted, for Christ's sake, and we took her to the hospital as a precaution. This whole thing is totally trumped up."

"I'm not a reporter."

A reporter was harmless enough. A reporter would leave when asked.

"Well, it doesn't matter ... you're not supposed to be here."

"I'm her grandfather," Albriton said.

Her face lost all expression. She seemed dismayed.

"My name is Lee Albriton, and I'm her mother's father. I need your help."

"I, uh, don't know what you mean."

"Look at her."

Yvonne glanced down at Kitty, still busy with her pegs. She saw the watery eyes, the skin, the dark circles. She came around the table and put her hand on Kitty's forehead. The child did not feel warm. "She looks tired," Yvonne said. "She probably should have stayed home today. But ... I don't understand why you're here."

"What can you tell me about Kathy? About her father."

"I don't get it."

"What about her mother?"

Kitty got up and ran over to a shelf of dolls. She pulled one out and dropped it into a wooden cart.

"You mean your daughter ..."

"Peter McKusick returned to this area with this child alone, right?"

"Yes. As far I know. Now would you please—"

"I've never seen Kathy before. Mac's kept her away from us. He kept her a secret since she was born. Can you help me understand that? I never even knew she existed until last night when I heard about her on television. Do you know anything that would account for that?"

Her eyes widened. "Margaret! Margaret! Oh, God . . ." The other woman came rushing over. "Please bundle up the children and take them outside."

"Right now?"

"Right now."

Albriton stood up. "Young lady, please. I can tell that I'm frightening you. I'm not some lunatic. I'm just a little upset about what's happened."

"Please go," she said. "Honestly." She was begging now, not commanding.

Two little girls ran into the room. Then a young man appeared behind them in the doorway, holding two child-sized jackets. He said, "Can I help with anything, Yvonne?"

"Yes!" Her eyes lit up. "Yes you could." She smiled all too earnestly. "This gentleman heard about Kitty on television last night. He's discovered that she's his granddaughter."

"Ah." The young man dropped the jackets onto a chair and came over. "That's very interesting. Maybe I can help you."

Albriton heaved a sigh. "Listen, son . . ."

"No," he said with a smile, "I'm not your son." He winked at Yvonne. "I'm a policeman. And if someone has taken your granddaughter away from you, I'm the one to talk to. Why don't we let the children get on with playing, huh? I'll give you a lift."

Albriton sensed defeat. He lowered his head and stepped toward the door. "I'll be back to talk to you, miss. I need to see my grandchild."

"You need a rest, pal."

Yvonne called out, "Thanks, Mr. Giacconi."

He nodded. "Good we were late," he said. Then he added, "My wife'll pick 'em up at four."

Walking past the graveyard, Albriton tried to get his wits about him. That was the issue, wasn't it? This cop thought he was crazy, some deranged pensioner following the news for his long-lost child. Once the assumption was made, it was impossible to disprove. Especially when the facts as you knew them were just as crazy.

"So look. You got a wife or anything? Someone who looks after you?" He kept one hand loosely on Albriton's arm. "Let's give a call, what d'ya say?"

The morning was still breezy, but warmer now.

"Your name's Giacconi. Are you any relation to that man on the news? The councilman?"

"That's right, my friend. You're in good hands."

Albriton walked along without questioning. He was at a loss. They were nearing the end of the high iron fence. Maybe it was best. Better to be in police custody for something he did not do than for what he might.

"Does he know what he's talking about? Giacconi? Is it true that Kathleen is sick?"

"Hey. Not to worry. I'm sure your little granddaughter is fine."

Maybe there was an advantage to being a

mental case, some sort of harmless fool, Albriton thought.

They approached a plain green Ford sedan. "Lean against the car, Mr . . .. What's your name?"

Albriton was startled, but he did as he was told. "My name is Lee Albriton, and I think this has gone far enough." His heart was pounding. "I'm from out of town. I'm not some lunatic laying claim to children on TV." Giacconi's hands were patting up and down his body. "I had to talk to you, but what I have to say . . ." The steel flicked and snapped around his wrist.

"Stand up and bring your other arm down behind you."

"This is unbelievable!"

"I'm sure it is. You're under arrest. You have the right to remain silent, you have the right to an attorney . . . If you cannot afford an attorney, one will be appointed for you. Anything you say can and will be used against you. Just like on TV, huh?"

Giacconi opened the back door and helped Albriton into the seat. "Sorry about the cuffs, but it's a regulation, you know? Not too tight are they, pal?"

Albriton was fuming, but it was too late now for pithy explanations. He stared through the windshield up ahead and waited for Giacconi to come around. "Why are you doing this? What are you arresting me for?"

"Criminal trespass, if you wanna get technical. But it's for your own good, pal. Trust me. Now, you got a wife?"

"Yes, her name is Nina Albriton. She's in room 912 of the goddamn Parker House Hotel, and I am not crazy!"

"Parker House. That's a nice place, huh? You got good taste, Mr. Albriton. Good taste."

16

CHARLIE WHARTON WAS waiting in the secretary's office when Kluer came through the door, scowling like a wrathful god. Mrs. Nichols seemed appropriately intimidated. "This gentleman insisted on seeing you, Dr. Kluer. He doesn't have an appointment—"

Wharton was on his feet. "Charles Wharton, Dr. Kluer. From the CDC in Atlanta."

Kluer continued his pace, passing in front of the man and into his office without saying a word. Wharton glanced at the secretary, then lingered in the doorway. Kluer had already covered the considerable distance to his desk. He threw down the papers he was carrying and spun back around. "You now have a paratroop corps?"

Wharton smiled. "I was in New York," he said, stepping forward into the room. Kluer stared at him from the other border of a red and gold Oriental rug. "I came to see you because you're the head of the lab. We're not officially involved yet. I simply—"

"Dr. Warren—"

"Wharton."

"Do you have psychiatrists on your staff?"

"No. No we don't."

"I suggest you hire one and send him to Cambridge. There is a certain local politician you should be talking to. The only malady I'm aware of lies entirely within his head."

Wharton nodded. "May I sit down, Dr. Kluer?"

Kluer made a faint gesture to one of two wing chairs facing the couch.

"I realized that your man Giacconi's track record runs toward the sensational. As I said, we're not jumping to any conclusions. We simply don't want to be caught off guard."

"There seems little danger of that."

"Now the little girl. She's the child of one of your researchers?"

"She is."

"Has she actually been in the lab? Do you know?"

"Dr. Warren, her father is not even working with recombinants."

"But you have everything under the sun going on here. Has she spent any time in the building?"

"She has a cot. Her father, who is without a wife, brings the little girl here in the evenings as a matter of routine."

Wharton sucked his teeth and made a note on his pad.

Mrs. Nichols appeared in the doorway behind him. "Dr. Kluer, the president is on twenty-three."

Wharton raised his eyebrows and watched as Kluer made a nonchalant cross to his desk and the phone. He picked it up and said, "Hello, Tyson. How are you?"

Wharton relaxed. It was the president of Harvard.

Kluer's denials came as no surprise, and Wharton knew that Kluer was probably right. Still, men like Kluer were filled with the smug assurance that science was a lens of infinite resolving power. They had never felt, quite as he had, their pathetic vulnerability when confronting exotic infectious agents. For all that science had brought under control, there was so much more waiting to be discovered.

Trying to remain politely uninterested in the conversation on the line, Wharton stood and glanced out the window. Below him he saw what looked like a sandbox outlined by railroad ties. A tricycle lay overturned in the dirt beside a rusted swing and a kitchen stove. It looked like some redneck's front yard back in Georgia.

Kluer hung up the phone and began reading something on his desk. It was as if Wharton had ceased to exist.

"Dr. Kluer. Excuse me, but do children play out there?"

Kluer looked up at his visitor, glanced at the window, then back at his desk. "I have the privilege of overlooking the Harvard Yard Day-Care Center," he said.

Wharton was dismayed. He stood at the window now, pushing back the drapes to take in the whole scene. "Dr. Kluer . . . I don't get it. After all the flap about biohazards, what on earth is a day-care center doing next door to this laboratory?"

Kluer continued reading. "Space is at a premium, Dr. Warren. I believe their choice was either here or next door to the cyclotron. Which neighbor would *you* prefer?"

17

Nina Albriton was pale and trembling when she came into the station. But she was wearing her fur jacket, and the pearls he had given her, and the look of a dissatisfied patron at Neiman-Marcus. Albriton was ready to clasp her knees and kiss the hem of her garment.

"God, Lee, I knew you were going to get in trouble! What on earth . . ."

He stood up and hugged her. She smelled of powder and Estée Lauder. The mink was cold to his touch.

Albriton saw Giacconi looking at them from across the room. He was coming over now, dropping a folder onto a desk top as he passed. He looked slightly sheepish. "Hi," he said. 'I'm Detective Giacconi." One glance at Nina and he saw his case slipping away.

"I'm Nina Albriton, and why are you detaining my husband?"

"Why don't we step into my office, okay? You want some coffee?"

*   *   *

Nina sat rigid on the edge of the chair and Giacconi sulked behind his desk, peering over his clasped hands. He picked up a pencil. He tapped it against the blotter on his desk. "Why don't we, uh, take it from the top?"

"I think you're the one who needs—"

"Nina, honey." Albriton placed his hand on her arm. "Maybe I better explain." He gave Giacconi a tired look, still rubbing his wrists.

"Our daughter and Peter McKusick lived together. They went off to Colombia together."

"She was an anthropologist," Nina interjected.

Albriton went on. "We didn't hear too much from them. Then one night we got a phone call. It was McKusick sounding out of his mind. I had to piece it together that what he was telling us was that she was dead. He kept saying that it was his fault. He was torn up." Albriton sighed heavily. "They'd cremated her down there, and he flew back to Texas with her ashes. He spent a few days—it was like he was part of the family—and then he went back. He said he was going to complete some of the work they started together. And that was the last we heard from him for about four years.

"But what about the little girl?"

"That's the point. Apparently he came back with her a few months ago. A friend of Kathleen's passed word back that he had returned to Harvard. We had dinner with him last night! That's the incredible part. We spent all evening making small talk, and never once did he mention a child. You just don't keep secrets like that. Even if he had met another woman . . .

But I mean there's no doubt about it. This little Kathleen is our Kathy's." He turned to his wife. "You should see her, Nina. It's Kathy all over again. The same hair, the same eyes. Her little face is even the same."

Giacconi was drumming a manic beat with the pencil.

"And now this talk last night. Your uncle. We discover a granddaughter we never knew we had, and in the same breath they tell us she has some disease from all this gene-switching business."

"Look. You gotta understand my uncle. He's sort of a showman."

"I've seen her."

Giacconi laughed. "The whole thing is a bluff. He's desperate. That's just his style."

"The little girl is sick."

Giacconi grimaced and closed his eyes. "Mr. Albriton, my uncle is a hack politician. He gets in the limelight for fighting Harvard and for being outrageous. He's been after this stuff for years with no luck, and now . . ."

"Mr. Giacconi!" Nina leaned forward. She glanced at her husband and then back at the detective. It seemed so obvious to her. "The boy who cried wolf," she said. "There was finally a wolf."

18

WHEN MAC SAW LIZ'S face he knew things were grim. She was standing outside her office with a copy of the *Globe* in her hand.

"I saw it," he said. "I saw it."

She fell in step with him, heading down the corridor. "Do you *always* take your phone off the hook?"

"Force of habit. What is this? A court martial?" They were walking hurriedly toward Kluer's lab.

"Could be," she said. "They were packing up when I passed by. The reporters. What did you say to them?"

"Nothing. I didn't even know what they were talking about till I saw it in the paper."

"Bayard is very upset. We all are."

They breezed past a flustered Mrs. Nichols, into Kluer's inner sanctum. He was at the far end of the room, standing behind his desk. He dropped his glasses on the blotter, then gestured to the couch and chairs nearer the door.

Liz moved to the couch and sat down facing the fireplace. Mac lingered a moment, uncertainly, then followed suit.

"So what is this all about?" Kluer said bloodlessly. He lowered himself into one of the matching wing chairs.

Mac looked at Liz, but she sat motionless. He was exasperated. "You were there," he said.

"I mean with your child. What is the nature of her illness?"

"She isn't sick. The day-care center took her to the hospital because she fainted. The resident examined her and found nothing wrong. I don't know why he filed a report with the biohazards committee, but I guess he played it by the book."

"That's all?"

"That's all."

Kluer leaned back, crossed his arms, and stretched out his legs. He was silent. He was thinking. McKusick knew that these periods could go on indefinitely. Kluer did not subscribe to the usual social conventions. He made no effort to entertain employees, and Mac, like everyone else who worked with him, had learned simply to sit and wait. He looked at Liz, who was leaning forward with one elbow propped on her knee. She was watching her husband.

"A man from the CDC was already here. We've worked out a plan. I want Larry Rycliffs over at Children's to look at her this afternoon. For what it's worth, he currently heads the Pediatrics Society. That will look good in the story. We'll hold a press conference and we will call this fool's bluff. Then we can get back to work."

McKusick was burning. It was as if his daughter were a malfunctioning piece of equipment.

"My secretary will set up the appointment. I'm sure Larry will oblige."

McKusick nodded. For Kitty's sake he had to tolerate this man. He needed the lab, if only for a few more months. He knew he was getting agonizingly close to the answer.

Kluer called in his secretary and began instructing her. That was how an interview in his office came to an end. You simply left.

As he walked out of the outer doorway, Mac realized that Liz was behind him. He turned, and she placed her hand on his arm.

"Sorry about all this," she said.

He smiled. "I always wanted to be a famous scientist," he said, and started toward the stairs.

"Listen. I'm also sorry I was such a bitch the other day."

"We're all under a lot of pressure. You especially."

She jingled the key ring in her hand. "After this blows over, and it will, take a few days off. The rest of this is up to Bayard, really. The business side, and the university politics."

"Maybe."

"Get out of here. Take Kitty and relax a little."

"I can't. I'm behind on my own stuff."

"Surely a couple of days isn't going to matter."

He shrugged and said, "Maybe." Then he added, "I wouldn't even know where to go."

"Use our place," she said. There was something familiar in the tone. "At Woods Hole. It's quiet. It's on the water."

He looked at her carefully. He remembered this face. These eyes. From a long time ago.

"Getting better all the time," he said.

"We haven't really closed it up for the season. It's not quite L.A., but if you're lucky it'll still be warm enough to walk on the beaches. Kitty doesn't swim anyway, does she?"

"No, but she likes to splash. Thanks. Maybe I'll do that."

"Here." She began to remove a key from the set. "Take it now." She held it out to him. "There'll be no one else around to bother you. Believe me."

He took the key, smiled, and then turned away. She watched him as he walked slowly down the corridor, thinking how different it might have been back in L.A. if only she had seen the staff doctor first. It could have been over and done with and he never would have known. They would still be together, working together at Harvard, or UCLA, it didn't matter. But it had been the Friday before Labor Day, and the pulling pain would not stop. She remembered the uncertainty on the resident's face as he blurted out, "You're pregnant." Then, even before the shock could settle in, he'd added, "But don't worry, it's not normal." She could laugh about it now. He thought it was ectopic. Then the second apprentice came in and declared it a fibroid tumor. The diagnostic lab was closed already, and the little boys were playing guessing games with her life. She had felt bruised and abused, and she had expected Mac to share her outrage at their incompetence. Instead, he was oddly silent. He seemed awestruck. He had

no faith at all in their guesswork about complications. He had such a look of tenderness on
his face while she sat beside him feeling like
some high school girl who had been caught in
the act. "What are the odds," he'd asked, "that
you're simply pregnant?"

19

HE STOOD IN THE DOORWAY of the lab, his hands in the pockets of his windbreaker. He looked confused, out of place, like some tourist trying to find the Glass Flowers.

McKusick was working head-down at the laboratory bench. He was absorbed in the one problem that had filled his mind for years, and for the first time he felt as if it just might yield. Among the litter of spiral notebooks, chromosome maps, numbered bottles, and shallow plastic dishes, a pattern was beginning to emerge. But then the flask shaker humming behind him stopped. He looked up at the silent figure across the room. The one great incongruity in his life was staring him in the face.

"I went to the day-care center," Albriton said.

McKusick filled his lungs and breathed a sigh that carried the full weight of three years. Maybe if he just closed his eyes and waited long enough, Albriton would go away. But there would never be that much time. He placed the computer print-out gently on the counter and looked up again. The anger and bafflement in Albriton's face exhausted him. In three years he had been unable to come up with the explanation, and now it was time to speak.

McKusick put his hands in his pockets and walked over to the window. He looked down into the yard below, where the children were playing. It was so laughable. It all could have been so simple. Every day he listened to these kids. If one of them had been hurt he could have made it downstairs in less than a minute. But there had not been any vacancies at Harvard Yard, so Kitty had gone to Garden Nursery. And now, because of something so trivial, his whole world was coming unraveled.

"I saw her," Albriton went on. "She's Kathleen's child. There's no question about that."

He waited.

"Are you going to try to tell me something different? Are you going to say that she's not? Goddamn it, answer me!" Albriton reached for Mac's shoulder, but it was McKusick who spun around in a rage. He grabbed Albriton by the throat and rammed him backward into a wall of cups and funnels hanging from wooden pegs.

"Leave me alone! Leave me alone!" Mac was yelling. Albriton struggled for his footing and gripped McKusick's wrists. He was past his prime, but he was strong.

"You're meddling!" McKusick screamed, his face distorted with fury.

Albriton shifted his bulk and pushed, and the tug of war went back the other way, step by step, faster and faster until McKusick went crashing up and over a countertop, smashing through a wooden framework supporting glass tubing. He fell to the floor and lay stunned.

Albriton stalked around the counter and stood screaming. "You're crazy! You're a goddamn lunatic!" He shook his fists in frustration. "You came to our house! We took you in like family! And then you killed my daughter!" The big man's eyes were streaming with tears. "Why did you do this? Why?"

McKusick stumbled to his feet and sat on a stool.

"And little Kathy is sick. Anybody can see it." His teeth were clenched, his voice trembling.

"No." Mac shook his head. "She's not sick."

"She needs to see a doctor!"

"I am a doctor."

"Is that it? You arrogant . . ." Albriton grabbed McKusick again and they tumbled to the floor like a pair of brawling drunks.

"What the *hell* is going on in here!" It was Sandy, staring at them open-mouthed from the doorway.

Albriton glanced over his shoulder, then rolled to his knees. He looked at her as if she were a co-conspirator. "Who are you?" he said.

"You're asking me! I'm calling security, Mac."

Just then Watson came in behind her. "I already did," he said, then peered around her. "What the fuck . . ."

They all waited open-mouthed but silent. Albriton and McKusick were panting like Saint Bernards.

Mac said, "I think you better get out of here."

"Don't give me advice, you son of a bitch!"

"No! I'm going to give you some advice. Get back on your plane. Go back to Texas. It doesn't concern you. None of it has anything to do with you."

Albriton was standing, tucking in his shirt, pushing his hair back out of his face. "You're wrong there, boy," he said. He was still trying to catch his breath. "You're gonna find out just how wrong you are."

Albriton strode past the two stunned lab assistants and then out the door. McKusick stepped over to Kitty's portable bed and collapsed in a heap. Then he flipped back up. Kitty had left her stuffed donkey on the jelly-stained pillow. It was crawling with ants.

20

MICHAEL GIACCONI WAS scanning the sidewalks as
he drove toward Inman Square. He had his
police radio turned down to a murmur and was
listening instead to WHDH. In a flurry of
irrelevance, the governor had just issued his
civil-defense plans in case of nuclear attack.
Giacconi was relishing the details. When the big
one's on the way, everyone in Cambridge is
supposed to pile in the family car and head out
to Greenfield. Allston evacuates to Belfast; the
Back Bay up to Augusta; and so on. Terrific
plan, Giacconi was thinking. He could just see
the entire population of Cambridge making it
out Route 2 in fifteen minutes. That's what an
ICBM gives you, right? Fifteen minutes. He
wondered if there was some secret requirement
that people in positions of authority be idiots,
or if it just happened that way.

He parked in a loading zone in front of
DeVito's and cut the engine. His uncle was not

at home, and the only other place for him to be this time of day was at the restaurant. The traffic crawled past, loud and snarled. Too many people with not enough room, he was thinking. They could be living in Brockton for all it mattered to them. Cambridge was just another grubby little town, except for the eggheads making it a prime location for ground zero. Why do these guys have to be so damn smart? Draper Labs making bombs and missiles. MIT and Harvard with God knows what think tanks for the Defense Department. He could see Route 128 and then 495 farther out, like rings on a bull's eye, pinned to some wall in Moscow.

He stepped into the grease-specked dimness of the restaurant just as a strobe light flashed against the ceiling. A young man in a field jacket was squatting down in the center of the room, aiming one of his several Nikons at the booth where Vincent Giacconi was holding court. The councilor was surrounded by local guys in Knights of Columbus windbreakers who were hanging on his every word. A tape machine was on the table. On the other side of it sat a fey-looking man in a vested suit, bow tie, and New Balance running shoes. The *Globe*, Michael was saying to himself. His Honor is hot copy again.

Vincent scanned his audience, gesturing with his cigar as he retold the story. Michael waved his hand and ducked his head. Then he stepped back out into the daylight.

Diane had called shortly after the Albritons left the station. She was taking the kids out of school. The Garden Nursery mothers were all on the hot line talking about viruses, and she did not want to take any chances by exposing Nancy and Adele.

Michael's uncle emerged from the glass doors behind him, squinting in the sunlight. "Hey, what are you doing here?"

Michael turned. "Let's have a talk," he said, and stepped over to his car.

Vincent settled into the passenger seat and adjusted his weight. It was as if his paunch made it hard for him to fold in the middle.

"So what are you doing, Uncle Vincent?"

"You saw me on the news, huh?"

"Yeh. I did. You looked real good. You still got the stuff."

The older man puffed on his cigar, smiling.

"But what have you got? I mean really. Is it bullshit or what?"

"Hey! I don't go up in front of the public unless I have a—"

"TV camera. Come on, Unc. Don't shit me now. What gives?"

"So. Not much."

"That committee that reports on hospitals. I saw a copy of that. Pretty routine stuff."

"Look. It put those Swiss bastards on hold for a week. Maybe something else will come up next week. Who knows? I'm making a last-ditch effort here. I'm fighting 'em all alone. It's just me standing between the bigshots and all the little people they're trying to roll over."

Michael ran one finger along the cool plastic curve of the steering wheel, nodding his head, waiting until the barrage was over.

"You got Di scared shitless. And that kid's grandparents. They're up here on a visit from

Texas, you know. They're also a little worried about what you had to say."

"Well . . . Maybe they should be! Maybe I'm doing them a favor. Hey, I'd like to talk to them."

"Relax. You don't need to get them into your act."

"So how did . . ."

"They're nice people. They think this McKusick character may be a little weird. An unfit parent. They're talking about getting a lawyer."

"What'd you tell 'em?"

"I gave 'em a little advice. Told 'em to call Phil."

"Good. Good."

You know Uncle . . ."

"What?"

"It really surprises me. And I really hate to say it. But for once in your life, you may actually be on to something."

21

"NINA!"

Lee pounded on the door. There was no answer, so he fumbled for his key. A maid watched him surreptitiously from the other end of the long, carpeted hallway.

He knocked again as he opened the door.

"Nina?"

She had not returned. She was supposed to have come directly back to the hotel to wait for Marie's call. It had taken him more than an hour to pick up the rent-a-car and weave it back through Boston's narrow streets and kamikaze drivers.

He sat on the bed and reached for the phone. It was surrounded by cardboard placards— "Lunch at the Last Hurrah"; "Parkers—A Tradition of Elegant Dining"; "Instructions for Direct Dialing Overseas Calls." He knocked them all away and started placing his call to Houston.

"This is all a little hard to believe," was Jerry

Schoenbacher's first response. His mind had become more accustomed to the staid affairs of major corporations, the Byzantine but logical circuitry of antitrust. "And the child. How old?"

"Three, maybe. A little over."

"Born where?"

"Colombia. It'd have to be."

"But Kathy never actually married this fellow, did she?"

"No. Not unless they kept that a secret too. Which I doubt."

"Then his claim to the child is by no means absolute. But I wouldn't be the one to help you with this, Lee." Albriton waited. "But I'll tell you what. I'll call a friend of mine there at Frazier, Waterhouse. You need local contacts. Somebody who can mix it up down at the local courthouse."

"They recommended someone to me, Jerry. He's in Cambridge. Named Philip Pulchari."

"Well, I can check him out. I'll try to get back to you before lunch, okay?"

Albriton got up and stood at the window. Where was Nina? Maybe she was meeting Marie after all? Maybe they were having lunch downstairs. He looked down at the people walking briskly in the sunshine nine floors below. It was the same kind of day when Charles Whitman took his lunch and a steamer trunk up to the top of the library tower in Austin. It could be a pleasant way to spend an afternoon, he thought. Puffy clouds and blue sky. A highly accurate scope. He could well imagine lining up the cross hairs on the necks of those people so distracted and so far away. Simple decency demanded such control these days that psychopaths seemed to be the only ones not suffering heart attacks from suppressed rage. Whitman's answer had been provided by a six-ounce tumor pressing in on his brain. Albriton wondered what his would be.

He was not hungry, but he needed something to do. He called room service and ordered a hamburger and a pot of coffee. He did not like his train of thought. He needed to be back home where he could swing an ax into a log, or blast clay pigeons with a shotgun.

His food came and he ate a bit, but it was the wrong thing to do. His stomach began to boil. His throat burned with indigestion. They had brought it on a little cart, with a rose and a white tablecloth. They could have served it in wax paper soaked in grease, for all it mattered.

The phone rang and he picked up the receiver. It was Schoenbacher, prompt and circumspect as always.

"Uh, Lee . . . I don't know what to say. If you give me some more time maybe I can come up with a suggestion of my own. But I don't know that I'd want to get involved with this Pulchari. He's very well connected politically, so he's moderately effective. But he's a real ambulance chaser. Been damn close to an indictment more than once. I believe the phrase they used was 'ethics of a snake.' "

Lee Albriton was silent, conjuring the image of a snake following an ambulance.

"So let me keep at it, okay? As soon as Fred

gets back to me I'll call you. Okay, Lee?" There was still silence. "Lee?"

"Fine, Jerry. Thanks a million."

Albriton stood at the window once more. He needed to settle down, to think about Dean and Marie. He was not the only man in the world to have ever lost a child. He still had two fine youngsters, and he was proud of them. They would survive, and they would marry, and they would have children. The rest of the story would be played out as he and Nina had always thought it would. Except for Kathleen.

The phone began to ring again, and again he picked it up.

"Lee! Where have you been?" It was Nina. She sounded frantic.

"Well, where are you? You were supposed to come back here."

"I went to the center to see her, Lee. I couldn't help it."

"Did you? Did you get to see her?"

"No. And I went by the apartment, too. And Lee, I'm so upset. They were very rude to me. They treated me like . . ."

"What about the apartment? Why couldn't you see her?"

"Because of Peter. He came and he picked her up, Lee. Before I got there. And now he's gone. He's taken Kitty. He's left town."

22

PHIL PULCHARI'S OFFICE was on the first floor of a large Victorian house off Prospect Street near Central Square. It had been covered with siding of some unnatural substance painted royal blue. The porch on the ground floor was enclosed with glass and aluminum, and a series of bronze plaques listed three law firms and a real estate office. The Albritons climbed the steps uncertainly in the clear light of an autumn late afternoon.

Pulchari was concerned with real property and the real world—condominium conversions, tax abatements, bad marriages, bad drivers. His law degree was from the night school at Suffolk University, but for his particular calling his credentials were impeccable—three generations in Cambridge, and some form of kinship to virtually every person in a position of power in Middlesex County.

In the foyer, heavy gilt mirrors hung on opposite sides of a chandelier. The light dispelled the medieval gloom of wood paneling coated with a dark, syrupy stain. As the Albritons stepped inside, a man stood waiting by a pair of French doors. His tie was loosened and his vest undone. He was holding a clear plastic bag containing live fish in about a quart of water.

"Albriton?" he said.

"That's right."

Lee let the outer door close behind him.

"Incredible deductive powers, huh? I'm Phil Pulchari. Come have a seat."

Pulchari slid back one of the glass-paneled doors to let them pass through. Behind the stairway to their left, a secretary was putting the dust cover over her typewriter.

The only light in Pulchari's office came from a green-shaded floor lamp and from the aquamarine glow of a hundred-gallon fish tank. Pulchari gestured to a black leather couch, and the Albritons sat down. They faced an immense roll-top desk. Above it, somewhat incongruously, hung a teal-blue swordfish that spanned the office from wall to wall.

Pulchari walked over to his aquarium. "The boys are hungry," he said. "Hope you don't mind."

Inside this Olympic-size container, two immense pacu hung in languid suspension. Pulchari lifted the lid and began dropping in handfuls of the sparkling feeder fish. "Now what can I do for you?" he began.

Lee Albriton glanced at his wife. She was watching, not quite believing, as the lifeless mouths of the pacu slurped in goldfish after goldfish. They simply disappeared.

"Big fish eat little fish," Pulchari said. "Sort of an inspiration to me." He dropped in another handful and then closed the lid. Still holding the slightly deflated bag, he sat down in a black Franklin chair with the Harvard Veritas in gold seal on the back.

"You have a problem and you come to me as your hired gun. You're from Texas, right? The Wild West? You know about gunfighters."

Nina could not take her eyes off the huge, inert fish dumbly munching their live meal. A bloody head drifted down and settled on the bottom.

"I serve my client," Pulchari went on. "I get him what he wants, but I expect him to leave the details to me. Okay?"

There was only one feeder fish left. It was holding very still in the narrow strait between a decorative rock and the glass wall of the aquarium.

"So just tell me what you want."

Nina looked up. Her eyes drifted over to Lee.

"We want our granddaughter," he said.

23

THE HOUSE OVERLOOKED Nobska Point Beach. It was just below the lighthouse, set back from the water and the road by two hundred yards of salt marsh. When the fog lifted, the living room window offered a view of blue ocean and, farther off, the sandy hills of Martha's Vineyard.

When Mac pulled up in front of the house Kitty was asleep in her car seat. He left her there while he ran up to test the key Liz had given him. The door swung open into the musty stillness. The place had not been used since Labor Day.

He walked back to the car to get his daughter. The sea breeze, tempered by the Gulf Stream, was surprisingly warm. He went to the trunk and lifted out the one large suitcase he had packed for both of them, and then the duffel bag full of books and toys. This had been a difficult trip to pack for. He had no idea how long they would be staying.

He tried to close the lid gently, but, even so, the noise was enough to wake Kitty and start her fussing to be freed from her straps and buckles. He set down the bags and lifted her out. She was cranky, still yawning, and he carried her on his left shoulder, clutching both bags in his free hand.

Her eyes peeked over. "What is that?" she said.

"The ocean, honey."

They went up the walk and into the house.

There were clean sheets on the beds. The kitchen was stocked with dishes and cookware. One trip to the store would probably hold them. If Kitty would do her part they could eat most meals out. Mac was mentally cataloguing the larder when Kitty came running in from the living room.

"Daddy, Daddy! Come look. Come look."

"What's up, sugar?"

She took his hand and led him around the corner into the living room, pointing excitedly to the brick fireplace dominating one wall.

"Santa Claus!" she said. She had never seen a fireplace before.

"Santa usually comes only at Christmastime, but who knows? We'll build a fire in there tonight. Maybe we'll pop some corn. How's that?"

If they were going to go out at all it would have to be soon, before the afternoon wore on and the temperature began to drop. Mac dug out their sweaters, bundled Kitty, applied a thin layer of vaseline to her face and hands. It was just dry skin. That's all it was. He piled her up on top of his shoulders for the walk to the beach.

"I have Princess Leia," she said.

"Good, honey. She'll like the beach."

"I have her safe in my pocket."

"Great."

They followed the dirt road bordering the marsh. Some gulls circled over the still surface, then glided in for a landing. The smell of the ocean was getting stronger, the sound of the waves louder. There were half a dozen sailboats on the stretch of ocean that separated them from the Vineyard. Off to the right Mac spotted the car ferry chugging around the point from Woods Hole Harbor, heading toward the island. Occasionally a car would pass on the blacktop road behind them. But the beach itself was all theirs. It was a narrow strip of sand—not resort stuff—but off to the left the waves crashed onto the rocks below the lighthouse just as they did in every post-card picture of New England. He let Kitty take off on her own, scooping up sand and running down to the water's edge to scatter it into the wind.

He should have stayed in Colombia, he was thinking. He remembered her naked, brown as a berry, padding along in the mud and now and then giving it a taste. She squealed like mad while he probed her gums, soft and nearly toothless, to clean out the grainy mess. It could have all worked out there. They could have stayed forever, with no one to question anything. But now the Albritons were never going to give up, and he was never going to be able to explain it to them. Certainly not now, not in the middle of the circus the politicians were creating. He was not sure what he was going to do. He needed time to think.

"I want to swim, Daddy."

McKusick stuck his fingers in the water. It was probably no colder now than it was in June. "Okay, doll." He sat her down on his knee and stripped off her shoes and her corduroys. "Just up to your ankles, honey." She scampered off in her sweater with no pants, Princess Leia in her hand.

If she was coming down with something, she would come down with it anyway. The cloudy eyes had gotten no worse. There was no cough. At least she cold enjoy her afternoon. He watched her splash, and smiled as she screamed with glee. He did not like her in shoes and jackets, being penned up all day in the nursery school. It had been better in Colombia, with Kathleen's orchid-filled jungle as a playground.

He watched her now, stooping over to let the Princess swim. The surf was gentle, sweeping in over her feet, then gliding back out again.

Kitty stood up and, for a moment, looked around her in the wet sand. She seemed calm, thoughtful. Then in an instant she was shrieking in agony. Her face was contorted in grief and covered with tears. It was too late. McKusick could have prevented it, but now it was too late.

"Leia! Leia!" she was screaming. She looked up at her father, her body reeling under her loss. Mac felt sick. He ran over to her and tried to pick her up. She pushed his hands away. "Leia's lost and I'll never find her. She's lost, Daddy, and she's my very favorite!" McKusick stumbled a bit in the sand, thrusting his hand down toward a bump exposed by the retreating surf. It was just a shell. He waded out a few feet, soaking his shoes and pants legs, scanning the bottom for any sign of the doll.

Kitty was unconsolable. She was red in the face, crying herself sick. She fell down on her knees and put her head on the sand. Mac came over and picked her up. She was limp. There was nothing he could offer. He could not say that they would find her. He could stay up all night, he could strain a million gallons of water and a thousand tons of sand, but the ocean had him outclassed.

"Maybe we'll find her tomorrow, honey."

"No we won't. She'll never come back."

"Okay, honey. Okay. I guess she just wanted to go for a swim. She wanted to explore the ocean."

"Why?" There was fury in her voice.

"To see what's there. To meet the fish."

She began to sob again, worse than before. "What if a big fish comes and eats her!"

"We'll get another Leia, honey. We'll go to a store here and they'll have another Leia for you."

"No. She won't be the same. She just won't."

The wind was becoming raw, now, picking up grains of sand to add to the bite. Mac began trudging back across the beach.

They made it to the house, and Mac wished he could simply batten the hatches and hide for the night. But they had nothing for dinner or for breakfast. He shook the sand out of their shoes and coerced Kitty back into the car. In a moment they were whizzing down the beach road, up and over the hill on which the lighthouse stood, toward the A&P in Falmouth.

It was a difficult trip. Kitty was weepy and mopey, and burst into tears at the slightest provocation. She was sad, but she was also unusually tired. The circles under her eyes had deepened and become darker.

When they returned and had the groceries put away, Mac set about building a fire. "You want to help me gather some sticks?"

"Okay," she said. But the enthusiasm he had expected was not there. She followed him out onto the rear deck where he collected an armload of split logs. Kitty found some twigs and some leaves, and came in with two handfuls of kindling. She squatted beside her father and watched as he arranged the wood with her contribution at the center of the pile.

When he was satisfied that this was really going to be a fire, he closed the glass doors over it. Kitty was sitting back now. "You guard the fire while I cook us some dinner, okay?" A few minutes later he looked up from the stove to see her curled up on the hooked rug, sound asleep.

McKusick brought his plate into the living room and sat on the couch near Kitty. There was an afghan, and he placed it over her. The scallops, broiled in butter, were fresh and good, but he could always make more for her if she woke soon. He decided to let her rest. She looked so lovely lying there. He thought of Kathleen, of nights alone by a fire. And he thought how odd it was to be here with the memory of Kathleen in a house that belonged to Liz.

After dinner he carried Kitty into the guest room and tucked her in properly, lifting and maneuvering each pliable limb to get her out of her clothes and into her pajamas. She was sleeping soundly, clearly down for the count.

He lay on his back in Liz's big double bed and tried to sleep. He had probably downed one beer too many, and felt more uncomfortable than drowsy. He hoped Kitty would sleep through the night. He hoped they both would get a good night's sleep. They needed it. Tomorrow Kitty would awaken and be as good as new. The vague dread that was growing in his consciousness would be removed. And as for himself, he would awaken with a plan. A miraculous plan that would dissolve this horror that had crept out of some bad night and into his waking hours.

He got up once and padded through the strange house, moonlight guiding him here and there, and found her in her bed. He sat beside her and listened to her breathing. It was the most comforting sound in the world. He remembered his anxieties when she was first born, how he would go into the nursery and place his ear near her mouth, just to hear that sound. Just to reassure himself that she was okay. She was older now, he was a more experienced father, but that need for reassurance had not lessened.

He went back to bed, but still he could not sleep. His mind kept running down the list of anxieties. He tried to break the cycle by choosing an image to focus on. He tried to visualize the beach, remembering the waves and the sunlight, the endless repetitions, but his mind drifted back.

They had been on the ocean then, too, the weekend he and Liz sailed to Catalina. A dangerous electricity had surrounded them, a surface charge that made them afraid of touching each other.

He remembered a sky turquoise and pink in the west, gradually darkening behind them toward the same deep blue as the calm water they were riding on. They turned on the running lights, and in the twilight they could see the island rising up ahead of them and other sails converging toward its harbor.

"What if it turns out to be normal?" Mac said. His words seemed to trail off into the breeze. It was dark, and they had dropped anchor off Avalon. They had grilled a couple of steaks and were sitting out on deck with the lights of the town shimmering across the water.

"No point worrying about that. They were pretty insistent on the abnormal."

They could hear bits of distant conversation drifting over from other boats. He watched the lights of a small plane pass overhead.

"We've never talked about it. I don't think we ever believed it could happen. Some kind of immunity we might build up by knowing too much about the mechanisms involved."

"No such luck," she said, and got up to go below.

That night they were rocked by the gentle motion of the boat, both very much aware of the presence of the third party—the one growing inside Liz's body. He assumed that the diag-

nosis would be 80 or 90 percent accurate. The
talk of an ectopic pregnancy or of a fibroid
tumor seemed to him reckless speculation.
Chances were, then, that the embryo they had
detected was properly attached to the uterine
wall, was dividing and growing at a normal rate,
and would become some kind of human being
for them to contend with. He was surprised to
find that he did not feel threatened by the
prospect. There was no sense of an encroachment on his freedom, no worry about financial
strain. He was simply stunned and fascinated.
He wanted to find out who this person was in
there.

He turned toward Liz and whispered her
name. She must have heard him, but there was
no response. In the dim light of the cabin he
could see her lying on her back, her eyes open,
staring blankly at the ceiling.

It was a weekend spent in limbo. Two people
in a confined space with the same preoccupation,
but with divergent points of view. They took
turns at the helm, sailing through the Santa
Barbara Channel, but somehow Liz spent more
and more time sunning herself on the deck.
Their relationship had suddenly turned brittle,
and he wondered if the softness would return.

On Tuesday Liz saw the attending physician.
He was sure, but he ordered an ultrasound to
confirm it.

At noon she came back to the lab with a
three-by-five Polaroid image of her abdomen.
Clinging to the upper margin of her uterus was
the incontrovertible evidence, a perfectly placed
amniotic sac in the shape of a lima bean.

A note directed her to the courtyard cafeteria where Mac had gone to lunch. She appeared at his table looking lost, the Polaroid print in her fist like a useless set of directions. She sat down before he could suggest it, her dazed look spreading quickly to him across the table. He waited. The questions were too obvious to need asking.

"Pregnant," she said.

He still waited, reminding himself to swallow.

"End of story. Normal pregnancy. No complications."

He breathed out and then in. He wanted to smile, but he held it in check. Her reaction was so muted, so neutral. Some confusion was understandable. Wanted or not, deliberate or not, a pregnancy was never trivial. But the smile he wanted to share did not come. Her face remained grim.

"You want something to eat?"

She shook her head.

It was her body, her career, her decision. He knew that. Marriage gives the male some right to an opinion. The premeditated impregnation, contractual, socially acceptable. This one was an accident. His equity was slight—a milliliter of seminal fluid, twenty-three chromosomes carried on one championship spermatozoon who beat the odds. It was her decision, but it was *their* child.

"So what happens now?"

"I go in on Thursday."

"For what?"

"What do you think!" Her eyes were glistening with tears.

"You could keep it."

"Stop it! I do not want to discuss it!"

"I think it involves me."

"Since when did you get so interested in fatherhood?"

"So what? It's happened now. It was never an issue before. We never thought about it. That's all I want you to do. To think about it."

"Gimme a break. *You* think about it! It's my life that's gonna get fucked up, not yours!"

"I admit the timing is not great. But if it comes to that, I can drop out for a while."

"Oh, Jesus. Don't be ridiculous."

"Why is it ridiculous? People are doing things like that. We could put a crib in the lab. It could be . . ."

"I cannot believe you are being so asinine!"

"I can't believe you're reacting so emotionally. It's just fear. That's all I see."

"Oh, fuck off."

"It's life. You don't suddenly have to start baking cookies. We're not suddenly going to move to Glendale. We do what we do, and it tags along."

She stood up. "I can't deal with this." Her hands were up to her face, waving him away. Then she turned and ran across the courtyard.

Mac picked up the small black and white image she had left propped on the ashtray. It was the only picture he would ever have of their child.

It was light outside. McKusick looked at his watch. It was 8:15. For a moment the whole world was peaceful—the luxury of sleeping late. He lay back down and watched the ceiling as the sunlight radiated through the sliding glass doors. It was odd that he had not heard a peep out of Kitty. He threw back the covers and walked into her room.

She was lying with her face to the wall, her arms stretched out as if in the arch of a swan dive, breathing softly. She had kicked the blanket off on the floor, so he sat down on the edge of the bed and drew the sheet up over her shoulders and patted her tiny rump. He stroked her head, and a glistening mat of hair came off in his hand. He stared at it, then gazed down at her hand lying on the pillow. Her veins were sallow and protruding. There were liver spots on her skin.

"Kit-ty!"

He grabbed her shoulders and flipped her over. Her face was pallid, loose and wrinkled. Discolored pouches hung below her eyes. He shook her violently and her lashes flickered and he saw a dull glimmer of white deep within the blue of her eyes. "Honey ... Honey ..." He put his face close to hers and was overwhelmed by the stench of her breath. "God! God! What is wrong with you!"

Kathleen, 1976

24

HE WAS JOGGING ALONG with his head thrown back, trying very hard not to think about anything. It was a Thursday morning, early, and Peter Mc-Kusick appeared to have the path around Fresh Pond to himself. He watched the sunlight filtering through the overhanging trees. He was absorbing the luminous lime greens, the rich kelly greens, the dark forest greens, hoping the oxygen from all this photosynthesis would some-how clear his head.

Halfway around the pond, in the deep shade just beyond the golf course, he saw a woman running toward him, her strawberry blonde hair blown back by the wind. She wore a sleeveless T-shirt clinging to her chest; the split sides of her nylon running shorts flapped open to show the perfect contour of a firm, bronzed thigh. He stared as he turned to watch her go by, but her eyes remained fixed on some uncertain point in the path ahead.

He stumbled on his next step but kept running. The trees thinned and he passed an open field with a pile of large rocks and gravel, then came out alongside Fresh Pond Parkway with its jumble of gas stations. This was the kind of emotional counterpunch he really did not need at the moment. He was trying to run out his frustrations, not add to them, he reminded himself.

Like several thousand other people, he had just arrived in Boston, but his coming had nothing to do with tall ships and bicentennial celebrations. He was not even aware of the great bash along the Charles—Arthur Fiedler and a barge full of fireworks, with cannons and church bells ringing out the finale to the *1812 Overture*. Peter McKusick had come east to begin what he expected to be the most intensive period of work in his life.

It had been a year since the breakup with Liz. She had spent the time jetting back and forth to arrange for the transfer of their lab to Harvard. They were going to be working with the Nobel laureate Bayard Kluer on the creation of mammalian chimeras—living organisms containing the genetic programming of two different species. It was a fantastic opportunity. It would have to be, considering the price he was paying for it.

If the break had been clean, he might have been over it by now. But they had each invested far too much in the other to simply walk away. He had followed Liz from medicine into basic research. She said an M.D. alone would never carry him very far, and he had dropped his residency program to work with her toward a

Ph.D. And now he had totally uprooted his life to follow her to Harvard. Like cell lines or favored pieces of equipment, graduate students moved with the lab.

The trail dipped back into the woods along Huron Avenue, and a hundred yards away, coming at him with a perfect, graceful stride, was this blonde again, running at a pace that was much faster than his. She had eaten up far more than her half of the distance from where they had passed each other before. She seemed to be traveling in a private world, riding on her own endorphins. Her face was serene, oblivious even to her own exertion, except for the red flush on her cheeks, the tiny beads of perspiration on her upper lip. But this time as she passed she fixed him with a firm, dispassionate stare. It was absolutely neutral, but it was definite eye contact.

He had to assume that she would be coming to a stop around the bend at the parking lot, but he could not just turn around and head after her—she would think he was nuts, some rapist in running shorts. He had to complete his lap to make it look casual. So how fast could he do two miles?

Gradually, he began widening his stride. He pumped a little harder with his arms, and now each huge stride came more quickly. He sped through the grove by the water intakes, around past the golf course, and into the heavily wooded stretch where he had seen her first. He knew full well that this was absurd. He was probably going to kill himself just to see her driving off in a BMW with her husband and her dog, but he kept pumping. His lungs ached and his legs felt as if they were going to cramp. He was not in shape for this. He rounded a turn and cleared the thick overhang of bushes, straining for all he was worth, and then he saw her smile. It was modest at first, but as they raced toward one another, Mac locked into frantic pursuit, it grew wider and wider until, twenty feet away, she broke out in laughter. He could not stop. He ran right past her, laughing at himself, and finally broke his stride. He circled back, stumbling on wobbly legs, but she was still running, glancing over her shoulder with a curious grin.

"Hey! Come back here!" he yelled. "Please!"

She kept going, and he took a few steps, shaking his head. How could she do this to him? He tried to resume his pace, but he found himself limping along on tightened muscles.

25

THERE WAS STILL LIGHT in the midsummer sky as McKusick stepped through the granite portals and began climbing the creaking wooden stairs. The first floor was deserted, making the vaulted ceilings and pseudo-Gothic grandeur seem all the more out of proportion to anything that might ever go on there.

He stepped through a wood-framed doorway that was twice his height and looked into the council chamber itself. A perfect cube, the room had red and gold wallpaper covering even the ceiling. It was like a hatbox, gift wrapped on the inside. He pushed down on one of the red, plush theater seats and took his place. He was an hour early.

A television crew with minicams and floodlights was making small talk on the floor, while one council member relaxed with the newspaper in his high-backed swivel chair. Mac watched as the people of Cambridge drifted in through the doorway and settled into the gallery seats. About the only person he would be likely to know here was Liz, and he was thinking this might be a chance to talk. She had been acting strangely ever since he arrived. He tried to live with the fact that their relationship was strictly professional now. But on his first day at the new lab, she had acted as if she could not quite remember who he was or why he had come. That might have been a fairly clear signal, he supposed, except for past history. She had been just as distant in California at the beginning, right up to the very moment she planted that first, unequivocal kiss on his mouth. The door closing behind the last of the guests, the porch light going off, and then her walking calmly toward him while his blood pressure skyrocketed.

But even that weekend had not made any immediate difference. They spent fifty-six hours together, fifty of them in bed. They made love like teen-agers in a parked car. They made it tenderly and slowly, experimenting, exploring, drawing it out for languorous hours in her room. That Monday his testicles were throbbing and his inguinal muscles were aching all the way through his morning classes. But then he stopped by to see her in the lab that afternoon. He leaned his head through the door of her office only to face the puckered polyester backside of a man leaning over a stack of papers on her desk. They were wrangling over a grant application. She looked up from around her colleague without so much as a glimmer of light in her eyes and snapped, "May I help you?" The irritation in her voice sounded entirely genuine.

*   *   *

Liz stepped through the doorway looking very businesslike in a light-blue suit. And just behind her was Bayard Kluer, his bald head shining pink above a turtleneck and corduroy jacket. She and Kluer were very thick these days. The two of them huddled like conspirators just inside the door, their heads tilted toward each other. Kluer was speaking as if he were laying out the plan of attack, and Liz nodded seriously. Then Kluer began to drift toward the front of the room, and Liz turned to gaze up toward the gallery. She scanned the rows of seats, now nearly filled, and Mac waited. He lifted his hand, but only a little, and finally he caught her eye. She raised one brow and made a half-hearted wave of three fingers, but she completed her survey of the room. He wondered exactly what it was she was looking for, or pretending to look for. His neck burned with irritation. When she finally started toward him and the quite obviously empty seats on either side, he was tempted to tell her they were taken.

She sat down, brushed her skirt, looked around the room, then shook her head. "This is such a waste of time," she muttered.

It was a hot night without air conditioning, and the place was filling up. By 8:00 P.M. students in blue jeans were sitting cross-legged on every available inch of floor, spectators huddled in the doorway, and loudspeakers were carrying the proceedings to the crowd overflowing back onto the lawn. The first order of business, as ordered by the mayor, was a Cambridge high school choir, fifty adolescents in silver robes singing "This Land Is Your Land." From the lawn outside another chorus rose up—Science for the People singing "We Shall Not Be Cloned." The arc lamps of the television crews brought the air temperature inside to well over 100 degrees.

As the crowd fanned themselves like the faithful under a revival tent, Vincent R. Giacconi rose to the occasion. He brandished his copy of the *Phoenix*, shouting into his microphone, "Why does the mayor of Cambridge have to read an underground newspaper to find out what's going on at Harvard?" Then he launched his standard speech about all the property Harvard had tied up exempt from city taxes. He talked about "Frankenstein monsters" and "guys in white coats." Then with himself firmly established as the injured party, he called his first witness.

Lionel Bainbridge was a theologian, but he was married to a biologist. He came forward in a black turtleneck, a gold peace medallion dangling on his chest, his white hair fluffed like cotton at the back of his head. "These men are recklessly tampering with the core of our existence," he began in his priestly cadence. He was an old hand at righteous indignation. He had been a principal in the Movement, from civil rights to antiwar to ERA to antinuke. "The genetic code, written in the language of DNA, has been transmitted within species for three and a half billion years. It is the central mystery of evolution. It is not a message to be taken lightly. To violate natural law by mixing the genes of higher and lower organisms is presumptuous in the extreme! It is a sacrilege!"

The scientists in the room squirmed restlessly as "Bishop" Bainbridge reviewed the whole tale of recombinant DNA hysteria: how the scientists themselves, alarmed by certain of their colleagues' research plans, had prompted a fiery debate, a series of international conferences, and a self-imposed moratorium until federal guidelines could be drawn up. Harvard's plans to build a new maximum-containment facility for recombinant DNA had fired the same sort of debate within the Bio Labs. A number of highly respected scientists had insisted that their own labs be moved out of the building if the P4 facility was put in operation. In Bainbridge's telling of it, half the faculty were interested only in saving their skins, while the other half were madmen cooking up deranged combinations of life—tumor viruses spliced into *E. coli.*

By the time the old man stepped down, he had cast a spell over the entire audience. The issues involved were abstruse and highly technical, but the emotions were all right on the surface. It would take a master of patience and diplomacy to counter the spell, to explain the basis of the controversy and the true nature of the work, to ease the fears of the people in this room. Instead, the scientists at Harvard had as their spokesman Bayard Kluer.

Liz smiled faintly and nodded with assurance as he made his way toward the microphone. "Bayard will put him in his place," she muttered. Then, as a follow-up, she glanced at McKusick. "Just watch," she said.

Mac looked at her elegant profile, then glanced down to the gap between the buttons of her blouse, remembering the softness that was so well hidden now. He had never understood her eagerness to ingratiate herself with Kluer so completely. Sure, Mac valued the chance to work at Harvard, but he supposed he would have survived without it.

Kluer was chairman of both the Department of Molecular Biology and the Harvard Biohazards Committee. He was the only person in the room who could completely answer the question Giacconi insisted on asking again: "Why did no one see fit to inform the Cambridge City Council of the health-safety question being raised at Harvard in the last six months?"

Kluer cleared his throat behind his fist and then, with an air of indulgence, began. "First of all, I should like to call the attention of the Council to the various efforts that were made to inform the public, if the public chose to be informed. The following advertisement appeared in the *Boston Globe* as well as the *Herald American*. And I quote: 'Public Meeting. On Harvard University's intention to resubmit for federal assistance to renovate space within the Biological Laboratories for research on animal cells, tumors, viruses, and plasmids. Such a meeting—' "

Giacconi cut in. "Doctor, excuse me, but let me give you a little advice in case you ever wanna get into politics. Get somebody else to write your ads. That one's a real stinker, and it's a phony, too. A legal notice required by the EPA is not what I would call outreach. If you'll forgive my saying so, I think you insult the people of this city by trying to pass this off on them."

Giacconi leaned back and made an elaborate business of tucking in his shirt front. He was feeling good. He was winning one for the people.

Bayard Kluer sat motionless, staring coldly over the half-lenses of his black-rimmed reading glasses. When the crowd grew silent again he drew a breath. "'. . . will be held Thursday, February 26, 1976, at 8:30 P.M., Harvard Divinity School, Francis Avenue, Cambridge."

"What a pompous ass," Mac whispered.

Liz's eyes flashed at him.

Giacconi picked up a pencil and began tapping its point into the table top. The two men glared at each other while the crowd sat silent. Finally, Giacconi leaned forward into his microphone. "Okay, Doctor. I can see that you think I'm a foolish man. I'm a common man, I certainly admit that, but let me tell you something. When I was a little boy, I used to fish in the Charles River. I woke up one morning and I found millions of dead fish. And I read in this report here that you prepared, that you guys dump chemicals into the sewer system that overflows into the Charles! Now you say what you do in your lab is none of my business. I ask you if the chemical waste dumps out in Woburn are the business of those parents whose kids are coming down with leukemia."

Liz flipped her wrist, gesturing to no one. "This is totally out of line," she said.

Giacconi looked up at the audience. "I'd like a show of hands, here. How many of you people are actually for this lab? Raise your hands." Giacconi scanned the gallery. "Go ahead. Nobody's taking down names." Here and there a hand waved in the air. Mac was riding this one out. Liz seemed honestly confused, wishing to be counted but not wanting to play along with this fool.

Giacconi brought his focus back to Kluer sitting at the table in front of him. "Doctor. I have a memo here that you wrote having to do with ants. Seems you've had a little trouble with the exterminators over at the Bio Labs."

Kluer simply stared.

Giacconi held up the memo and smiled at the crowd. Then he read from it. " *'Monomorium pharaonis.'* That's the pharaoh ant, right Dr. Kluer? Give me a little advice in case I ever have the problem. How do you get rid of pharaoh ants?"

Kluer sighed. "The species is virtually impossible to eliminate by any known technique."

"That's what I've heard. And the fact is, the Biological Laboratories is overrun with them. Some genius brought them back from South America, and now they own the place. So tell me, Dr. Kluer. How are you going to handle the ants in your fancy new containment facility?"

"That is an internal problem with which we shall have to cope."

"How do you figure that?"

Kluer sighed again. "What you consistently fail to understand, sir, is that the principal purpose of the P4 facility is to protect the experiment. It is designed primarily to keep contaminants out, not in."

The crowd was dumfounded. It was as if Kluer were purposefully trying to alienate them. Giacconi called a fifteen-minute break, and McKusick sank down into his seat groaning, "What an idiot . . ."

Liz was totally exasperated. Through clenched teeth she gasped, "You make me furious!"

He threw up his hands. "Look, I'll work for the guy, but I still think he's a robot. He just set us back six years."

"It is not Bayard's fault that this whole thing is a circus set up to—"

"What is this 'Bayard' shit?" McKusick sat up. Now he knew what had been bothering him. "Ever since I got here that's all I've heard. He's really sucked you into this Harvard crap, hasn't he? You're really one of the elite now, huh?"

She stood up, but the crowd had her blocked in. There was nowhere to go. In frustration she sat back down.

McKusick watched her for a moment, then began to shake his head. Her distance was finally taking on a meaning. "Don't tell me you're sleeping with him?"

"Just be quiet."

"Naw. You gotta be putting me on."

He sat sideways, staring at her with his mouth open. Then he settled back in his seat. "That is really depressing," he said.

"He's asked me to marry him. The wedding is planned for September."

Mac continued staring at her. After a moment he said, "I really can't believe what's happened to you. You were actually alive there for a little while. Now you're back with the machines. Are you that desperate? Really?" He watched her for another moment. She had her eyes closed, but the tears were working their way through her lashes. She glanced toward the ceiling.

"I think I'm going to be sick," he said, and got up to make his way toward the door.

26

MCKUSICK HAD NEVER SEEN anyone over the age of nine quite so eager to see her parents. He and Kathleen walked together through the tubular passenger ramp, past Braniff's huge color posters of Machu Picchu and Mazatlán, then stepped into the terminal itself. The whole family was waiting for them. Mac watched as Kathleen rushed forward to hug her mother, then her sister and brother, and finally the large, solid-looking man who was her father. Mr. Albriton clasped his big hands around her back and drew her to him, burying his face in her strawberry-blonde hair. He held her as if she had just been ransomed. He closed his eyes. When he opened them once again, they focused on McKusick. The look was an assessment. Cold. Immediate. Thorough. Then it warmed. "So who is this, now?" he said.

Kathleen made a flustered introduction, and McKusick realized what was going on. He was just her traveling companion—someone from Harvard who was also going to the wildlife preserve in Colombia. For whatever reason, Kathleen had left the rest unsaid.

They had known each other for all of one month, but that did not include the weeks McKusick had spent at Fresh Pond looking for her. He had gone back at the same hour every day the first week. Then he began to vary his schedule, sampling various possibilities, ultimately spending whole days walking around the track and lying on the grass, waiting. The city council's moratorium on gene-splicing had shot down any hope of starting to work. Without transferable credentials, McKusick was simply stuck.

Then one morning, while wandering through Harvard Square, he heard half a dozen drums pounding on the traffic island a block away. The rhythm, echoing against the storefronts, was like a war dance. He started walking toward the crowd. Over people's shoulders he could see women in black leotards and tie-dyed sarongs twirling to the music. The drumming tribesmen were bearded and bespectacled graduate students, more choirboys than warriors. A sandwich board stood beside them—PEABODY MUSEUM ETHNIC FESTIVAL. And then he saw her smile again. She had her hands on her hips and her shoulders thrust back, rotating in a throbbing pivot that made her breasts vibrate to the rhythm. She was giggling with her teeth clamped down on a whistle. She finished the circle, blew the whistle, and the dancers whooped and began rolling their hips in raunchy circles, around and around, back and forth. "Your tribe come here often?" he had asked.

Mr. Albriton guided the station wagon out the San Antonio freeways and then over the county roads, going higher and higher into the dry, mesquite-covered hills. Kath's sister Marie rode in the back. Dean, who was just starting his freshman year at the University of Texas, shared the back seat with Kath and McKusick. Brother and sister carried on a high-intensity conversation about what Willie Nelson was doing to Austin, while Mrs. Albriton, peering through her dark glasses, chattered along sometimes parallel lines. Mac could see Mr. Albriton's eyes in the rearview mirror, his look of pride and satisfaction as he watched his daughter. Occasionally the gaze would shift to McKusick, and Mac was not at all sure what he saw in it then.

The house was stone and cedar, and it stood on the highest point for miles around. A wide verandah on all four sides offered a view of dry, dusty hills held in place by scrub oak and cactus. They went inside out of the heat and drank iced tea.

"So what takes you down south, Peter?" Mrs. Albriton had a warm smile. It was Kathleen's face, only fuller. Older.

"Research. The same monkey project Kath's involved in."

"So you're an anthropologist?"

"No. I studied medicine, actually."

"Oh ... A doctor." Mrs. Albriton seemed

pleased, but her brows furrowed as she strained to make the connection.

"I'm hoping to . . . trace the genetic basis for some of the behavior Kathleen's going to be watching."

She nodded, with a look of kindly but intense skepticism.

Mrs. Albriton gave Mac a tour of the house and showed him where he would be staying. It was a pleasant room at the top of the stairs, with a brass bed and furniture that was worn and comfortable looking. But there were no high school mementos pinned to the wall, and no clothes in the closet. This was the guest room.

Kath appeared behind him in the doorway wearing a khaki shirt and Levi's. "Let me show you my childhood sweetheart," she said.

He followed her down the stairs and out the screen door. It banged behind them as they left the shade of the porch and came into the sunlight.

It was late afternoon now, and the long shadows seemed out of synch with the heat. "Why didn't you tell them?" he said.

She winced and took his arm. "I chickened out. I've never brought any guys 'home to meet the folks' before. If they knew we were sleeping together they'd probably try to be liberal about it, and on the inside it'd be killing 'em. I'm their first kid, you know? You have to lead parents through these things gently." He felt the reassuring warmth of her breast pressed against his elbow.

Up by the barn they could see Mr. Albriton

in the corral with two quarter horses and an
ancient, swaybacked mare.

"There he is," she said. "Roscoe. Ain't he
beautiful?"

"Good-looking horse," McKusick said. He
smiled, but he was still having trouble with this
arrangement.

"He had an accident some years ago that
prevented the consummation of our love."

"Accident, hell!" McKusick let out. He watched
her climb the fence, the denim tightening around
her thighs.

She ran up to the gelding and kissed his
nose. Then she stroked his flanks and, with one
hand on his mane, swung herself up on top,
bareback.

Albriton squinted with a smile. "Missed him,
huh, baby?"

She took off for a couple of turns around the
corral, kicking up clouds of dust.

Albriton yelled out to Peter, "You know how
to ride a horse?"

"We got horses in California," he said, hop-
ping down from the fence rail.

"I'll saddle Clover for you."

"I can get it, thanks."

"California cowboy, huh?"

"Sort of."

Kathleen pulled Roscoe to a stop where the
two saddles waited in the dirt. She slipped off
his back and then reached up with the blanket
first. McKusick was already working under his
horse to cinch the girth. Meanwhile, Lee Albriton
sat sideways on his old mare, dangling his legs
like he was sitting on a fence. He had the face

of a twelve-year-old boy, only wrinkled now, his sandy hair fading to gray. He was laughing, muttering nonsense to his horse and feeding her carrots.

"Wait! Wait!" Albriton slid off his horse and came over to double-check Kathleen's saddle. "One fart and he's gonna slip you right off, honey. Let's tighten this sucker up right."

While he worked, his mare nuzzled behind him, nibbling at his back. He tolerated it until, for whatever reason, the old horse sunk her teeth into his back. He swung around with a haymaker punch and slammed his fist squarely into her nose. "You goddamn bitch!" It was a powerful punch. "It's glue for you, Rosebud. First thing next week."

"Jesus, Daddy! You've been saying that since I was in grade school."

That night they watched from a wicker couch on the verandah as the sun settled down into the hills. It was a clear evening, and as the sky blackened, the only thing competing with the stars was a huge new moon rising out of the east. Hand in hand, they left the porch and followed their shadows in the moonlight along the narrow blacktop road.

They talked very little. At times like this Mac was not sure what to profess. He did not imagine she would want to hear about his admiration for her. His close, protective feeling was not quite it, either. He wished he could give her more. He knew there was more, but something was blocking it in. And so he simply hugged her to his side, and they walked through the darkness where a clump of trees overshadowed the road.

Later that night, he lay awake in the silent house for what seemed like hours, eager to get back on the plane. He wondered how it felt to be a child surrounded by this tribal feeling of a home—parents, brothers, sisters—bedded down for the night. His mother had tried to provide it once. She picked a stepfather for him out of the mortgage applications where she worked. A widower with a good business, a fenced yard, all the Middle American virtues. Their union lasted a year. Her marriage to Mac's father had been an equally short-lived phenomenon. There was a joke that McKusick senior kept a standing account at The Palms wedding chapel in Las Vegas. There was a story that, after his broker's license had been revoked and he moved to Florida, he married and divorced the same woman so often that the judge said they were wasting his time and told them just to live together. Usually, Mac could laugh at it all, but not tonight. This joke was his genetic heritage, and tonight the whole business seemed utterly sordid. Even his affair with Liz—a relationship that had lasted five years—seemed sleazy now by comparison. He should face up to the fact that he simply wasn't right for Kathleen. And as he was formulating the thought, he felt her warm body sliding in beneath the sheets.

She was up and gone before dawn. McKusick stayed in bed as late as he could, just to be on the safe side. There was something a little too intimate about pajamas and toothbrushes. He was not a member of this family. He was an intruder, violating their morning rituals.

When the air was warming and he could no longer wait without making a point of it, he followed the breakfast smells down the stairway to the kitchen. There was venison sausage sizzling in an electric grill, and Mr. Albriton standing barefoot by the stove, dressed in khakis, attending a skillet of frying eggs. Kath and her mother were both at the table, grinning over their coffee. Kathleen jumped up and kissed him. "Good morning!" she said. The cat was out of the bag.

Lee Albriton looked up from his skillet and said good morning nicely enough. Whatever it was, they were being good-natured about it. They seemed as pleased as punch.

"So what d'you Harvard hotshots eat for breakfast?" Lee mumbled. "We got any croissants, Nina? Can we run down to Dalton and pick up some croissants?"

Kathleen went over to her father and threw a mock, slow-motion punch to his jaw. "My redneck father is just showing off, Mac. But he's a phony. He talks Wallace and then votes McGovern. Kerr County's only pinko." And she reached up to hug his neck and kissed him, nuzzling like a kitten, dangling one foot behind her as she did. It was a playful but nonetheless erotic gesture, a link between her girlhood and her future. Right there between the skillet and the kitchen sink a ceremony was taking place that was making this child his. This was the posting of the banns. He was separating her from her parents. He was unutterably complicating her life and her ambitions by going with her to Colombia. She deserved to have her year in Colombia, she deserved to have the next several years free and unfettered to grow and experiment and get wherever she wanted to be. He should go back and settle his affairs in Cambridge, or he should go back to California and start over. Going with her to Colombia was tantamount to using her, and his guilt filled him with a sense of dread.

27

IN THE HEAT, the black coating of the binoculars was gummy in his hands. He brought the glasses back up to his eyes, knocking water droplets off his brow, and turned toward the hilltop rising from the dense vegetation of the river bottom. His field of vision narowed to one black-rimmed disk of light. He nudged the focus wheel with his fingertip and resolved on the stark, solid structure commanding the highest point for miles around. It was partially obscured by the fronds of forest palm, covered over with bougainvillea, but he could still see the grim outline of cinder-block construction, the windowpanes rimmed in steel. It looked like a physics lab out of the Weimar Republic. It must have been inhabited, or it would have been absorbed into the jungle by now. Vines would have choked it, or some tropical termite adapted for concrete chewed it down. They had neighbors, then, even here. Neighbors with strange taste in architecture.

Mac lowered the binoculars and looked around. The troop of females he was supposed to be watching were still resting in the treetops grooming their infants. He was sitting on a rusted-out tractor, withering in the heat of the clearing. He lifted his canteen and took a drink, and even the water was hot. His T-shirt was sweat-soaked and sticking to his back. His arms and legs were glazed with bits of bark and leaves stuck to his skin, and he realized that, if he allowed himself to think about it, the moisture running continuously off his head and into his face, stinging his eyes with salt, was going to drive him stark raving crazy.

He scanned the troop again and discovered the presence of a newcomer, a thick-chested male with dazzling white teeth. There was a red splotch on his coat of black fur. It was the dye that Wendy, the other graduate student, had used to identify Gable, the new alpha. The monkey's eyes were darting about, and he gave a low growl as he neared the females. One of them sauntered over and began grooming him, but he was obviously in no mood for pleasantries. He bared his teeth again and grunted. Then Mac noticed that the monkey's penis was fully erect.

McKusick started the 16-millimeter Bell & Howell. Several feet of film wound through the machine as Gable growled and paced back and forth, but the scene was not going anywhere. The monkey stalked off the set and flopped down against the tree trunk, and Mac stopped the camera. But no sooner had he lowered it than the male flew back into the center of the troop and tore an infant from its mother. Holding it in his teeth, he had time to bash its head against the limb only once before two older females were on him, hissing and nipping at his throat. The baby broke free and ran back to its mother, who drew it under her paw and led it through the branches to a cecropius tree where she nursed it. There was blood around its ear. It was heaving and trembling as it gasped for breath. Gable stood off the old matriarch and her helper as long as he could, scampering up to the higher reaches of the canopy to howl at them. McKusick watched in disbelief. The sudden lethal fury had shaken him. He had been waiting for it for hours, yet when it came he had not been prepared.

That evening at the trailer Wendy and Kath interrogated Mac for every minute detail. It was growing dark outside, and he could no longer see their faces as they huddled around the small, built-in table. Wendy had known that something was brewing. Bogart, the old leader of the Plantation troop, had not been seen for days. At the same time this new alpha appeared, two of the troop's four infants had disappeared. Wendy had been sitting in the bush for four months filling notebooks with descriptions of nothing more dramatic than the theft of a ripe fig, and this male amateur had walked right off the bus into a brewing political storm.

"Just make sure you spell my name right," she murmured, "when you credit all my background data."

The next day all three observers went out together to try to find the mother and infant that had been attacked. They were following a trail where the sun never penetrated the canopy of leaves a hundred feet above their heads. It was like walking through a cavern, or a green-windowed cathedral, except for the ripe smell of compost. They were engulfed in rotting cellulose, steaming in the heat. It was difficult to tell where the vegetation ended and the soil began.

Wendy's cowboy hat was bobbing down the trail well ahead of McKusick. He was following Kathleen, her blonde hair stuffed under a Texas Rangers baseball cap, her slender legs emerging from work boots that must have weighed ten pounds apiece.

She stopped, giving a quick low whistle between her teeth, and Mac came up. "Is that them?" she whispered.

He focused his binoculars on a pair of howlers resting high above them.

"Yeh. You can see the caked blood around his neck."

"Judy and Mickey," Wendy said. She had made her way back and was gazing into her own up-turned field glasses. "Let's stay on them. If Gable's out for murder, he'll be back."

The three of them knelt down and watched the two monkeys reclining on their limb, nearly lifeless. Occasionally Wendy or Kath would note the time and jot something down. Mac simply watched and waited and swatted at the sand flies. Off to his right a muddy stream washed by, widened and deepened by the partial dam of a decomposing log. He glanced around at the primordial landscape of wet and rot, thinking about armadillos and three-toed sloths. This place was a time capsule, isolated through the millennia as the continents drifted apart. He would not have been surprised to see a pteranodon gliding past the green arch of a brontosaurus's neck.

Settling into a new position, he snapped a twig and rustled the leaves. Wendy turned toward him. "Uh, if you've got something else to do . . ."

The honeymoon, such as it was, had come to an end. He and Kath had been floating in a world of their own on the way down, landing on a new continent, careening through the Andes engulfed by clouds. But now they had reached the river bottom that was their destination, and they were no longer sharing a lark. He had come to be with Kathleen. She had come to work.

The next day McKusick wandered into the village to drink some beer and try to think things through. He had always known he might be a fifth wheel down here, but he had never expected the awareness to come so soon. He strolled along the Wild West main street between the low buildings. They were shaded by mango trees encroaching from the jungle that was always just a few feet away. He could hear music from a radio coming out of the darkened lair of a tavern. The wooden tables of its dirt courtyard sat empty at this hour. The only sign of life was a rooster stalking brazenly between two narcoleptic dogs.

McKusick did not go in. Instead, he followed

the mud street to its only destination, the docks, where a small riverboat was being unloaded. He could see some sort of commotion up ahead.

A gray-haired man, shirtless and swaggering like a pirate, was yelling curses at the stevedores in strangely accented Spanish. One of the workers had dropped a crate and broken the glass tank inside it. The big man was damning the peasant's ancestors and all his descendants for the next three generations.

"Agua salada!" the man was yelling. He wore blue jeans, rolled up to the knee and belted under a paunch. "Agua salada." Mac looked more closely at the crates and saw that the tanks inside each held some kind of marine organism. What the hell was this guy doing trafficking in sea urchins on the Putumayo River?

McKusick walked a little closer. "Pardon, señor. Soy un científico norteamericano estudio los primates neotropicales . . ."

"Good God, man! If you can't do any better than that, you bloody well better stick to English!"

McKusick was dumbstruck. But then the man gave a watery smile. "One of these spics will slit your gizzard for desecrating his mother tongue! I'm Jack Stasson," he said, extending his hand. The blond hair on his arms shone against skin as red as if it had been boiled. His whole body seemed swollen and inflamed. "Happy to see another gringo . . . and were you trying to say something about being a scientist? Not a linguist, I take it."

McKusick did not know how to respond. Stasson's energy was overwhelming, after so many silent days watching monkeys.

"Hold on here a minute. Let me get this shit onto my truck and I'll treat you to some of the local swill."

They went back to the tavern with the courtyard, stepping over a pig lying all but submerged in a puddle, its snout glistening with purple flies. Like a transmission beamed in from another planet, the urgent rhythm pulsing through the radio made the white heat and midday desolation all the more forlorn. Mac inhaled the odors of mold and heavy seasoning as he approached the door. The interior was dark and the walls were covered with fishnet and seashells. He had the sensation of stepping inside a crab.

"So you're down here for the monkeys to piss on? Watching them fucking in the treetops?" They took a table and ordered the local beer.

"I'm a molecular biologist, really. Just helping a friend. She's the primatologist."

"A woman! Now we get to the truth."

McKusick stumbled through an explanation of why he was in Colombia. He thought it peculiar enough himself to require explanation, but in the telling, the moratorium on DNA research sounded like a plausible excuse for a vacation. He left Liz out of the narrative completely.

The tavern was run by an Italian, and the specialty was spaghetti with calamari sauce. As the man set the food on their table, Stasson launched into his own biography, and Mac wondered what significant details the Englishman might be choosing to leave out.

"It was straight from the slums of Leeds to the RAF," Stasson began. "Math prodigy, you know. Did statistical analysis of the German bombing. Then up to Oxford, supported by a grateful nation, where I trained under Blain. Early embryogenesis. Took a year with Gurdon at Cambridge ... control of gene expression ... then back to Oxford with Edwards and Steptoe."

Mac cocked his head slightly. When he'd first heard Stasson's name there had been something vaguely familiar ...

"It was a bit of a 'midlife crisis,' as your pop psychologists call it. We had a general falling out, you see—future direction of our work, and so on. I thought they were taking it a bit far, really, and I was ready for a change. Ready to leave the old-boy crap well behind me. There was some flap in the press, and it attracted the attention of one Carlos Bustamonte, late of these parts. He *owned* these parts, I should say. The entire Parque Nacional, including the plantation where you're chasing monkeys. He made me an attractive offer. He made me lord of my own little realm, is what he did! I have the big house— you and your lady will have to come to tea—and a good percentage of the oil royalties to support my work. And no MRC to contend with! No pressure for the least publishable unit. Young Bustamonte was a bit vague on science, but he was quite sure Colombia ought to have some. A dear man. Owe it all to him."

The Englishman went back to work on his food, and Mac finished his beer. It all sounded a bit too good to be true. Rich men simply didn't pick names out of the newspapers and set up independent research foundations. As Mac watched Stasson swirling pasta onto his fork, he made the connection. There *had* been a "flap," but as he remembered it, the ethical issue was not Stasson's qualms about Edwards and Steptoe but their qualms about Jack Stasson.

When McKusick returned from the village with a dinner invitation, Kath was not sure what to make of it.

"Does he have a pith helmet?" she asked, raising her T-shirt over her head. Her body was glistening with sweat.

"Not that kind of Englishman," Mac said. He was sitting on the edge of the bed watching her undress. Wendy was still in the field, and for once they had the trailer to themselves.

"You think he'll have ice?" she asked, stepping out of her shorts.

He placed his hands on the smallest portion of her waist, testing for the hundredth time to see if he could reach all the way around. "What would you do with it?" he asked.

"Pour it down your pants."

"No you wouldn't."

"Oh. Maybe not. How much time do we have?"

"He said six."

She kissed his forehead. "Save the ice for the drinks," she said, as he traced the tiny copper grains of pigmentation to where they stopped at her breast. He fell back on the bed, carrying her with him, and they made love in the afternoon heat, gliding on a glaze of sweat.

True to his word, Stasson was waiting at the appointed spot, sprawled out across the front seat of his jeep reading a week-old copy of *El*

Tiempo. He saw them coming up the trail, hand in hand, and sat up, muttering " ' ... with wand'ring steps and slow/ Through Eden took their solitary way.' " He waved. "The monkey lady! Good God, Mac, she's bloody beautiful! Kathleen, is it?"

She walked up smiling and shook his massive freckled hand.

"Don't mind if I gawk and stare a bit. Really quite a shock seeing you tramping out of there. Stunning. Absolutely stunning."

She smiled. "I'll believe anything you say."

They settled into the jeep, Kath in the front and McKusick in the jump seat, and went scrambling up the hillside in four-wheel drive with Stasson chattering away.

"All of this was a rubber plantation, you see. Started up in the twenties by Bustamonte père. Bit of a visionary. Hated to see all this land going to waste, as he put it. Wilderness as wilderness. Didn't care much for the value of the gene pool."

The jeep was ripping into the roadway, leaving a shower of dust on the bordering vegetation.

"Transportation problems overwhelmed him," Stasson went on. "After the war, the scheme fell apart. Bit of an embarrassment to his son. Certainly a headache." He grinned at McKusick, then let his eyes linger on Kathleen for a moment. "This enormous house in a sea of leaves and crawling things. Son moved to Bogotá and refused to come back. When the old man died he gave the place away. Hated the house. You'll see why when we get there. Not far ahead of us now."

They were climbing a steep hill, winding back and forth on zagged switchbacks to reach the summit. After weeks on the jungle floor, this rush of air was like a dose of adrenaline. Mac watched Kathleen as she leaned forward like a bowsprit, her eyes closed, her hair blowing free. He felt the thrill of having her all over again, followed quickly by a twinge of guilt. He had come a long way since that first time when he felt he was corrupting a child. Her throat reddened and raw from his beard. Her eyes completely trusting as she urged him on. Still . . .

Up ahead they began to catch glimpses of the house through the flickering of the trees. It was the massive gray structure Mac had seen from the clearing. It looked more lifeless the closer they got, as homey as an electronics assembly plant.

"Bauhaus," Stasson shouted. "All the rage in the twenties. The old man was true to his faith in form and function, and he built himself a very expensive prison, eh what?" Stasson pulled the jeep around to the side and killed the engine. He lowered his voice, taking them into his confidence. "One thing I forgot to warn you—there's a race of pygmies about. Red hair, green eyes, quite exotic for these parts. But the blowguns are deadly. Poison-tipped."

Just then a long reed extended through the fronds of a bush. There was the sound of spitting. Then a small face popped up from the bush and a tiny form darted away.

"Missed, you bloody bastards! We'll be armed next time! Shoot to kill!" Then Stasson turned to face his slightly awed passengers. "My son and heir," he said. "Chip off the old block. That's what we call him. Chip. Afraid we dote a bit, but all in all he's a good lad."

They walked up the gentle rise from the driveway to the level of the front door. "Amazing diversity of flora and fauna," Stasson was saying, gesturing to nothing in particular. "You could support a team of botanists right here in this yard." Or a team of Japanese gardeners, Mac thought. Anthurium, bird of paradise, torch ginger, bougainvillea, all growing wild. "But you're not really a naturalist, are you?"

"An anthropologist," Kath said.

"And you're a molecular type."

Mac nodded. "Right."

"Couldn't have come to a better place."

They entered a tiled foyer from which they could see the Spanish courtyard. A lush garden grew in the center, green and alive, softening the austerity of pipe railings on the stairway and verandah. Out of this domesticated jungle a small, mahogany-skinned woman came toward them.

"This is Pia," Stasson said.

She looked at them with dark impassive eyes. Her long black hair was pulled back into a clasp at the nape of her neck; the bridge of her nose and her high cheekbones were delicately tattooed with what looked like a butterfly's outstretched wings.

"How do you do?" She smiled. "I assume you've met our son, Nigel?"

The red-headed pygmy from the driveway hid behind her pleated gray skirt. Above it she wore a plain white blouse; below it, sensible shoes.

"I'm afraid Jack encourages him to revert to the aboriginal, despite my efforts to civilize him." She extended her hand with the propriety of a librarian in the British Museum. "We're so pleased to have you as our guests. It's time to put Nigel to bed, and then I'll come down to join you. Say goodnight, Nigel."

The boy brought his fist up to his mouth and blew an imaginary dart into each of them. Then his mother led him away.

"I'll be in for a kiss," Stasson yelled after them. Then he smiled. "Afraid I've ruined the poor girl with six months in London. But if you could only have seen her—barebreasted, gliding down the river . . . Ah, it was a vision. Now it's 'Lie still and think of England,' you know."

They sat in the courtyard drinking gin—with ice provided by a mestiza girl of thirteen or so.

"So what do the monkeys have to tell us?" Stasson said. "Why are ya down here invading their privacy?"

Kathleen rubbed her glass against her neck. "I'm trying to understand infant killing. Dominant males in some species systematically murder the children. It's suspected among howlers. Mac almost got some of it on film the other day."

"Don't bring *that* up," McKusick said.

Stasson stuck a finger in his drink and gave it a stir. "Bloody stuff, eh?"

Pia was coming back through the garden. Stasson said, "I should probably go give mine a bite now, if you'll excuse me."

He stepped away and Mac and Kath waited a moment in silence, exchanging smiles with the woman. She seemed to be studying their faces as they searched agonizingly for small talk. Suddenly she snatched at Kathleen's neck, pinching away something small and black, then popped it politely into her mouth.

Dinner was served in a screen-porch dining area that looked out onto a swimming pool with a guest cottage behind it. A man and woman were walking along the edge of the pool. "The Nakamuras will be joining us," Stasson said. "My research associates. Usually have one or two passing through at any given time. What with cutbacks everywhere, it's amazing who you can pick up with a half-inch squib in *Nature*."

The mestiza girl and a woman who looked to be her mother served up a very British roast beef and Yorkshire pudding, with Stasson opening bottle after bottle of claret. The Nakamuras spoke very little English. Pia's was fluent, but only when she was affecting the niceties of a British hostess. Whenever she strayed into spontaneous remarks, the accent faltered and her vocabulary failed her. Stasson kept pushing Kathleen to talk about her work anyway.

"So what's your hypothesis about the infanticide? Population control? Malthusian monkeys?"

"Sexual politics. The male doesn't want females wasting time on any children other than his. He wants them ready to bear his children, to be sure his genes are represented in the next generation. So he takes over the troop, he drives out the old alpha and kills the kids. Then he has to stay on top long enough to protect his own children into maturity."

"Tidy. Tidy."

"Yeh. It works out fine for the males. The theory, I mean. What I want to know is, what's in it for the female?"

"She endures it like an Irish fishwife!" Stasson insisted, glancing around grinning.

"No. I have a few hunches, and that's not one of them."

"This is good stuff," he declared. "Not just stamp collecting after all." He pushed and probed further while everyone else strained to follow. "Marvelous! Marvelous!" he kept shouting. "Now maybe we'll get somewhere. You're catching on to what we lab types have known all along: The individual is nothing more than DNA's way of making more DNA. It's all in the genes. Deoxyribonucleic acid, the alpha and omega, world without end amen."

The Nakamuras retired to their cottage early. Stasson grabbed up another bottle of wine and insisted that Mac and Kathleen bring their glasses along on the grand tour. Stasson wanted Mac to see his laboratory. Pia begged off with the excuse that Chip would have her up early enough.

"Perhaps we should be going," Kath said.

"Nonsense! Even if I were capable of driving, you'd be eaten by something quite large ten minutes into that jungle path. You'll stay the night here."

They climbed the smooth cement steps. Once into the laboratory area Mac was awed by the sophistication of the equipment. A Digital MINC system with a W/PDP-11/23 microcomputer filled one wall. Another was taken up by a gorgeous ISI DS-130 scanning EM. He had a Beckman L8 ultracentrifuge, an LKB vertical electrophoresis, a Varian 5000 liquid chromatograph, and an Ortho Cytofluorograf. State-of-the-art gamma counters, beta counters, incubators, scintillators—the works.

"How did you get this stuff here?"

"Ah. Logistics. The one bugaboo in my kingdom. Some of it came down the river. With some of the heavier pieces I had a bit of assistance from the Colombian Army and a very large helicopter."

Mac was still perplexed. "Why here? Why not at the university in Bogotá?"

"I've tried notoriety, my boy, and I've tried obscurity, and I find I prefer the latter. Frees the spirit. I lecture in the city occasionally. But here I have complete control. No academic taskmaster. No political observers. This is a Catholic country, after all, with touchy political sensibilities."

"A passive contraceptive?"

"That's what Bustamonte is supporting. But I've lately been branching out. Taking it to the opposite end of the life cycle."

Stasson mounted a hardback chair, straddling it in reverse with his arms folded across the top.

"Before there was sex there was no death, you see. The cell simply divided and divided. Then along came this bright idea of the individual to carry the genes through each generation. But individuals don't keep dividing like daughter cells—they hang around cluttering the landscape. You need to get the message—time's up!

Selection acts on us and then we're expendable.
We're like spawned salmon, you see, only it
takes longer."

"I don't see the connection," Kath said. "What
does this have to do with embryogenesis? That's
your field, isn't it?"

"The switching! 'On' and 'off.' Our DNA ar-
ranges to have us bumped off, just as cells in
the developing embryo are instructed to die to
sculpt the body. It's necrosis. Programmed cell
death."

Stasson smiled and finished off his glass.
"Fascinating, eh? Taking on the grim reaper."

He focused on McKusick with bloodshot eyes.
The wine had made him chummy. "I could use
a molecular type. Why don't you come help me
in the lab?"

Mac looked at Kathleen. She shrugged with a
smile.

"Give me a hand and put your time to good
use. What are you, some kind of amateur out
stumbling around in the bush? There's a super-
visor's cottage down by the landing strip. A little
dust at the moment, perhaps, but all in all not
bad accommodations. Just at the foot of the hill.
That puts our primatologist close enough to her
monkeys, and you can motor back and forth in
the jeep."

Mac was thinking about Wendy Myers back at
the trailer. This meant a place of their own, and
the chance to get back to work—without NIH
guidelines. But there was something a little too
eager about Stasson's invitation. "Why don't we
have a look at the cottage tomorrow?" Mac said.

"I'll stock the larder and the cellar. But there's

no sending off to Harrods for a change of drapes, you know."

Stasson walked them to a guest room and, like a bellhop, pointed out the amenities of running water, windows that opened and closed. Then he left them to themselves.

It had been a strange evening, a colloquium in the middle of the rain forest. They weren't quite ready for bed. Still whirling a bit from the wine and the conversation, they stepped back down the stairs for a look at the pool and then a look at the stars. They wandered down the hillside behind the cottage, amazed at the blackness all around. There was not an electric light within five hundred miles to dim the view of Alpha Centauri and the Southern Cross. In the moonlight they came upon a low chain fence strung between iron spikes. A white marker stood in the center, distinct and pale. It was in the shape of a lamb, a fine piece of carved granite. On the pedestal they could read, PIA OCHOCO IBEÑEZ STASSON, 1970–1973.

28

"ANGEL OF MERCY," Stasson said, clasping his brief-case shut. "Bringing the wonders of science to these benighted souls." Then he bolted from the room.

McKusick watched from the laboratory win-dow as the Englishman splashed through the downpour, bareheaded, his son splashing along behind him. Mac looked out to the crest of the hill where streams of water were cutting deeper into the roadway. It had been raining since well before daylight, when the "whoop-whoop" of the howlers had called Kathleen out into the bush. He scanned the blackened sky and the saturated canopy of green, wondering where she was.

He turned back to the lab and resumed his browsing from room to room, trying to get his bearings. He had no plans to stay down here for the long haul, and yet in the last couple of days he had been ordering thousands of dollars worth of restriction enzymes and gene-sequencing equipment. "Just set it up for me," Stasson had said. "Don't worry about it gathering dust."

The day before, Mac had observed Nakamura working diligently in his own corner of the lab. The Japanese was investigating the rapid phase of protein synthesis that follows fertilization. He was focusing on the rise in intracellular pH that signals cell division—hardly the lunatic fringe, Mac was thinking. McKusick had stood around watching, now and then asking a follow-up question that led away from the lab bench and onto the subject of their host's personality. But Nakamura's English was mostly technical jargon. He smiled earnestly, even eagerly, but always brought the conversation back to the sex lives of sea urchins.

McKusick sat down on the stool near the sink at the far corner of the room. A ten-liter fermenter filled with powdered leaves was sitting on the bench in front of him. He leaned forward and winced at the smell of sulfuric acid. A filtering stand stood on the countertop and, clustered around it, reagent jars of benzene, sodium carbonate, potassium permanganate, and hydrochloric acid. He lifted the wax paper from a large Petri dish and found inside a brown paste of what would have to be cocaine hydrochloride.

Kath was bundled in a wool sweater underneath her parka. The rain was coming down, a great gray curtain limiting her visibility. She followed the path through the dripping leaves, following the sound of Gable's voice. She had learned to distinguish his call from Bogart's. It was higher in pitch, faster paced. Carol, the new student who had replaced Wendy, was following the Llano troop and keeping up with Bogart. She had seen him with five nomad males, hanging around on the fringe of the troop but never trying to copulate with any of the females. At least not yet. From time to time Gable would reappear and send the nomads lumbering off. For now he had control of both bands, but he had his work cut out for him.

Splashing through the mud, Kath saw a matted lump of fur lying in a deepening puddle. She walked closer, leaned over to shelter the corpse from the rain, and set her jaw, attempting to remain the cool, detached observer. It was the body of a howler infant, scarcely six weeks old. The neck was a mass of botfly swellings. The tongue protruded from a mouth caked with blood. The eyes were fixed in a wide stare of astonishment now gone blank.

Kath stooped under the weight of the downpour and examined the wounds. The brain case had been punctured. There was a long gash along the back of the infant's neck, raw and red.

That afternoon, after the rain had stopped and the steam had begun to rise from the forest, she noticed the female known as Ginger lounging in the crotch of a tree without her infant. Her baby and the corpse Kath had found that morning were roughly the same size. The dead infant must have been hers—there were very few other possibilities.

Kath watched the monkey for almost an hour

as she groomed, and was groomed by, one of her troopmates. The female appeared especially listless, even dazed, like a mother grieving for a lost child.

As twilight was coming on, Gable appeared, brachiating through the deep-green canopy. He came to rest on a limb just above Ginger's, and the female immediately got up and presented her hindquarters to him. Responding to cues too subtle for Kathleen to catch, the male mounted the female and began pumping his body against hers while her troopmates gathered around to watch. As the sexual excitement rose, the other females began leaping onto the copulating pair, nipping at Gable's neck. They were merely playing the genetic game—protesting Gable's attention to a competing female— but Kath was outraged. She wanted to bash both of them in the head. How could this mother brazenly solicit the same male who had just murdered her child?

That night Kathleen and Peter lay in bed and talked through the stifling air, too hot to sleep.

"It worries me about women," she said. They could hear the rasping of insects against the window screens. "I mean, human males do not routinely kill and devour their children . . ."

"Except in the *National Enquirer*," he muttered.

She ignored the joke, shifting her weight in the darkness. She was deadly serious. "All those millions of years of evolution have to mean something in making us what we are," she said.

The bed was soaked with sweat. McKusick said nothing, and for a while they listened to the bugs. It was obvious to him that this was a dangerous topic. It was also obvious that, given half a chance, the insects were going to take over. They had always been here—always would be. On the evolutionary scale, just as in this forest, humanity was simply passing through.

Her hand came to rest on his shoulder. "Tell me about you and Liz," she said.

"Liz who?"

"No, really. About how it ended. The abortion and all that."

"You *are* in a rotten mood."

She came closer, wrapping her arms and legs around him. "Don't say that. It's just that this whole baby thing is on my mind. Out here that's all there is. Living long enough to mate. Trying to keep the ball rolling. So what does it mean for us to have gotten so far away from that? Everyone being so cautious. Deliberate. Trying to stay in control." She traced the line of his jaw with her finger. "Why aren't people like us making babies?"

Mac slid his hand down her belly. "How about if we just go through the motions?"

She smiled and raised her head as he burrowed into her neck. "We should definitely make a baby."

"Someday we will."

"But you wanted one then. You must want one now."

"Not necessarily. I just wasn't afraid of it—she was. We didn't have the relationship I thought we had."

"What about us?"

Mac smiled. If he had to use words, he was

not sure which ones he would find. She kissed him, and then she took him inside her, but for all the passion and sweat and mingling of cells they did not create life. There were still barriers to that, chemical as well as emotional, still membranes that had not been broken down. Then they slept, huddled together, while in the darkness all around them billions of creatures shuddered, hiding from each other, seeking one another, intent on surviving one more night.

29

IT WAS THE "smock . . . smock" of the tennis ball that broke into Mac's thoughts. He was in Stasson's library, doing the only thing he could do until his equipment arrived— reading. He strolled over to the window, munching the last of the sandwich the mestiza girl had brought him, and saw Stasson and Pia hacking away in the shade of a dozen tall eucalyptus trees. Stasson was hitting ball after ball down what remained of the center line as Pia worked on her forehand. The court surface was cracked and broken, and weeds had exploited every opening. Stasson was barefoot and shirtless in his blue jeans; Pia was decked out like Margaret Court in a white tennis skirt and floppy white hat. The skirt was yellowing and too big for her. It drooped down to her knees. Her sneakers were high-top basketball shoes, black.

Now Jack was hitting to the other side and giving Pia a chance to test her backhand. She was catching the balls with everything but the strings, sending them flying off to all sides, dribbling back under the net, shooting straight up. Chip let out a groan and shook his head. He was the ball boy, waiting at the net, barefoot and shirtless like his father. He was standing with his hands on his hips just as Stasson had stood that first day on the river docks. On his face was his father's warm, broad smile.

She found Judy resting on a lower limb swallowed up in lianas and epiphytic orchids. Kath fully expected to see her alone, with Mickey dead, one last victim of Gable's takeover. But as Kath came closer, she saw the baby scampering about, batting and chasing an unripe fig, frisky as any kitten. Obviously his wounds were healing, and Kath was relieved. Somehow she wanted this kid to make it, to slip through as the exception to the rules of the game. It was not his fault that he had been born in the wrong season, during a time of war.

For a while, Kath simply relaxed and let her note taking and her critical judgment lapse. She felt guilty for letting her emotions in, and guilty for spending so much time focusing on behavior that was not central to her study. But she needed a break from the tension. She felt like being a tourist for a while.

After an hour or so she heard a roar coming from a treetop to her left, and her stomach muscles tensed. It was a male howler, approaching quickly, limb to limb. Maybe this was it. The bloody end to the game. She watched Judy for her response, but there was none. The mother remained impassive, even when the male approached within a few feet. Then Kath understood why. This monkey was Bogart. He had been the alpha male of the Plantation troop before Gable—he would have to be Mickey's father. The two adults, male and female, watched each other at a neutral distance. There was nothing Bogart could do now for his former consort or for his child. The only strategy left to him now was to try to gain control of the Llano troop while Gable's attention was divided. The children of past seasons would have to fend for themselves.

Kath came back from a midday rendezvous with Carol to find the troop feeding quietly in the tree where she had left them. She settled in for a long hot siege, hunkered down on the aluminum camp stool she carried with her. After a few minutes she noticed agitation. The females were casting furtive glances as they milled around. Kath tensed up, preparing, trying not to be caught off guard. Then she saw Gable making his way toward the center of the group. Kath trained her binoculars on the male and watched how, as he approached, each female would scamper just out of his reach, then stop to feed again. Gable stopped and stretched tall, as if to peer off into the distance. But his curiosity was merely a feint. All at once he leaped from his perch and landed on Judy's back. Bette and Joan were on him immediately, driving him off, but not before he had gotten a good swipe at the infant. Kath saw a tuft of fur flying out, and then a splotch of blood.

Gable retreated, but not too far. For fifteen minutes he watched from a nearby limb, howling and barking his threats. Then he attacked again, only to be driven off once more by the older females. This time they carried the counterattack back up the tree. He found a good, solid limb and stood his ground, barking at them until they backed off and gradually returned to feeding at their original positions. Kath's pulse was racing as she looked for Judy and then Mickey, trembling as he clung to her side. Garbo, Ginger, and Patch moved to a post nearby. Gable appeared to calm down, and Kath tried to relax for a moment herself. But Mickey, the center of all this deadly attention, began to grow restless, and after a while he squirmed away from his mother, venturing out on a limb about three feet away from her.

Gable was making his way back toward him. The alpha was on a higher limb, keeping his eyes on the bystanders as if they were in some way the objects of his interest. But he kept coming closer, slowly, casually, until he was directly over Judy. Mickey scampered out on a smaller branch that cracked and broke. He fell through the air and Gable dived down after him, but Bette was already there. She scooped up the child and began clambering up the tree toward Judy. By now this stand-off had lasted an hour and fifteen minutes, and Kathleen was exhausted. She watched Judy with Mickey back at her side as Gable brachiated away. The mother was panting, a diarrheic ooze dropping down beneath her.

*   *   *

That evening Kath ran the Englishman from one corner of his rubble-filled tennis court to the other until he was red in the face and glazed like a ham. Sipping gin, Mac watched the rout from the sidelines with Pia and Chip. It had been Stasson's idea to get her out with a racket ever since Mac had mentioned her having won some kind of championship at Radcliffe. She was accustomed to playing with men, and she was accustomed to coming out on top.

"She's out for blood!" Stasson gasped. "The girl has no mercy in her."

Kath was not in a charitable frame of mind. She could not bash out a certain monkey's brains, so she was bashing a tennis ball instead.

After dinner, McKusick and Stasson went up to the lab. Kath shared a smile with this other woman, so different from herself. She said, "Pia, forgive me if I'm bringing up a painful subject, but . . . Nigel isn't your first child, is he?"

"No. We had a girl."

"We saw a marker. The little graveyard."

Pia nodded, smiling faintly.

"I can't imagine that kind of loss. I mean, I see you and Jack doting on your little boy . . . Do you ever get over it?"

"No. I feel it very much."

"Can another child fill the gap? The longing?"

"For me, no. Another child is different child. You love him, but he is not the child you lose."

"How did she die?"

"Very tragic. Not even Jack knew what to do. A healthy baby, happy, pretty. Then everything falls apart." She crumbled an imaginary leaf in her hands and let it fall to the floor. "Very fast."

"Nigel is a beautiful child," Kath said after a moment.

"Thank you. A good boy."

"It's amazing how much he looks like his father."

"Yes. Averages out, Jack says."

"How so?"

"Pia looked just like me."

On the way home that night, Mac was winding down the hill as if it were the Santa Monica Freeway. Kath looked out at the darkness looming over the edge and said, "Mac! Slow down! You're gonna kill us."

"Sorry." He eased off the accelerator and shifted back down into second. He knew she was edgy. He also knew that by now he could make it down this road blindfolded.

"I talked to Pia tonight. About the grave out back. About losing the little girl."

"What happened to her?"

"I don't know. She made it sound like the kid just sort of withered away and died."

McKusick nodded, but he seemed to be focusing on something else.

"What's wrong?"

"I don't know."

"No. Come on. What?"

"I don't know. As much as I like Jack, I don't trust him. There's something fishy about what he's doing out here. What he's doing every other day down in that Indian village."

"So what do you think?"

Their headlights swung past the bone-white cottage, illuminating a family of coatimundi scampering by. In the mimosa tree out front a family of opossums, pink and naked, hung upside down, the mother's eyes glimmering. Mac shut off the lights.

"I haven't a clue," he said.

30

SOMETIME NEAR THE MIDDLE of February, Ginger gave birth to a new infant, the first to appear in the Plantation troop since Gable's takeover. This new child was so small it was difficult to see as it nestled against its mother's black fur. But for the moment, Kath was more interested in Gable, resting tranquilly beside mother and child, acting very much the proud father. So this was the other side of the coin, she was thinking. Not the wrathful Herod but the watchful, protective male, tolerating the infant's occasional forays across his head and shoulders. The difference, of course, was the genetic link. But Kath was doing a little arithmetic while she watched—simple enough, but far more than the howler's primitive brain could handle. The normal gestation period for howlers is at least six months. The copulation she had seen—the shameless cow-eyed humping that had seemed so disgusting to

her—took place only in October. This was not
Gable's child. It had to be Bogart's.

McKusick was rummaging around in the file
cabinet trying to find the service manual for a
protein analyzer that was malfunctioning. Stasson
was off on one of his "clinical days," and it did
not seem likely that the rep from Hewlett-
Packard was going to be in the area anytime
soon. There in the middle drawer, neatly arranged in chronological order, were files containing Stasson's lab notebooks for the preceding
half-dozen years. For a moment, Mac rocked the
drawer back and forth on its metal rollers.
Stasson had given him the run of the house and
lab. Why would his host mind if he made a brief
review of the lab's progress up to this point? He
reached for the folder in the back of the drawer,
the oldest, and flipped through. Nothing very
extraordinary leaped out at him. Stasson had
been working on infertility, just as he had said.
The lab notes appeared to be cross-referenced
to other files containing epidemiological data.
Mac pulled out another drawer and reached for
the thick manila folder labeled "1969." He pulled
off the heavy rubber band and left it dangling
around his wrist. These were case studies. The
file gave off a moldy smell as he thumbed the
pages.
    Stasson had written up, in excruciating detail,
the sex lives and reproductive histories of a
succession of Indian patients, all infertile and
all from the Yonomo village. How could you get
so many cases from one small group of people?
At the back of the thick folder was a smaller

file. It was labeled "Pia. Age: approx. 15 yrs." Given the physical description and the age correlation, he knew that this Pia had to be Stasson's wife. If she had been part of this epidemic of infertility, then obviously Stasson had found a cure. Mac noted a reference and page number leading back to the lab notes. He dug into the file cabinet again and found the spiral booklet labeled "1969 C." It was devoted entirely to the endocrinological and gynecological condition of "Pia. Age: approx. 15 yrs." Mac flipped through it, spot-reading as he went, until he came across a passage that looked out of place.

Oocytes obtained by injection gonadotropic hormone. Stored in culture medium 2% cysteine hydrochloride at 18 C, brought to pH 8.1 with NaOH.

10 ml Sendai virus inactivated by UV light as per Okada and Tadokoro.

Oocytes combined with Sendai at 4 C, raised to 37 C. Fusion occurs.

He closed the book. He replaced the file in its proper place and slid the drawer along its rails back into the file cabinet. Maybe he did not want to know after all. He left the lab and went downstairs and out into the hazy sunlight to clear his head.

31

KATH WAS THE FIRST to see the tarantula. It was crawling along the back of the couch toward Stasson's outstretched hand. The two couples were sitting in the parlor, sipping brandy in the candlelight, when she saw the furry, eight-legged shadow projected on the wall in horror-movie proportions.

"Jack!" she shrieked. She pointed, unable to articulate, and Stasson calmly brushed it away with the back of his hand. The spider fell to the tile floor, and Stasson splashed it with brandy. Then, matter-of-factly, he reached over with the glowing candle. The creature reeled momentarily in its cloud of fire, then curled into a smoldering cinder. The stench rose and filled the room.

Mac and Kath sat with their hands to their mouths, and Stasson began muttering apologies. "Life in the tropics," he said. "Something's always creeping and crawling."

Pia stood and turned up the lamp. "I'll get a rag," she said.

Kathleen nodded. "I'll go with you."

The two men looked at each other and settled back into their chairs.

"I can't see it," McKusick began. He was studying Stasson's face. "I mean, how much privacy can a person use?"

Stasson shrugged and poured himself another brandy.

"Your explanation for this setup, Jack. I wouldn't call it a complete crock, but let's just say I don't think you've given me the whole story."

"Really?"

"It's an awfully damn inconvenient place to do research, pal. Why are you here? What are you up to with these Indians?"

"Ah, reality is never as intriguing as we'd like," Stasson said with a sigh. "I do have my reasons for a bit of secrecy, old man, but it's simple proprietorship." He edged forward in his seat, the light sparkling in his eyes. "The Yonomo are a bloody natural laboratory, and I have them to myself! No one could do any more for them than I've been doing. At least I'm protecting them from everyone else coming in and mucking about."

"Mucking about in what?"

Stasson swirled the amber liquid once around his snifter and then leaned back. "The Yonomo have been declining for decades, which is not surprising. Habitat's being destroyed for all the Indians. Missionaries. Booze. Developers. But it isn't that these people are being squeezed, so much. They have the rest of Amazonia if they want it—the only encroachment is from the west. The oil people. River traffic." He cleared his throat and then wet his lips with brandy. "This tribe was dying off simply because they weren't having babies! I mean they fuck and fuck and nothing happens. Pia was virtually the only member of her generation—to give you some idea of what I'm talking about. Some anthropologist wandered in with the oil companies and pointed it out to Bustamonte. He was intrigued. Whatever afflicted these people, he wanted more of it. Spread it around. So he brought me here to look into it. Saw my name in the papers during the flack at Oxford and rang me up from Bogotá. Of course I thought he was mad, but he offered inducements to come for a look, and here I am going on ten years later."

"But what about the infertility? Pia's borne two children."

"Oh no. Didn't affect her."

Stasson drained his glass, and Mac sat bristling at the lie. He had just skimmed a file two inches thick describing her infertility in clinical detail.

32

IT WAS MARCH, and the troop was gradually migrating farther and farther from the plantation. Kath began driving Mac up the hill to Stasson's, then using the jeep herself to cover the distance along the trail before taking off into the undergrowth on foot. Each day she scanned the treetops with the binoculars until she found Mickey and Judy. Surely within another couple of weeks the child would be weaned and on his way.

She was an anthropologist, not a naturalist, but more and more she was feeling at home in the jungle. She had come to like the dank smell of the vegetation, the rotting stench of compost. More and more she was coming to accept it on its own terms. She had watched calmly one morning as a rainbow boa crushed an unlucky cottontail. She had seen eagles drop from the sky to snatch capuchin infants from the trees. That was life. There were no guarantees, and every individual was somebody else's next meal. She had to watch what was crawling at her feet, but when she had the chance she could relish orchids dangling from the trees and parakeets streaming through brilliant shifts of light. The jungle was one great organism, an infinite series of living membranes through which the same energy was passed back and forth. The beauty of it made her optimistic.

The boy was playing at the computer terminal, banging away at it as if it were some kind of video game. McKusick was trying to work at the lab bench behind him, but the erratic clatter coming from the keyboard kept distracting him. The boy was getting angrier and angrier as his frustration grew. Finally he brought both fists down on the terminal and started to cry.

"Daddy! Help me!"

Stasson came over immediately. This was the ultimate only child, Mac was thinking. Not another kid around for five hundred miles.

"What's the trouble, old Chip? Nothing to cry about, I'm sure."

"This bloody display keeps rounding off my numbers!"

"What are you doing, son?"

"Euclid's primes."

"What are you in?"

"Assembly."

"Well, look, old man. The memory can only accommodate so many digits. You'll have to . . ."

"Okay!" he cut in angrily. "I've got it."

Stasson drifted away and the boy went back to his clattering.

Fine, Mac was saying to himself. A five-year-

old on the computer is not that unusual. His
father was a math prodigy, why not the son?
Mathematical ability is an inherent trait. It does
not take any hocus-pocus to pass it on to offspring.

Mac went back to work, and after a few minutes the clattering stopped. Chip had reverted
to being simply a boy, drawing felt-tip dragons
in a Spanish-language coloring book.

McKusick had set a sterile flask on the lab
bench and then stepped away. When he returned,
the flask wasn't there. He looked around, thinking he was losing his mind, and noticed that
Chip was also unaccounted for. He walked over
toward the windows, circling the area, and saw
a flash of red hair dart from under a table into
a lower cabinet.

"Chip!" Stasson bellowed. "What have you
taken, boy? Give it back. That's not a proper
game." Stasson made his way to the cabinet and
leaned down. "Chip!" No response. "You'll hand
it over this minute, or there'll be no pudding."
A small hand emerged holding up the flask.
Stasson took hold and offered it, apologetically,
to McKusick. "Sorry, old man. Bit of a hellion,
he is." Then Stasson slapped his knee. "All right
now, lad. Out of there. Let's go get some lunch."
The boy crawled out scowling, and Stasson
turned to Mac. "You ready for a break?"

"Not quite. I'll come down for something a
little later."

McKusick sat for a moment in the now-quiet
laboratory, staring at the flask. Then he pulled
down the large magnifying glass mounted overhead. He flipped on the fluorescent tube that
circled it with light, and began searching the

surface. He found two clear thumbprints, one large, one small. As far as he could tell, they were identical.

He swung the glass back into place and let out a deep sigh.

As Gable slowly approached, swinging from limb to limb across the canopy, Kath glanced around for Bette and Joan. But Judy and Mickey had wandered off to the edge of the feeding group. They were alone. Gable was moving swiftly, silently. He appeared confident, making no effort to camouflage his purpose. When he came to the branch just above them, he swooped down like a panther, knocking Judy off her perch and snatching Mickey away. He sunk his teeth into the infant's neck and swung to the next tree. Then he stopped. Kath saw a line of red appear on Mickey's flanks. She saw the pink of intestines unfold. The baby shrieked, then fell, and Gable settled onto his branch to lick himself. He glanced down, as if to satisfy himself that the job was done, and then brachiated away. Judy ran over to her child, too late. She took the nape of his neck in her teeth and climbed back up the tree. He was washed in blood, hanging limp in her jaws. Kath kept carving away with her ballpoint, until she realized that her notes were not making any sense. Her tears were wrinkling the paper, blurring the lines of script. She was crying out loud, now, with no one in the forest to hear her.

McKusick stood in front of the house watching the rising cloud of dust as the jeep climbed up the hill. The sun was melting down into the treetops. The day had simmered until it was done.

He eased himself down the sloping lawn to wait by the parking shed. He heard the roar of the engine and then saw Kath rounding the last curve. He could see from her face that something had gone wrong. He stood in the shade of the banana tree and let the dust rush up and envelop him. She skidded to a halt, pulled the brake, and killed the engine.

"What happened?" he said.

She climbed down and circled the fender. She had washed her hair and left it still wet, parted in the center and hanging straight. Her eyes were red-rimmed, and her skin had a translucent quality, like paraffin.

"How about some gin?" she said.

He took her under his arm and they began climbing together. "Tell me," he urged.

"Gable finally got him."

McKusick winced. "Did you see it?"

She nodded. "The tough-minded primatologist does not sink down during the splatter scenes. I'm okay now. I've been sitting in the damn jungle crying all afternoon, and now I'm fine. I've worked it out. And some good stuff's come out of it. It really has."

"Tell me!"

"I'm thirsty."

She sat in a wicker chair and McKusick poured gin and tonic water into tall glasses filled with ice. His own revelation could wait. Maybe it should wait indefinitely, he was thinking. He turned back to Kathleen and saw the stunned, visionary look in her eye. Maybe they were both sliding into some kind of tropical craziness. He had the momentary dread that she was going to start describing some voice that had spoken to her out of a burning bush.

She took the drink from his hand with a half-hearted smile. "I was so depressed I just sat there and cried," she said. "And it wasn't just sadness, it was anger! I kept thinking about all those pathetic females, meek and mild through the millennia, wringing their hands, hoping the old boy won't eat the children. Hoping maybe he'll come from the hunt and have a kind word for her." She brushed back her hair. "And then I realized what a load of bullshit that was. Nobody's been paying attention! They've all been watching the males and making up theories to explain male behavior, as if that were the whole story. I couldn't understand why Ginger offered herself to Gable right after he'd killed her kid. The reason was, she was already pregnant. She duped this sucker into spending the next couple of years protecting Bogart's child. It's an end run around superior male force. She's competing to get her genes into the next generation just like he is. And can't you see what this means about the evolution of concealed ovulation? And my God! —orgasm . . ."

Stasson came into the room with eyebrows raised. "Dinner is served," he announced. He pinched his nose, then headed for the bar to pour himself a quick gin.

Kathleen waited. She was impatient. McKusick said, "Right, Jack. We'll be in in a minute."

Then they stood up, and Stasson drifted back out with his drink.

She began to laugh. "The point is—I'm going to have a brilliant thesis! Female-female competition. The selective advantage of promiscuity and sexual deception. That's why female orgasm emerged—not to make her ready for her mate, but because sleeping around was the best strategy for *her* genetic advantage!"

He hugged her to his side as they walked through the courtyard. " 'Kathleen Albriton, noted authority on orgasm . . .' "

"Damn right! On all the talk shows. The Joyce Brothers of the clitoris."

He grasped the screen door and pulled it open for her.

"And I want you to impregnate me," she whispered.

"Well it's about time!" Stasson bellowed. "I'm hungry!"

The door slammed shut behind them, and Mac wanted to pivot with her and go back out again.

"All I hear from these two is clitoris and orgasm! Decent people don't converse about such things until after dinner. And we'll have no groping under the table!"

Pia smiled a slightly blurred smile. Mac noticed that the top three buttons of her blouse were undone. There must be something in the air, he was thinking. The empire was losing its grip.

"Tonight," Kath whispered.

Mac glanced down at the table and saw cassava, grilled fish, and chicha, the beer Pia made by chewing corn and spitting it back out into a bowl to ferment.

"Going native," Stasson said. Then, grabbing Mac's arm with an air of confidentiality, he said, "All I can do to gag the stuff down. Have a snort," and he slid over a Petri dish filled with dazzlingly white, very nearly pure cocaine. "The freeze will get you through the first course," he said. "Wretched stuff."

Kath took a pinch, and then Mac. It was bitter, uncut, and, in Mac's state of mind, redundant. Stasson was already coked up, and Pia was clearly bombed on something from her native pharmacopoeia. Kath sat leaning against Mac with her hand gripping his leg just above the knee, her elbow teasing him into an erection.

They began to eat, and Jack began badgering Kath about her new theory. "But that's the same old crap!" he said. "Sexually insatiable female. Schoolboy's dream, old man's nightmare."

"No! It's a fine distinction I'm making. The whole damn story of human culture is nothing but an attempt to control female sexuality so the male can know the baby she's carrying is his. This is not a trivial issue!"

"Agh . . . If you're talking about pair bonding—"

Pia began waving a finger in the air. "I know about these things," she said, and everyone else grew quiet. For once, she would settle the argument.

"I can tell how it all began." She rubbed her mouth with the back of her hand. "The women know," she continued. "The women begin it. Little boys have their penis sticking up, but they don't know what to do with it. When I was a child they used to grab me and hold me down and try to practice on me, but they never knew.

"The women had a village, you see, once, in the early days, all to themselves. One day the men discovered it. They sit and eat, and at night the one man goes to the woman, the other to the other. He tries to put it in her mouth and she says, 'Not like that.' He tries her ear and she says, 'Not like that.' He tries her eyes and her nose and she says, 'Fool. My mouth is for eating. My ears are for hearing. My nose is for breathing. This' "—Pia hitched up her skirt—" 'this is for fucking. You fuck this.' And he did. And the next morning the men went out and told all the other men, 'Last night we found the secret place. Now we know what fucking is.' And so then everybody started fucking like that. And that is the true story, because my mother told it to me."

Stasson rolled his eyes and said, "Darling, let's keep your little treasure trove out of the dinner conversation, eh what?" Then he buried his face in her neck, muttering, "We'll have it for dessert in the parlor."

Kathleen pushed back her chair. "Jack, Pia, thanks very much, but we got a baby to make." She took Mac's hand and stood up. "Doctor, I need your assistance."

McKusick put his shoulder into her belly. "This may be an emergency," he said, and hefted her up with him.

And with that he ran for the back door, Kathleen dangling over his shoulder. They stumbled out into the night, giggling, and just beyond the light from the window they fell into a bed of geraniums.

"Professor Albriton, what are the chances of achieving orgasm by spiritual union?"

"Nil. Don't waste the jiz."

"Let's do it right here."

"No, no. It's gonna rain. Let's get home."

They leaped up together and ran hand in hand toward the jeep. "This may take some trying, you know. You're over the hill. Live sperm count's dropping."

"Don't sweat it."

They piled into the machine and he started the motor. "I want big, swelling breasts," she said, "streaming like a fountain."

Mac threw it into gear and the tires dug into the mountain. "What is this fixation?"

They cleared the overhanging trees and saw a huge, rising moon poking through the clouds. "I'm gonna do it all!" she said. "I'm not going to be some harpy on the sidelines. I wanna know what it's all about, inside out. We're gonna be back in Cambridge in six months. Settled in . . . and you get to work, son. Support your family even if it means practicing medicine! I put the crib in the study. Never have to leave the house. Go right from the dissertation to the book."

He laughed and started singing "The Book of Love," while she chattered and the vehicle ground along in second, picking up speed as gravity pulled them down and the transmission held them in check. She threw her arms around him and started singing too. Mac was popping the brake to the doo-wop rhythm of the song, glowing with the warmth of her body pressed against his.

He hit the brake too hard and the wheels grabbed and the jeep went into a skid. They veered toward the crumbling shoulder, a slow-motion carnival ride. Kath was laughing, wild-eyed but ready, until the driver's side began to rise and she screamed. There was nothing in the darkness to stop them. She slid away from him and her spine slammed into the armrest. The roof crushed on the first roll. She fell across the seat, her knees landing on his chest. He reached for her, but they rolled again, and then again, faster and then faster, and all Mac could do was grip the wheel and watch Kath being thrown from side to side and top to bottom, screaming. Her face hit the dashboard and her nose snapped, splattered her face with blood. Then the passenger door slammed into a boulder with an explosion of glass. They had come to rest.

Liz

33

THE SMELL OF SAWDUST and fresh lumber could not disguise the odor of thirty years' worth of motor oil permeating the low brick building on Kirkland Street. It had been a foreign auto repair shop before Kluer's attorneys had leased it, with considerable foresight, from the Harvard Management Corporation. The place was gloomy, the only light coming from the raised garage door that was still the only means of entry or exit.

Liz Altmann's heels echoed on the hard concrete floor as she made her way across the large open space where the fermenters would be. She was there to check on the massive refrigeration system that was supposed to have been installed the day before. The new ceiling looked complete, though the electrical fixtures were not working yet. An office had been framed in off to the right, and in the back was space for refrigeration and storage, packaging and shipping. She stumbled over a 2 x 4, and the "plonk" of the lumber echoed all around her. She kicked it out of her way. Through the opening she confronted the stainless-steel walls and double glass doors of the unit. It looked right. She came closer to check the model and serial numbers against those on the purchase order. They matched up.

She turned and began to make her way back out. A man stood silhouetted against the daylight, framed by the open garage door. She could hardly see his face.

"Hi there," he said. He stepped forward and Liz began making contingency plans.

"You Dr. Altmann?"

"Yes."

"Scared you a little bit, didn't I?" He was coming toward her out of the sunlight. His hair was long and blown dry. He wore a cheap-looking suit with the vest unbuttoned. "I'm Phil Pulchari," he said. "I'm a lawyer. And you're a very good-looking lady scientist."

He seemed to be enjoying making her feel uneasy.

"What do you want?" she said flatly.

"I'm representing a couple from out of state. They're related to your friend Peter McKusick. I guess you could call them his in-laws, though I understand the young couple never took the benefit of clergy."

"So what is the point, Mr. Pulchari? This is a little removed from my concerns right now."

"Yeh. I hear you got your hands full with 'his honor' on your ass." He winced. "You'll have to forgive my language. I'm not used to—"

"Cut the crap and tell me what you want."

"My clients would like to have a little talk with Peter McKusick. Seems over the last three or four years he forgot to mention a little detail to these people. Seems he forgot to mention to them that they had a granddaughter."

He waited a moment for her reaction. There was none.

"They're not too happy with the arrangement. They're making noises like they think he may be a little off his rocker. Maybe some of this DNA shit seeping into his brain, huh?"

She had never given it a thought. There was no family in California. Mac had always been alone, and ever since he had come back with Kitty he had sealed himself off with her, almost indulging himself in isolation. Of course there would be grandparents. Of course there was more to the story—she had simply never taken time to think about it.

"How do you know they're the grandparents?"

He shrugged. "We just want to talk to your friend. That's all. Just talk. It's not going to help him any if we have to go for a subpoena. That's the next step."

"These are Kathleen's parents . . ." Liz thought a moment. "There could have been some other woman, you know. He was down there a long time. They're simply assuming that Kitty's her child."

"Why is he hiding?"

"Because there's a goddamn circus going on around here with that bastard Giacconi!"

"Yeh. And it may be that he's got something to hide. Look, I'm not out to nail this guy. I'm just trying to serve my clients. All they want is access to the kid, and to be sure that she's not in any danger."

"Look. I'm sick of hearing about 'dangers' from people like you. You don't even know what recombinant DNA is. You toss around the term as if it—"

"Hey! Lady!" From somewhere within, Pulchari managed a look that was workably condescending. "I don't mean from the bugs. I mean from her father."

34

THERE WAS A NOTE sticking up from the dial of her telephone. It was Kluer's distinctive scrawl, on Kluer's distinctive memo paper. "See me," it demanded. A loving touch from a loving husband.

Mrs. Nichols nodded assent as Liz passed by. "There's a gentleman with him," she said. Liz had thought there might be.

She entered without knocking. The gentleman stood up, while Kluer sat sulking on the couch, picking at a seam on the armrest.

"Ken McCarthy from the *Globe*," the man said. He extended his hand, big and pink and moist. He looked like a minor official in some forgotten branch of the federal bureaucracy. His suit was rumpled. His shirt was unironed. His belt was too long, and six inches or so flapped loose at the end.

Liz sat down in the center of the couch, and McCarthy regained his seat. He smiled and waited, as if Kluer might want to fill her in. He soon realized that it was up to him.

"We were just talking a bit about Peter McKusick," he said.

Liz nodded.

"He sounds like a very interesting man."

"Perhaps."

"Now ... As Dr. Kluer was saying, I know there's been some irresponsible reporting. Our friend at city hall is always out to make headlines, and so far the television people have complied. Still, I have to ask the obvious questions—it's an occupational hazard." He tapped his notebook against his knee. "I mean, is it recombinant DNA? Is the child's illness related to some outbreak from the lab?"

"Categorically not," Kluer said.

McCarthy smiled pleasantly and shifted in his seat. "How can it be categorical, Dr. Kluer?"

"There is absolutely nothing to implicate the lab beyond Vincent Giacconi's hysteria. There've been no accidents. No errors. No other reports of illness. Nothing."

Kluer sat glaring as McCarthy took a moment to jot something down.

"Dr. Kluer," he said quietly, still looking at the notebook. "There's another little story here that interests me. Something else that seems a little out of the ordinary."

"And what might that be?"

"That McKusick has dropped out of sight. That there's a couple here from out of state claiming to be the child's grandparents. Claiming that they never knew of the child's existence until they heard about her from the councilman."

He paused, and Liz began to understand the method behind this man's sloth. He looked so harmless—comfortable, cautious, a little bored; just the sort of sleepy uncle you might want to confide in. She kept silent.

"What can you tell me about Peter McKusick? I mean, what sort of man is he?"

"He's a very good father. He's a very good scientist," she said.

"What's his role here?"

"He's a technician," Kluer volunteered.

Liz glared at the lie. Their entire commercial operation was because of Mac. His contribution was absolutely fundamental.

"Whatever his personal peculiarities, this entire predicament has nothing whatsoever to do with the supposed hazards of genetic engineering. The work he's assigned to does not even involve genetically altered life forms," Kluer said.

"Right. But he does work on the same floor as Goldman and some of the others. I understand he even brings his daughter up here a lot. Beds her down on a cot while he works late at the lab, that sort of thing."

"That's right," Liz said. She had seen them coming in together so many times as she was leaving for the night. How many times she had wished she could stay with them instead of going home to hostess for Kluer, or to attend a meeting with Kluer, or simply to wait for Kluer to come in from the airport.

"What was he doing up here in the evenings? I understand he had his own little research program."

"He was working on the major histocompatibility complex as a factor in senescence. Culturing old and young cells. Comparing genetic transcription. He started it while he was in Colombia."

McCarthy smiled helplessly and shrugged his shoulders.

"The MHC," she said. "It's part of the immune system. It controls a number of responses involving cell-cell recognition."

"A possible link to the child's illness?" McCarthy offered.

Liz simply stared, curling her lip disapprovingly.

"I see." McCarthy made a note. "Well. I don't suppose you have any idea where Peter McKusick might be?"

She shook her head.

"Or any background on his relationship with these people? Why he would act so strangely?"

"None whatsoever. But if you people would stop jumping to conclusions and simply wait until you hear his side of it; it probably won't seem very peculiar at all."

"I couldn't agree more. But to do that we have to find him, and he is not being very cooperative."

She had nothing to say to that.

"It's a shame, too. Because in the meantime he's letting his opposition line up some fairly influential support. They already have a hearing scheduled. And the courts have been known to go against the natural parents in this kind of dispute, especially in what they might consider an 'unnatural' home environment. From what I understand, Peter McKusick's homelife is hardly what you would call 'natural.' "

                    *   *   *

Liz spun out of Kluer's office in a daze. She did
not wait to see what he had to say, much less
wait for him to dismiss her. She walked down
the corridor simply because it was long, and it
was dark, and it was bounded by two walls. As
she passed the departmental office a grad student at the phone desk called out, "Liz! It's the
Phoenix. They want an interview."

"Tell them to read the *Globe*," she said.

She saw a man standing outside the door to
her lab. A younger man. Good-looking. Nicely
dressed.

"Are you Dr. Altmann?"

"If you're a reporter, I don't have time to
talk."

"I'm not a reporter, but I would like to talk.
I'm with the cops."

"Delighted to meet you. Come in."

"Detective Giacconi," he said, flashing a badge.
He stepped through the doorway.

"Giacconi?"

"Right, right. He's my uncle."

"Christ!" Liz dropped into the chair behind
the desk.

"That has nothing to do with this. I'm simply
trying to locate Peter McKusick."

"Why?"

"Missing persons. A missing child. Complaint
was filed by the grandparents."

"This is official business?"

"Absolutely."

"That means if I lie to you or don't cooperate
you could lock me up?"

"More or less."

She leaned forward, resting her elbows on the desk. "Then maybe you'll believe me, Mr. Detective, when I tell you that I haven't a clue."

35

LIZ WAS HEADING OUTBOUND on the Southeast Expressway, just ahead of the afternoon rush hour. Orange barrels and wooden barricades guided her through the only lane not blocked by construction. She took it like a toboggan run, swerving through the narrow spaces, suprised to be feeling so happy. She had the top down but the side windows up, and the wind was bracing as it swept over her head. She felt like a woman racing off to meet her lover. Maybe she was.

As she passed the gas tanks in Dorchester she cleared the last of the construction and slipped into fifth gear and cruising speed. It felt good to be in the Porsche. She and Peter had picked it out during her Polynesian restaurant phase, her "learning to live in L.A. and like it" phase. The Porsche was all that was left of that time, now. It was also one of the few things in her life that Kluer had not somehow appropriated, catalogued, and diverted to his own uses. He had never driven it. In four years he had never even ridden in it.

She roared down the highway past the shopping malls near Hingham. There was life beyond Route 128 after all. Chevy dealers and Sears Auto Service Centers and six-screen shopping-mall cinemas. America! She had forgotten. She was an intellectual, a New Yorker, a Jew one generation out of Europe, yet it felt perfectly natural to be on a six-lane freeway heading for the beach.

She punched in a rock station on the radio and thought about L.A., and the beach. She simply needed to talk to Peter. She trusted him when he said Kitty was not sick, but she had to admit that this business of the grandparents worried her. It sounded strange, what Mac had done, if he had done it. But she didn't believe he'd been driven over the brink quite so easily. The important thing for the moment was that she felt herself coming back to life. She was going to be able to help him.

She thought about all the dead spaces she and Kluer had inhabited for so long. Whenever they left their incredibly focused little world, the half-mile lying between the Bio Labs and their home, it was to jet cross-country to some conference center or to hop onto the shuttle to New York or Washington. It was all airports and Marriotts and folding chairs in windowless rooms. They never drove anywhere like this, the way real people do, to see the real world. They remained insulated, which was Kluer's natural condition but not hers. And certainly not Mac's. But being with Kluer had deadened her, and it was the tension that was most deadening of all, the tension of loving Peter and yet cutting back and cutting back, trying to convince herself that it was not true; so much so that her entire emotional fabric was worn thin. She was feeling old again.

A prefabricated apartment complex appeared on her right, its aquamarine tennis courts looking like swimming pools with nets strung across the middle. She wondered what kind of people built their lives around such a core. She and Kluer went away for the summers, but it was only so that they could get more writing done. They had their summer home on the Cape, but they had chosen the site not for proximity to the beach but for proximity to the library at the Marine Biological Laboratory.

She crossed over the bridge near Pembroke, and suddenly she was in the country, traveling through cranberry bogs and marshes. It was so easy to forget the textures of the land, to forget the special signature of the region, of New England. She was ready to slow her life down now, to make some attempt to settle into this place. Her major ambitions had been achieved. Now maybe it was time for minor accomplishments, little endeavors meaningless to anyone but herself. She wanted time to read, to plant a flower garden, maybe to take piano lessons again after twenty years. She wanted—she broke off the thought before it could fully form. She had carried his child inside her once, but she had not been ready. That much was understandable. But why had she been so rash, so absolute and irreversible in having the tubal ligation? There was no back-up. No fail-safe. What was done was done. And yet in Peter's case she had been so cautious, so foolishly sentimental. She had enough of his sex cells frozen away in the lab to repopulate the earth.

After the rotary at the Sagamore Bridge she was on the Grand Army of the Republic Highway, four lanes of undivided traffic alongside the Cape Cod Canal, flanked by Cape Cod Charlie's Bait and Tackle, Ye Olde Homestead Motel, and The Herring Run. After a mile or so of this, the Bourne Bridge lifted her higher and higher over the canal until she felt airborne. A tugboat was nudging a line of barges hundreds of feet below. Through the erector-set steel of the railing she could see Buzzards Bay in the distance off to her right, the familiar outline from the map made visible now in three dimensions. She found herself playing with the gearshift, stroking it self-consciously. She laughed at her own eagerness.

She had to get McKusick back for the hearing. That was primary. He would be able to sort out all the confusion with Giacconi tomorrow afternoon, and then they could see about the rest of it. But there was no point starting back, of course, until the morning.

She spun around a rotary and went flying off on the tangent marked South 28, toward Falmouth–Woods Hole. A green sign pointed her to "The Islands," just as the Bourne Amusement Park gawked at her from the roadside. A carnival tent with minibikes, bumper cars, a driving range, and a roadside restaurant specializing in waffles. It was a grotesque idea of fun,

just as Los Angeles had been grotesque, but at
this moment she totally approved. After another rotary, the road narrowed to two lanes
through the coastal forest. Again, a sign promised "The Islands."

The antique shops and guest houses along
the way appeared ready for winter hibernation.
There were no busloads of tourists leaving the
Island Ferry parking lot for the docks in Woods
Hole. Even the summer scientists, the only vaca-
tioners with no interest in the Vineyard or Nan-
tucket, were gone now, leaving just the oceano-
graphers and the permanent staff of the Marine Biological Laboratory.

Just before the Coast Guard harbor she was
there, turning left, heading out toward Nobska
Point and their private road. She crossed the
narrow wooden bridge, passed by the Church
of the Messiah with its graveyard. The Porsche
hugged the curves as the road wound past the
expensive year-round homes, and Liz swayed
back and forth in the leather seat. The sun had
made it hot, and the leather burned her legs
with each slight shift in position. At the top of
the hill she could see the water. She felt another
rush of excitement, one remembered from
childhood, at that first glimpse of ocean. The
road dropped down quickly to shore level, a
row of telephone poles jutting out of sand drifts
giving it the look of a Dust Bowl highway in the
thirties. Between the clumps of grass and the
dips in the road she could see the house back
behind the pond. She looked for his car. She
was eager for any sign of him, but she would
have to wait.

Just before the rise toward the lighthouse she turned off. She rumbled along the dirt road, studying the house looming ahead of her. There was no car. She stopped in front and let a cloud of dust catch up with her. There was nothing lying about. The doors and windows all looked shut and locked. She got out, walked up to the porch, and reached under a flagstone for the spare key. Everything was silent, except for the faint sound of the ocean behind her. The door had been left unlocked. She pushed it open and felt the stillness that had settled in again.

"Mac?" she said. The sound echoed dully in the silent house.

She looked in the refrigerator and found it stocked with food. There were dishes in the drainer and fresh ashes in the fireplace. She went down the hallway and found a trickle of water running in the bathroom sink. She twisted the tap and turned it off. Then she stepped into the bedrooms and found the beds they had slept in rumpled but the closets empty. There were no suitcases. There was no other sign that anyone had been here, or that they ever planned to return.

36

KITTY WAS SLEEPING as the 747 lumbered down the runway. Mac grasped her hand through the torsion and queasiness of liftoff, eager for the pilot to level out and the stewardesses to start serving alcohol. It was going to be a long night, with a stopover in Miami.

The No Smoking sign disappeared almost immediately. As they banked in a wide turn, he looked out the window and saw Manhattan Island outlined by the eerie glow of vapor lamps. Which was harder to believe—that this warehouse was now thousands of feet in the air, or that his child might be dead in a matter of days?

He listened to the hydraulic groans of the aircraft as it maneuvered, then the gliding whine of the engines as the pilot cut them back for noise abatement. This night, a graceful dive into Sheepshead Bay had a certain appeal. But Kitty was still *alive*, he told himself, her deterioration was not that advanced. He had started

her on thyroxin that morning, to try to stabilize
her metabolic rate. The drug would balance the
build-up of glucocorticoids until he and Stasson
could get to work. Like the passengers on this
plane, he had put his faith in technology, and
now there was no backing out for any of them.

The Fasten Seat Belts sign disappeared. The
stewardesses wheeled their carts up the aisles
and he bought two miniatures of Jack Daniel's.
He unscrewed the cap and downed the first
bottle. Then he slipped off his shoes and settled
back, nestling Kitty under his arm. He leaned
down to kiss her as she sighed in her sleep, and
the smell of her breath turned his stomach. He
opened her mouth and swabbed the reddish-
brown excrescence along the edges of her gums.
He ran his finger along the row of tiny molars.
They were coming loose in their sockets.

Approaching the immigration and customs barrier, Mac had a momentary panic. All along, he
had carried the dread that someone in authority was going to question him. His own nervous
distraction was suspicious enough, and impossible to hide. But one glance would tell anyone
who cared to notice that this little girl was very
sick. McKusick nudged their bag along with his
foot as Kitty slept in his arms. He held up his
passport and waited. There was a two-sentence
exchange, and the small, dark man slammed
down the rubber stamp. He was utterly indifferent to this norteamericano and his child. They
were accepted into the country.

Mac drifted along with the flow of travelers.
He was groggy and disoriented. He felt threat-

ened by the crowd he saw squeezed behind the aluminum barrier up ahead. They seemed to be jeering at him, holding up their placards. But they were not there to antagonize him. They were waiting to greet friends and relatives from Miami. He scanned the line for the familiar, debauched face of Jack Stasson, but that spark of recognition and relief never came.

The air-taxi service would not reopen until dawn. Mac sat upright on a couch in the starkly lit terminal, his daughter sleeping in his arms. He held her hand in his and tried to ignore the grotesque pattern of senile keratosis that was now recognizable on her skin. The wrinkles and discoloration might be reversible. He had to believe that they were. It was damage to her brain and nervous system that he dreaded hopelessly. He knew that lipofuscin had to be intruding everywhere, dissolving her cells into bags of yellow-brown pigment.

He lifted his eyes and gazed across the expanse of empty floor, still gleaming in the swirling pattern left by the buffer. Airports and hospitals. The all-night places. He had been on duty through many a sunrise as a medical student and resident. Then as now, he had wished the night would end. He felt like the cancer patient who had cried out when Mac mindlessly closed the door on rounds. He needed the light to keep hoping.

McKusick did not trust the pilot, but he had been up all night and was too tired to find someone else. The man had behaved like an idiot, staring in open-mouthed horror as he looked into Kitty's face. Couldn't he tell that the child was awake, that she would see? Mac tried to distract her as he buckled her into the rear seat, wishing the half-wit would pay attention to his radio and his controls. It came as a relief when the man settled in and started to whistle and chatter about his women as they waited for clearance. When the signal came, he gunned the engine and the plane raced forward, gaining speed, hurtling them into the cloud hovering over the end of the runway. They broke through it quickly and continued to climb.

The day was overcast, but the ceiling was high. It was like flying indoors, beneath a huge vaulted dome. Once they reached the river it would be up to Mac to give directions, but to him, every square mile of rain forest had always looked the same.

Kitty had just enough energy to be restless throughout the long trip. Mac tried to point out sights along the way—a rugged peak, a waterfall—but once they cleared the mountains the landscape became tedious. They were flying over endless grasslands, and Kitty started singing "The Wheels on the Bus Go Round and Round." Mac joined in with her, making the motions for each verse—the wipers on the bus going swish, swish, swish, the money on the bus going clink, clink, clink. She had been coming home and teaching him new songs ever since she started at the nursery school. At least Cambridge had been good for her in that respect—she had been around other children.

The airplane kept up its monotonous drone, and Kitty sang "The daddies on the bus go 'read, read, read,' " as she held up an imaginary newspaper, "all through the town." Then in a high squeaky voice she mimicked, "The babies on the bus go 'boo hoo hoo,' " and dabbed at imaginary tears. She did not seem to notice that the tears in her father's eyes were real.

Off the left wing, Mac saw the gray bunker projecting from the hilltop. He tapped the pilot on the shoulder and pointed. The man nodded, then threw the plane into a slow spiraling path downward. They glided low and made a pass over the villa. Mac could see nothing moving except their own dark shadow and a swirl of tropical birds rising up to meet them.

The pilot let the plane roll to a stop in the middle of the landing strip but did not even kill the engine. He claimed to be in a rush to get back to Bogotá, and remained seated at the controls as Mac lifted out their bags. Mac counted out the last of his cash and placed it in the man's creased palm. They were utterly and completely alone now. Mac took Kitty in his arms, and the sound of the propeller grew louder and the plane rolled away.

Mac watched the Cessna taxi to the opposite end of the field. From this point on they were stranded, with no money and no one to help them except Jack. He had put all his faith in Stasson. The plane started racing back toward them, lifting off at the point where Mac had left their bags in the center of the field.

Kitty said "We're home, Daddy," and the pilot tipped his wing in a gesture of farewell. Mac did not notice. He had already begun the long walk up to the villa.

They passed the cottage where he and Kath had spent their months together. It was overgrown now, slipping into a hopeless state of disrepair. The sound of the airplane was growing fainter and fainter, but McKusick was listening to his own ghosts.

It took a little over an hour to climb the hill up to the house. It was a steamy day, and sweat ran across his face. His scalp was burning and his shirt was soaked. And all the while he had an appalling sense of déjà vu as he made his way up the winding road.

What if he had come all this way, spending his last dollars, simply to have Kitty die in sweltering discomfort in this godforsaken place? Whatever might have kept Stasson from coming to Bogotá for them, at the very least he should have been roused by the plane. He should have driven down to the airstrip to collect them.

"Stasson!" Mac began shouting as he climbed the steps that led from the road up to the front of the house. The only response was the wind, the buzzing of cicadas, and, occasionally, the loud, piercing whoop of one of Kathleen's howlers.

They walked across the yard and up to the verandah. The front door was open, the screen unlatched. Mac made his way inside and peered through the gloom. The only light came from the windows facing the courtyard, and was diffused through the heavy vegetation of the inner garden.

"Stasson!" Mac let out.

"Where is Uncle Jack, Daddy?"

Mac glanced down quickly. Then he checked

his irritation. "I don't know, sweetheart. How do you feel?"

"Kinda sick," she said. The heat had added a red blush to her face.

He walked down the flagstone hallway that led to Stasson's sleeping quarters. He turned the corner and saw the man coming toward him in his underwear. His eyes were blurs of red and yellow. The deep lines of his face came together like the rubble of an orogenic belt, all faults and fracture zones.

"You said you'd help me," Mac began. "Didn't you get the cable?"

The Englishman padded by on bare feet and staggered out toward the courtyard. He pushed open the screen door and said, "I got the cable."

Mac followed him out, then let Kitty down to play with a tennis ball that had been left behind.

"I'm sorry, old man. I just couldn't face it. Not again." He fell into a wrought-iron chair and worked his fingers through his hair.

"We could have used some help at the airport."

"Shit. I'm sorry, Mac. But Madam Bottle seduced me. She fucked me good, to tell the truth. I'm still pissed."

"Where's Pia? Chip?"

"Back to the village. She said she'd leave the next time I got like this. I did . . . and she did. It surprised me."

"We've got to get to work."

Stasson glanced up at him, still refusing to look at Kitty. "Is it worth it?"

"What the hell do you mean, Is it worth it! This is my child we're talking about!"

"Worth the pain, old man. To her. To you. It

simply doesn't work with females. It worked with Chip. Chip's fine. But our baby girl . . . Now Kitty . . ."

"Jack, this isn't just an exercise. I haven't just been jerking off the past three years. I've sequenced the gene! I can save her, dammit!

"Come on, Mac. You can't be sure of that. The chances of isolating it, much less correcting it, are so fucking slight . . ."

McKusick's eyes silenced him. "I'm sure," Mac said.

Stasson dragged his hand once more over his damaged face. "Get me some coffee," he said. "Just let me get straight."

They would perform the splenectomy that afternoon. Mac could either try to suppress Kitty's rampaging autoimmunity with anti-B cell reagents—Nisonoff, mercaptoethanol—or he could simply remove her spleen, the primary site of autoimmune cells. The drug treatment was risk free but slow, and time was one of the many luxuries they did not have. Any surgical procedure, however commonplace, involved a degree of risk. The conditions he would be working under here pushed those risks well beyond an acceptable level, but there was no choice. He had to set his course of action and then see it through. Time was running out.

While Kitty napped and Stasson sobered up, Mac scrubbed down the small surgical unit Stasson maintained in one corner of the lab. Unlike the rest of the villa it was air-conditioned, cordoned off by heavy drapes and mosquito netting. It had been months since it had been used, and Mac went over every surface with soaps and disinfectants. He broke open the sealed packages of instruments and sterilized them again. He set up the Mayo stand, then tested the monitors and the anesthesiology equipment.

Mac ate a little, then tried to rest. He dreaded the fine line he was going to have to walk between autoimmunity and infection. The hypersensitivity of Kitty's antibodies was what was killing her, so he had to suppress them. With her immune system suppressed, she was fatally vulnerable to any and every microbial threat. Infection in the tropics was a matter of serious risk even without a massive surgical invasion of tissue. The smallest cut left untreated could turn a foot, and then a leg, black within a matter of hours.

He knew he was violating every canon of medical ethics by operating on his own child, but that seemed the least of his transgressions at this point. He had entered this nightmare one small step at a time, yet it had all been waiting for him from the first moment panic or love or pride had allowed him to slip over the edge. His only consolation now, and it was not much, was confidence in his technical skill. He could handle the surgery and he could handle the rest of it. Stasson's competence as anesthesiologist was a much more immediate concern.

37

When Lee Albriton saw the story he was livid. He had gone downstairs for the newspaper and a cup of coffee and was scanning the headlines. There on the bottom of page one was a picture of Phil Pulchari standing at a microphone. Next to him, pounding his fist and flapping his tongue, was Vincent Giacconi. Albriton threw a dollar on the counter and hurried back to the elevators.

"Mr. Pulchari, this is not what we had in mind."

He had called the lawyer's home number. He had reached him at the breakfast table.

"Mr. Albriton. How are you this morning?" The sound of crunching toast was coming through the wire. "Now let's slow down. I'm afraid I don't understand the problem."

"We are not after publicity."

"Your name's not mentioned in that story, Mr. Albriton."

"That's not the point. There's just no need to

sensationalize. This man Giacconi would have
her touching off an epidemic and McKusick
some sort of lunatic who kidnaped my daughter.
I just don't like it. I don't see how press conferences are going to contribute anything."

"Look. A little public opinion on your side
has never been known to hurt. I do favors for
my friends and they do favors for me. You said
you wanted to nail this guy, and I'm gonna nail
him for you. It's like Sinatra. I do it my way."

"We didn't say anything about 'nailing' anybody."

"Mr. Albriton, don't bullshit me. Then just
what were we talking about?"

38

LIZ WAS RACING UP the steps of the Middlesex County Courthouse, stepping over beer bottles and newspapers blown by the wind. She had wasted half an hour trying to find the building, and then another fifteen minutes circling the block looking for a place to park. Just as she reached the massive red-brick columns, thick as smokestacks, she saw the sign— USE SIDE DOOR ONLY. "Christ!" she let out. She was miserably late already.

She ran around the corner toward the ground-floor entrance of the crumbling old building. There she found a far less grand doorway with "Family Court–Probate Court" stenciled on the glass. She bolted through, startling the pair of uniformed guards just inside the narrow hallway. They were sitting on either side of a metal detector. One of them, old and frail, glanced at her purse distractedly and waved her on. Another flake late for her divorce, they must have been thinking.

She flicked a comb through her hair and tried to catch her breath, then passed into an airless waiting room that looked like a railway terminal— oak benches, white pillars, a coffee counter closed down for the afternoon. To her left, the first of four flights of stairs. She started climbing. It was so easy to forget the fabric of laws that bind our lives. She was accustomed to dealing with natural laws, elegant and precise.

The smoke from a hundred cigars seemed to rise with her as she climbed. She passed under a sign—REGISTRY OF DEEDS ... REGISTRY OF PROBATE— with stenciled hands pointing in opposite directions. There were phones ringing and the echoes of a dozen conversations as the lawyers and bureaucrats wandered the tile hallways.

She was out of breath when she reached the fourth floor. Above her, a stained-glass dome covered with a century's grime let in a lurid light. But down the hallway to her right was an intense white glare hovering over yet another crowd of film crews and reporters. She was too late. The proceedings were over.

As she came closer she could see that the lights and cameras were focused on a short, rumpled pensioner wearing a polyester suit and vinyl shoes. It was Vincent Giacconi.

"I have no idea," he was saying. "They may have taken him out of the picture. Got him in one of their hospitals someplace, who knows? Maybe they dumped him in the river. That's the way these Wasp Harvard types operate, you know. Cement overshoes. But only the best brand!" The reporters laughed. Liz could see how Giacconi must brighten up their lives. He had to have been the first person out the door, making sure they "caught" him first.

"Why'd he hide her from the grandparents?" someone yelled.

"Probably 'cause he knew there'd be a hearing just like this one to take her away from him. It is not healthy for children and other living things around here, with these tin gods on the loose. What they're doing in their laboratories is a sacrilege. I just hope we all don't have to atone for it."

Liz let them pass on toward the stairway. The double doors had been thrown back and the rest of the crowd was coming out. She could feel the suction as the air rushed toward the huge open windows of the courtroom. The walls and ceiling here had a fresh coat of light-blue paint. She saw a well-dressed couple coming toward her past the rows of oak benches gleaming with shellac. The lawyer Pulchari walked behind them, until a tall man with a briefcase tugged his sleeve and he lagged behind.

Liz stood in the doorway confronting them. "I'm Liz Altmann," she said. "I work with Peter McKusick. You're the Albritons?"

Both of them focused on her intently. Nina said, "Do you know where he is? Do you know what he's done with Kathleen?"

Liz shook her head. "I wish I could help you. But I'm sure there's a reasonable explanation. I know Peter pretty well. I can't believe there was any malice in anything he's done."

"Just what kind of explanation do you think

he could offer, Miss Altmann?" Lee Albriton
stood to one side as the women stepped through
the doorway ahead of him.

"I don't know. He may be disturbed. Maybe
the accident was too much for him—who knows?
But he lives for Kitty. I do know that. I don't
think you have to worry about her safety. Or her
health. I'm a scientist, and I can tell you that
these people, this Giacconi, he's simply in it for
himself. He doesn't know what he's talking about.
The government has been easing the restrictions.
There was a rash of hysteria, and a long close
look—years have gone by—and there's simply
no danger to be found."

"I hope your faith is justified," Lee said. "On
all counts."

The Albritons walked on out, arm in arm, and
Liz was left standing just beyond the door, holding steady against the current of people still
leaving the courtroom.

The policeman from the day before was coming out. He noticed her and smiled. "You missed
the feature," he said.

She forced a smile. "What was decided?"

"He's been ordered to present the child before the court and to show cause. Either the
court or the Albritons could be made guardian.
I'd bet on the Albritons."

"But why? How can they do that when he
hasn't done anything? He hasn't even been able
to tell his side of it."

"Look. Courts protect children, not fathers. A
father without a marriage license is nowhere.
The mother's solid-citizen parents will win out
every time."

He took her arm and guided her to a bench surrounded by ashtrays. "Got a minute?" he said. She sat down. "You know, I'm really not a bad guy. I got a couple of little girls myself."

She nodded. She liked this man.

"You sure there's no way you could help me locate her father?" He studied her face for a moment. "It might be doing him a big favor," he said.

She looked into his dark brown eyes. It was the same question he had asked before, and her answer would have to be the same. Only this time it was the truth.

39

"WHAT'S THE STORY on Bogotá?" Detective Giacconi asked her over the phone.

The Immigration Service computer had recorded Peter McKusick and a minor child passing through the international terminal at Kennedy. His car had turned up at the airport in Providence. He had left it there, collecting parking tickets at a meter until it was towed, and boarded a commuter flight for LaGuardia. He had helicoptered to Kennedy, then boarded an Avianca flight bound for Bogotá, Colombia.

Liz tried not to show any emotion. She had already pulled Mac's letters from the file, looking for the address. She knew he had either gone to California or back to the jungle, and his choice came as no surprise.

"There's a private research institute near there. That's where Mac worked for the last few years."

Giacconi made a check mark on the scratch

pad in front of him. "Anything else you want to tell me?"

"That's all I know."

The only address was a post office box. She had been trying all day to get a telephone number, but with no luck. "It's run by an Englishman named Stasson. Somewhere in the south. Near Peru."

"Sort of what you'd call the middle of nowhere."

Liz nodded, thinking. "So what are you going to do?"

"South America is a little out of my jurisdiction."

"What about the FBI, or—"

"He hasn't committed a crime. Yet. But I'll tell you this, he's going to be up to his neck in hot water if he ever wants to come back to Cambridge."

"I doubt that he's worried about court orders right now. But Mr. Giacconi, who else knows about this? You haven't told the Albritons, have you?"

He waited a moment. There was no point in lying to her. "They were here when I took the call."

40

AT 2:30 MAC GOT UP, washed his face, and put on a scrub suit. He checked Kitty. The Phenergan and Demerol he had given her were working well. She was sleeping soundly.

He walked down the hall and stuck his head into Stasson's room. "How is it, Jack?"

The Englishman sat on the edge of the bed wearing an identical suit of surgical greens. He sat bathed in the afternoon sunlight, dust particles swirling around his head. He was leaning forward, gripping a coffee mug positioned evenly between his knees. "Sorry about before, Mac." He looked up, then let his focus drift back down to the floor. He seemed drained of all energy except the downward pull of regret.

"Are you up for it?" Mac asked him.

Stasson nodded. "I'll be fine."

McKusick watched him drink from the cup. He'll have to be, he thought. There's no one else.

Mac walked into the room where Kitty was sleeping and scooped her up in his arms. She still felt like a child, naked and small. She *was* still a child. He made his way toward the surgical unit with her wrapped in the sheet. How many times had he carried her to her bed like this, only to realize that he did not want to let her go? He would simply stand in the dim glow of her night light, swaying back and forth and humming a lullaby. That feeling was reinforced a thousand times now as he held her over the surgical tray. She was sick, but she was warm. She was alive, yet the surgery risked it all in a matter of minutes. The normal anesthetic risk was daunting enough. Under these conditions, with Stasson assisting, the risk doubled. But it had to be done and done now, or there was simply no hope at all.

He lowered her onto the cold, hard surface of the tray and wheeled the IV stand into position. He scrubbed the back of her hand with disinfectant, then inserted the needle into the vein. He glanced up and saw Stasson by her head now, inspecting the equipment that McKusick had already checked out. Mac taped the rubber tubing to the back of her wrist, then turned the stopcock to start the flow. He moved to the other side and began attaching the adhesive disks of the electrodes, encircling the tiny unformed breast. He flipped the switch and watched the reassuring signature of her sinus rhythm traced across the screen.

Stasson assisted as Mac scrubbed. Then the Englishman came around to Kitty's side with a syringe of Pentothal and injected it into the tubing of her IV. Kitty was gradually being lowered into a deeper and deeper sleep. Stasson adjusted the regulators over the cylinders of halothane, nitrous oxide, and oxygen, then placed the mask over her face, forcing her to breathe the mixture of gases that would sustain her in an anesthetized state. Mac stood by, his gloved hands motionless in front of him. He watched Stasson inject the *d*-tubocurarine. Almost instantly her breathing stopped. Her skeletal muscles were paralyzed. Quickly, the Englishman inserted the endotracheal tube, inflated it to form a tight seal, then squeezed his hand around the ventilating bag. Her chest rose slowly and then fell. For the next few minutes she would be depending on Stasson for her every breath.

Mac bathed the upper left quadrant of her abdomen with disinfectant. Then he picked up the scalpel. He glanced at the ECG monitor, then at Stasson's bloodshot eyes peering at him over the surgical mask. He took a deep breath, and as he released it made a left subcostal incision, tracing a line of red across the pale white skin. He had to override all but the most conditioned responses as he made the deeper cuts through the viscera. It made no difference how many times he had tickled this belly. He listened to the steady rhythm of her heartbeat and let his training carry him through the work at hand. He severed the splenorenal, splenocolic, and gastrosplenic ligaments. Then he placed his left hand on the spleen itself and applied a gentle pressure. With his right, he transected the splenophrenic ligament, revealing the short gastric vessels, which he then ligated and cut, each in turn. Finally, he was left with the pedicle of the splenic artery and vein. He tied them off, he cut them, then he lifted out the organ itself and placed it in a stainless-steel bowl.

The surgical suite became the recovery room. Mac moved Kitty to a cot where she could be more comfortable, but kept her within the aseptic confines of this one corner of the lab. He made a bed for himself on the floor where he could be at her side around the clock.

After twelve hours the wound was draining properly and there were no immediate complications. He started her on dimethylaminoethanol. He had to assume that her lysosomes were overloading with lipofuscin. The drug would stabilize the membranes of the organelles and prevent toxins from leaking through and doing further damage. He gave her centrophenoxine to retard the formation of lipofuscin in the brain, and Gerovital to activate the brain cells' own scavenging mechanisms. He kept her caloric intake down to practically nothing. He had to retard her metabolism in every way possible until he could reverse the genetic switch that was speeding her toward the end of life.

While Stasson watched over Kitty, Mac rummaged through the kitchen, the storage rooms, the garage. He needed a watertight tank in which Kitty could rest immersed in water and ice.

Mac stumbled down the cement stairway leading to the cellar. The exposed bulb overhead was filthy and cast a sickly half-light over the cardboard cartons and jumbles of discarded furniture and equipment. A pair of scorpions backed away from him to stand their ground in the corner, defending a mound of dust and grit.

A series of large wooden crates were leaning near the sliding doors that led outside. Mac came closer, ducking his head to avoid the exposed water pipes. Branded into the wooden slats of each of the crates was the emblem of the Colombian Oil Corporation. McKusick looked inside one of the crates to inspect what looked like a large metal cabinet. It was an aluminum coffin. There were four of them, two adult size and two much smaller. Stasson's lab was simply the nearest thing to a hospital in this isolated place. In case of emergencies, this is where the workers would come. In case of death, this is how they would leave. McKusick gripped the last crate, one of the smaller ones, and lowered it to the floor. He found a length of pipe nearby and used it as a crowbar to pry the boards loose. When he was finished, he lifted out the small, highly buffered aluminum box. It was much too large for Kitty, he told himself.

Upstairs, McKusick sterilized the coffin and lined it with a layer of sponge rubber and then a layer of rolled towels. He placed it on a cart and wheeled it into the surgical area where Kitty was resting.

She was still heavily sedated. Mac coated her body with a thick layer of Vaseline to protect her skin. He gave her an injection of chlorpromazine to temporarily knock out the hypothalamic thermostat in her brain, then lowered her into the bath. They would need a level of hypothermia bordering on hibernation to lower her metabolic rate and bring down the number of misguided lymphocytes circulating in her blood. The water temperature was 4 degrees Celsius. He inserted a rectal thermometer to monitor her body temperature, which would now align itself with the temperature of her surroundings. At 34 degrees Celsius she began violent shivering, the body's last defense against cold. He gave her an injection of morphine and heparin, and the shivering stopped.

They kept her at 30 degrees Celsius for four days. On the fifth, she was showing increased tolerance to the chlorpromazine, so Mac discontinued the drug and replaced it with crude marijuana extract mixed in a Tween-80-saline medium. He would still have to wait another forty-eight hours to begin the gene transfer operation. She was responding well. All they needed now was time.

41

LEE ALBRITON WAS WAVED through the gate by a uniformed guard and by a small, stylishly dressed man he took to be an immigration official. The man smiled faintly and extended his hand. "Welcome to Colombia, Mr. Albriton. I'm Jorge Estaban. Call me George." Estaban led Albriton toward a pearl-gray Mercedes 380 where a middle-aged chauffeur stood by the open door. "Jesus is trained in evasive driving," Estaban said. "We're in good hands in case you're being followed." Once inside the car, Albriton said, "I can't imagine anyone would be following me."

"You're here to take back your granddaughter?"

"That's right."

Estaban shrugged, smiled behind his tinted glasses, and lit a cigarette with a slim Cartier lighter. After a moment he said, "How is my friend Mr. Schoenbacher?"

Albriton glanced up as if he'd forgotten

something. "I haven't seen him in a while," he said. "How do you know him?"

"Coffee. My firm represents the growers in this country. His firm represents them in the States."

Albriton nodded, and the silence returned as the cigarette smoke swirled around their heads. They were on a modern, multilane highway. Just beyond the right-of-way on either side were hovels made of scrap lumber and tin.

"We'll take you to your hotel," Estaban summarized. "A good dinner, a good sleep, and tomorrow we will fly to the Putumayo."

The Colombian mentioned several fine restaurants they could try, but Albriton begged off. He did not want to be wined and dined as a client—this stopover was merely a necessary inconvenience. He ordered dinner from room service and ate it alone, looking out once again at the lights of a strange city. The clouds hovered low over the urban landscape shimmering outside his window. It was not the jewel of the Andes he had expected. It was Dallas with mountains. It was Denver.

For a moment he felt swallowed up in the depth of his anonymity. He did not know another soul on this entire continent. He remembered the same sort of feeling—the mild titillation of it—from his traveling days when he was young. Even in places like Tulsa and Houston he could have found some pleasure, swept along by the hedonism of good hotels and restaurants. But he had kept himself in check. He was a family man, even then, and he had willingly made the sacrifices. He had made a commitment to Nina, and he had been investing in it for thirty years. Now he wanted the payoff. He wanted to sit back and enjoy the family they had raised together. He wanted to enjoy the grandchildren he had sacrificed for.

The next morning Estaban was waiting for him with the same car and driver. The sky was clear. The air felt clean, rinsed by the night's rain. Still, Albriton had not slept well, and at this hour his senses picked up nothing but irritation.

"Do you like flying, Mr. Albriton?" Estaban's face reflected the glow as he lit an early-morning cigarette.

"Enough, I guess." He did not feel like making small talk. He was nervous. He had a queasy stomach. But it was not the flight that worried him. It was what they were going to do when they landed. He had the feeling of being swept along by forces he had initiated but over which he had long since lost control. He had even lost touch with the emotions that had started it all. He had lost Kathleen once already. Why was he torturing himself?

They rode in silence to the airport, a different one that was devoted to private aircraft, executive jets. The sky was still red in the east. The tarmac was wet. The orange windsock atop the hangar hung limp.

Albriton and Estaban sat behind the pilot, who hardly looked old enough to be out with a car. Albriton studied the back of his well-groomed head and tried not to think. The lift-off through the early-morning air was smooth and gentle. Estaban smoked, and Albriton rested his head against the curtained window. His eyes burned and his stomach churned. Below, the Andes dropped away, allowing the small plane to gain altitude without climbing. The earth remained green, only less rugged. Albriton could see the morning sun reflected in the Guayabero River, a thread he had to follow.

"Do you speak Spanish, Mr. Albriton?"

"A little. None of it well."

Estaban nodded thoughtfully. "I don't know this man in the district, but I'm sure he is a reasonable fellow. I'll try not to spend more of your money than I have to."

"It doesn't matter."

"You're probably right. Two or three hundred dollars would seem like a fortune to him."

They were flying over the eastern savannahs now, the sea of grassland that washed up on the foothills of the Andes.

Estaban crushed his cigarette in the ashtray beside him. "The district police, you know ... In these rural areas, they take the largest and stupidest oaf in the village, give him a gun, and let him dress up in a uniform. It's mostly to keep him out of trouble. He is a very tractable public servant, loyal to whoever pays for his food and his aguardiente. But he is still a peasant, hardly in shoes and dulled by the parasites. He has ... how shall we say it ... rather base instincts."

Albriton nodded uncertainly.

"I have heard of men castrated. Disemboweled. Fed to dogs."

Albriton's nausea increased. "I see what you mean."

The oil-company airport first appeared as a dry stripe in a hay field. The pilot had radioed ahead, and a car was waiting for them. A white 1962 Chevrolet, parked alongside the fuselage of an ancient P-38 the color of molted skin.

A crosswind made their descent bumpy. In the rising heat, the plane simply did not want to go down. But then they were hovering low, then magically rumbling along the ground.

Albriton stood stiffly for a moment in the sunlight. Then he was bending down again, into this relic of a Chevrolet, which roared off in a blast of smoke as if it were powered by coal. The driver turned his head from time to time and rattled away at Estaban through a mouth of jagged brown teeth. The Spanish was coming too quickly for Albriton. He simply looked out at the sun-baked vegetation threatening to reclaim the roadway. He glimpsed a cloud of dust up ahead and then saw a herd of jabalinas galloping across the road. The driver surged forward, yelled something back over his shoulder, and with a wild burst of laughter caught the last of them under his right front wheel. There was a squeal and a thump, and then the animal was rolling over and over in the dust behind them.

"Why did he do that?" Albriton asked.

Estaban shrugged. "For kicks? Is that still the term back in the States?"

After a kilometer or two Albriton could smell the agua negra alongside the road. Wooden houses appeared in the distance, a town from out of an Italian western. The car sped through the jumble of buildings and stopped in front of a café.

"The man is having lunch," the driver said.

The cafe itself was made of timbers that seemed to be gradually easing themselves down into the gully that ran alongside. A pile of Coke crates was the only buttressing. A huge shade tree covered the roof. Estaban and Albriton walked in from the low verandah.

Two uniformed policemen sat at the bar drinking aguardiente out of the same bottle. Their sergeant sat at the most distant table, at the side of a man wearing a loose-fitting white shirt and wraparound sunglasses. The civilian's face was leathery, dark, reptilian. His thin mouth seemed frozen into a lipless smile.

"Mr. Estaban," he whined. "You made good time. Welcome to the prize of the river."

Estaban returned his greeting. They were approaching the table. Neither of the men stood up, but both studied Albriton closely.

The mayor said in a slow, slurred manner, "You are bringing us foreign aid? Welcome. Sit down." His wiry arms hung down like vines.

The newcomers ordered refrescos, and Estaban began to tell their tale. The mayor continued with his lunch—mazamorra, arepas, and tamales. The sergeant sat with one hand resting on the stem of his aguardiente bottle.

The mayor slowly scraped his plate with the native bread. Then he shoved back his plate and his chair and made a ceremonial gesture of wiping his hands and face. He took a final sip of beer.

Estaban offered two hundred dollars to help defray the expenses of the police in carrying out this action. "A donation for the good of your town," he said.

The mayor took a final sip of beer, sucked his teeth but said nothing. The sergeant leaned over to spit at the base of a palm tree potted in an oil drum.

By the end of the conversation the price agreed upon was an even thousand dollars, and the mayor was nodding with satisfaction and patting his stomach. Then the sergeant reached down to the empty chair beside him and retrieved the handgun lying there. It was a German automatic, large enough for a caisson. As he stood and stuffed the weapon into his holster he said, "Mr. Albriton, do not worry about this man who kidnaped your granddaughter. I will make him a soprano."

The Chevrolet was waiting as they came back into the sunlight. Estaban, Albriton, and the mayor got into the back seat; the sergeant took the wheel, with the two policemen beside him fondling the small Uzi machine guns in their laps. The driver was left on the verandah, scowling as the men pulled away.

The mayor gave directions, and then began to discuss tactics. Estaban calmly lit another cigarette, while Albriton reeled from the nausea he had felt all day, compounded once more by the smell of sweat and tobacco in the hot, crowded car. Fortunately he was by the window, which was open to the breeze. He looked out and saw the land rising slightly. There was a ravine below them now, and Albriton thought of the accident. He looked down at the boulders protruding from the side of the hill and he wondered which one of them Kathleen had been crushed against. Then again, that entire story could have been McKusick's fabrication. What kind of fear would have made her keep her baby a secret from them? What kind of pressure? In this place, Kathleen could have been kept a prisoner. Anything could have been going on. Kathleen was dead, and McKusick was responsible. Albriton wanted his grandchild.

The house was just beyond one more bend on the winding road, but the sergeant pulled over against the hillside and stopped the engine. Albriton could see a series of stone steps in the high grass. "A little exercise," the mayor said. Behind him the doors slammed shut like cannons.

42

STASSON PUSHED BACK the drapes, and a narrow swath of warming sunlight lay across Kitty like a blanket. He took her pulse at the carotid. He listened to her chest with the cold stainless-steel stethoscope that gleamed in the light. There was no change. The signs that he hoped for each day simply were not coming.

He lifted the clean white sheet and confronted her small withered frame. The subcutaneous fat of childhood was gone. She had lost seven pounds—one-fifth of her total body weight. Her ribs protruded, ghostly reminders of his own daughter just before she died.

He was supposed to be a bloody genius, wasn't he? He had chosen to live on the edge because genius could not wait for the normal channels, the peer review, the checks and balances. He had rushed ahead assuming that any damage he might do along the way would be offset by the glorious fruits of his brilliance. He had never imagined that the people bearing the cost would be those he loved most.

It was too early now to tell if anything they were doing for Kitty was having any effect. She was alive. That in and of itself was remarkable. But they were working in the dark. For all Mac's confidence that he had found the answer, they were not even sure of the question. Why did the error affect the girls and not Chip? Was it true aging, simply too early and too quick, or was it autoimmunity, as Mac insisted—antibodies no longer able to discriminate between self and nonself; subtle cellular changes making "self" no longer the same—mimicking the degeneration of old age? Ultimately, was there any difference?

He followed the clear tubing that lay across her belly to the plastic bag hanging at her bedside. He changed the reservoir, setting aside the contents for urinalysis. Then he scrubbed his hands.

McKusick had traced the defect to a single gene on the MHC, and so they had taken a bold gamble. They had extracted marrow from the bone in Kitty's thigh and altered its DNA, tightening the histone bond to turn "off" the damaged switch. But to give these cells an advantage, they had combined them with a syngeneic strain selected for resistance to the cancer drug methotrexate. They then irradiated Kitty's entire body, suppressing what was left of her immune system, and after that reinserted the marrow cells. They began treating her with heavy doses of the drug. If Mac was right, and very lucky, Kitty's entire population of marrow cells would be transformed in time, because the altered cells, with their advantage of drug resistance, would thrive and return her immune system to a normal level of activity. If Mac was wrong, or unlucky, she would die.

The incision where they had removed the marrow was fine. Stasson changed the dressing and then sat down at her bedside. He cleared away the few additional strands of hair that had fallen onto her pillow. She was virtually bald now. It was a sorry sight, and he took full responsibility. He remembered the stunning features of the young woman McKusick had brought to his house. This was not the idea at all.

From the second-story window Stasson's line of sight extended far into the green jungle surrounding him. The cool insulation of the room was deceptive. His gaze traveled downward to the rim of the hill, where he saw three men climbing the last of the steps. One was Baptista, the mayor of the village. The other two he did not recognize. What he had not seen was the three armed policemen preceding them. As it was, Stasson felt a surge of tension in the pit of his stomach. The small man had the look of a Bogotano, an official of some sort. The tall, fair-haired man behind him looked decidedly American.

Stasson padded down the stairs in his bare feet. He was tired, worn out by the work and the strain and the guilt. He slowly descended the last of the steps and rounded the corner into the vestibule, where the policía stood star-

ing at a grotesque modernist statue. He came
forward shaking his head and said, "All right,
mates . . ."

The policía spun around.

43

McKusick was at the edge of the jungle behind the guest house, raiding a beehive that had taken over the hollow of a massive, dying oak. He was capturing workers to extract the royal jelly from their pharyngeal glands. They secreted it to feed to the queen larvae. McKusick was feeding it to his daughter to try to keep her alive.

He stood and turned toward the house. Did Stasson have a gun? McKusick began walking. He dropped his collecting jar gently to the grass and began to run. He wanted to be there now, but his legs would not move fast enough. He rounded the side of the cottage and gained his first clear view of the house. There was no sign of anything amiss. He raced across the flagstones that bordered the pool, stumbling as he vaulted up the steps leading to the inner courtyard. His voice echoed, "Jack! Jack, what's going on?"

His momentum carried him across the garden and into the dim light of the entryway, where he confronted six men and the body of Jack Stasson. One man spun around to face him, yelling "No more! No more shooting!" It was Estaban, kneeling by Stasson's head. Lee Albriton stood pale and silent, staring at the blood making its way across the intricate tile floor.

The three men in uniforms descended on McKusick. "Echate al suelo! Agache la cara! Pon la cara contra el piso!" Uncomprehending, he was slow to respond, and the sergeant gripped the back of his neck and brought him down. Three machine pistols were trained at his head.

"This was not necessary," Estaban was saying.

The mayor shrugged and removed his sunglasses to blow a speck of dust from one of the lenses. "They lack training," he responded.

Estaban looked up at Albriton. The American was still staring at the corpse, and both were equally motionless. Estaban stood and walked over to McKusick. "The man is not armed," he said. "Let him up."

McKusick was dragged to his feet, the muzzle of a machine pistol still pressed into his neck.

"My name is Jorge Estaban. I'm an attorney acting on behalf of the Family Court of Middlesex County in the Commonwealth of Massachusetts. That body has awarded temporary custody of Kathleen Albriton to her maternal grandfather. We're here to take the child."

McKusick stared in disbelief. He looked at this controlled little man, then turned to face Albriton's pale look of disgust. Then he began to laugh.

The lawyer continued. "Why don't you take us to your daughter?"

McKusick, his eyes closed, began convulsing. Estaban sighed and adjusted his tinted glasses.

McKusick was shaking his head, tears rolling down his cheeks. "You killed Jack," he said.

"Take us to the girl. We want to help her."

"I'm the only one who can help her!" he screamed.

"I think there are sufficient doctors in Boston to handle whatever is wrong with her." He said something to the mayor in Spanish. Then he turned and said, "Mr. Albriton, why don't you come with me."

McKusick lunged forward and the policía pinned his arms.

Albriton turned away toward the stairs.

McKusick was struggling. "Listen to me!" He wrestled one arm free and took a step before the sergeant's baton cracked into his skull. His knees buckled. "Albriton!" There was a kick in the groin and another blow with the club, and McKusick fell to the floor.

44

"SHERRY?" the president asked.

Bayard Kluer took a seat on the sofa underneath a portrait of John Winthrop. "Thank you, Tyson, but no."

Tyson Bates seated himself in a straight-back chair by the window, the late-afternoon sun framing him like an illuminated text. He was the twenty-sixth president of Harvard, the latest in a line that had begun a century and a half before the United States Constitution was even dreamed of. Whatever indignities befell the presidency in Washington, and however many fools the people were forced to abide there, this was an ancient office still worthy of respect. Even Bayard Kluer could summon up some vestige of social grace in Massachusetts Hall.

"Now what's all this about ants?" Bates asked.

Kluer smiled and shook his head. "A young man with troubled sleep. This Watson, a post-doc, got it into his head that he caused the child's illness. A virus carried out of the lab on the backs of pharaoh ants."

"And?"

"Preposterous."

"You're sure?"

Kluer nodded slowly. "Our entomologists recently concocted a treat of synthetic juvenile hormone mixed with peanut butter. They spread it, as it were, throughout the building. The pharaoh ants are no longer an issue at the Bio Labs."

"Well, what *is* the problem then?"

"I think we can have an autopsy soon. That's the only hope of resolving this."

Bates clicked his tongue. "Who's looking after her?"

"Rycliffs at Children's."

"Good man?"

"The best. I made the arrangements myself for this Texan couple. I wanted to make it perfectly clear that we at Harvard were cooperating fully. That we have nothing to dread."

"And what is the state of play?"

"As soon as she's dead—"

"That's a bit hard, isn't it, Bayard? I mean, a three-year-old child?"

Kluer half-smiled. He allowed a moment to pass before he continued. "A good pathologist should be able to demonstrate that this Giacconi fellow has once again made a fool of himself. I should think that will keep him quiet for a while. Then Biota will be able to move ahead, and with that precedent established, I think it would then be prudent to announce the Harvard Plan."

Bates uncrossed his legs, adjusting his weight

in the chair. "Actually, Bayard, that's why I wanted you to drop by. Lew Williams from the financial office is going to join us in a moment, and I thought we could go over the details once more."

Kluer nodded, sensing rightly that there was more to come. Bates stood up and for a moment gazed out the window toward Widener Library. He was longing to return to his Chaucer and the soothing irrelevance of the fourteenth century.

"Frankly, Bayard, my reservations are growing." He turned back to face his guest. "Which is not to say that Harvard does not appreciate your family's generosity. I, of course, admire the inspired quality of the innovation. I simply don't know if the overseers, not to mention the faculty, are ready for the University's direct involvement in a commercial venture on this scale."

Kluer smiled tolerantly. "The University publishes and sells books. The University is the largest landlord in the city. With a one point six billion dollar endowment, we are hardly—"

"Yes, yes, but . . . This is *industry*, Bayard. It's not just the propriety of it that troubles me. I'm simply perplexed about the feasibility of the plan itself. The incentives for the researchers involved."

"We can make it attractive."

"I'm not so sure." Bates returned to his seat and leaned toward Kluer. "Your willingness to, essentially, donate your own commercial enterprise—as well as your family's largesse in offering to fund the institute . . . Well, it's quite unusual. For the other scientists we would be asking to cooperate, it would be the denial of an opportunity to make a great deal of money. And you must admit, Bayard, that the plan, endowed by the Kluer family, would place what might be seen as an excess of power in your own hands."

Kluer was nonplused. Of course there would be power. Money bought power. "I think my feeling is shared by most of my colleagues," he said. "None of us wants to see the academy dissolve in a vulgar scramble for profits."

Bates sat back and stroked the underside of his chin with a delicate forefinger. "You may be wrong there, Bayard. I simply think your colleagues are being secretive. In the past weeks we've learned of two more corporations being formed. Fredericks is behind one of them. Monoclonal antibodies. And Rosen. He's forming a company with Shields from MIT."

Kluer sat perfectly still, displaying no emotion.

"You were counting on both of them, as I recall."

Still no response.

"The point is, these fellows can now become quite rich from the proceeds of their science, and we cannot blame them for trying. This fellow McKusick, for instance, the one behind your cell-culture technique. Are you so certain he is going to be inspired to such altruism?"

"He's placed the negotiations entirely in my hands."

"You personally control the patent, then."

"There is no patent. I advised against it."

Bates cocked his head ever so slightly, and Kluer went on. "There are myriad variations, so a patent would be useless. The key to success is in getting contracts, and that I have done. Until after the clinical trials there is only one customer for interferon anyway—the National Cancer Institute—and we have their commitment."

"I see." Bates was laboring to conceal a growing discomfort. "Suppose Harvard is not permitted to accept your offer and you simply follow through and incorporate privately. This young fellow will be a principal in the firm, will he not?"

Kluer smiled faintly. "From what I've been able to glean, young McKusick, like the ants, will be troubling us no more."

45

"SO WHAT HAVE YOU got, Hughes?"

The young resident cowered against a file cabinet at the nursing station. Rycliffs was leaning toward him, physically intimidating him.

Charlie Wharton watched as the boy scratched his brow, inflated his cheeks, and then blurted out, "Hell if I know!"

The boy glanced at Wharton, then at his boss, who was scowling at the sudden burst of candid ignorance.

"It's not infectious," Hughes assured them. "I know that."

Wharton nodded. "I think the CDC would like to be the judge on that one. Why don't you just describe the case to me a little. Tell me what you've found so far."

The resident made his way around the counter, trying to regain his composure. "Well, as for physical findings, it's hard to know where to begin. She has the incision on the right thigh.

Her skin is thin, nails atrophied. Scleroderma and ichthyosis on both hands. We've got complete hair loss, loss of subcutaneous fat, but no enlargement of joints. I mean, this is not classic progeria."

"Right." Wharton nodded, leading him on.

"Blood cytology's normal. Serum calcium, phosphorus, cholesterol normal. Normal ECG, glucose tolerance, and urinary seventeen keto-steroids."

"You've gone through a complete battery of tests?"

"Absolutely. X-ray showed normal sella turcica, no coxa valga. The lungs are congested—a touch of edema. But the eyes give it away. She's got senile miosis! Pupils down to 2.8. Dilator muscles are atrophied, cataracts in both eyes. Dr. Rycliffs"—the resident turned pleadingly toward the Chief of Service—"I mean we've used amino acid racemization, psychomotor indices, adipocyte function, and a CAT scan. That's the end of the line."

He looked at Wharton and shrugged. "What we have here is a three-year-old girl with the body of an eighty-year-old woman."

46

"SERIOUSLY ILL" was all the newspapers were saying. Liz could find no indication whether the sickness was a new, unrelated development, or, in fact, the same condition that had brought on all the attention in the first place.

The Children's Inn was not putting through calls to the Albritons. She tried Detective Giacconi's office, but he appeared to be out on some never-ending investigation. She was growing frantic for the one piece of information the papers were glossing over completely—the whereabouts of Peter McKusick.

Congressman O'Neill's office had put her in touch with a Latin American specialist at the State Department. He promised to pursue the matter through the embassy in Bogotá until something turned up. Liz had decided to give them another twenty-four hours. Then she was going to fly down herself.

* * *

At the hospital she met a wall of indifference bordering on hostility. She was dismayed. "You can't even tell me what room she's in?" she said. Behind her the automatic doors opened and closed with an urgent rhythm.

The clerk touched her finger to the bridge of her eyeglasses. "That's what I said." The woman was entering a brittle middle age, and she did not like her job. She looked down, and Liz felt as if she had just become invisible. She was at a loss. There was no more to say.

She drifted past the long information desk and into the lobby itself. She passed shelves of picture books, available on loan for the patients. The patients here were all children—eleven floors of them. Liz was suddenly undone by the forced cheerfulness of the place. Behind her was a gift shop with candy and toys. She could see a bright rainbow made of tufted fabric, a clown suspended from red balloons—each destined to hang over a hospital bed. What if Kitty *was* sick because of the lab? What if she was only the first?

There were dolls in glass cases, a play kingdom of wooden barriers with doors and windows and crawlspaces, a terracotta path leading to a carousel of tiny unicycles linked together under a polka-dot awning. She studied the faces of the adults in this waiting area. She felt an obligation to put her own fears into perspective, but she could not be expected to worry less about Mac because Kitty was sick, or because there might be other dangers, or because anxiety was commonplace. She had practically destroyed him with her callousness. She could admit that. She had distanced herself from him for years, but that made no difference now. She loved him and he needed her.

She walked back to the desk. "Look. I want to leave a message."

The clerk slid a pad and pen toward her and went back to her file cards.

Liz clicked the ballpoint up and down while she tried to think. She made it as far as "Mr. Albriton." At this point, expressions of sympathy would be artificial. "Where is Peter McKusick?" she wrote. "Please call me." Then her name, and then her number.

Just beyond the glass doors of the lobby was a newspaper machine. She dropped in a quarter and took out a copy of the *Globe*. Then she walked down the winding entry ramp and around the corner to the Children's Inn, determined simply to sit and wait.

There was a sofa on either side of the door and a walkway in between. She sat down. She held the paper up in front of her, stage business to conceal her distraction, but her hope of remaining inconspicuous was a joke. Behind the desk, fifteen feet away, the hotel manager watched her like an inept predator, smiling awkwardly each time their eyes met.

She scanned the front page for the dozenth time, struggling to focus her attention. There was nothing about Mac, nothing new about Kitty. Genentech's stock had just soared from $35 to $89 on the first day of trading. Bayard would be ecstatic. And word had leaked of Harvard's plans for a biotechnology firm of its own. This was news to her. ". . . a major commercial venture in partnership with the University." There had been nothing said about this at the last faculty meeting. ". . . research supported by its own commercial applications . . ." The humanities people would go berserk. ". . . a financial hall of mirrors put together by Ruggles Professor of Biochemistry Bayard Kluer." Her jaw muscles gradually eased their grip as she stared dumfoundedly at the page.

A man entered and would have tripped over her if she had not drawn back her feet. His jacket was over his arm. He was disheveled and unshaven.

"Mr. Albriton!"

She dropped her paper and ran over to him. He looked up, blinking. His eyes were tired.

"I'm Liz Altmann. We spoke at the hearing."

He gazed at her without recognition.

"Where is Peter McKusick?"

His focus shifted beyond her head and he began to walk away.

"Wait! You've got to tell me where he is!"

He shook his arm free from her grasp. "Peter McKusick was detained."

"What do you mean 'detained'? Detained by whom?"

"The authorities in Colombia."

"Why? What are they holding him for?"

Albriton continued toward the elevator.

"Just how did you get Kitty out of the country?" Her voice was brazen with suspicion.

He stared up at the floor indicator, mute and immovable. The metal doors rolled back and he leaned forward. She grabbed his arms and tried to shake him. "Tell me where he is!" But her grip had no more effect than her screaming. She started pounding on him. "Tell me!" she insisted, and she caught him on the side of the head with her clenched fist. A shard of pain shot up her arm.

He grabbed her shoulders and gave her a jolt. His face was red, his neck distended. "You need to get hold of yourself," he said. Then he released her and stepped into the elevator. She burned with humiliation as he glared back at her from beyond the closing door.

There was a message on her machine from Mr. Curtis at the State Department. Her fingers were clumsy as she flipped through her book for his number. Frantically, she stabbed the digits for the call to Washington.

"It's not much," he began. "But maybe it's good news. They just found the Englishman. Jack Stasson."

"Yes?" she said. She waited. She did not understand. "What did he say?"

"Oh . . . No. I mean they found the body."

"What! What do you mean? How is that good news!"

His voice was matter-of-fact. "There could have been two," he said.

47

A SOFT TOUCH ON HIS eyelids, a tickling of the lashes. It was Kitty again, teasing him, trying to pester him awake. He smiled faintly in his sleep and went down deeper.

He saw himself surrounded by thirty dead and naked bodies lying spraddled in varying degrees of dismemberment, their feet in the air. The lighting was an intense white glare. The air was chilling and reeked of Formalin. He sat up to scratch his nose with the inside of his elbow—his hands were covered with embalming fluid and human fat—then leaned forward again between her knees. He inserted his right hand deep within the pelvic cavity to trace the obturator nerve. With his left he felt along the abdomen to correlate the nerve's location with surface structure. A blue stocking cap was pulled down over the lifeless head, covering it completely. That was very important to him. That was essential.

He felt the tickling again, and the air was amazingly hot. Amazingly still. He opened one eye. Over his head was a low roof of thatch. The faint touch was not Kitty's. The pressure was divided evenly among six delicate legs scampering across his face.

He bolted up, swatting at the cockroach, and felt a thundering pain in his head, a foul taste in his mouth. His back was stiff. His hip ached. He had been sleeping on hardpacked dirt.

He lay back down and looked toward the hazy glare of light in the doorway, but he could see nothing beyond the evenly spaced steel bars. He glanced around him. There were the flies, a little straw, and two ten-gallon paint cans. One was filled with water, the other with vomit. Near the cans the dirt had been brushed away, exposing the bars running underneath him. He followed their line up the mud wall and into the thatch. He was in an animal cage covered over and plastered with dirt—the municipal jail of the town of Arepas. He remembered now. The men with dark glasses. The guns. Stasson lying in a pool of blood. He rolled over onto his side with his knees drawn up. He did not know why he was still alive, but he did know that this was where his life would end. Where was Kitty? Was it over? It was beyond his control. He was not going to be able to save her now, and beyond that overwhelming fact he was indifferent. He would spend whatever was left of his life in this hole. His life was over.

He woke again with an incredible thirst and the feeling of having been baked. The lowland sun was full in the sky now, and his cage had become an oven. He heard footsteps in the dirt, and then saw a brown uniform at the door of his cell. A guard, a boy of maybe twelve, was unlocking the door.

"Hey, American," he said. "Your lawyer's here."

McKusick wondered what kind of a joke this was supposed to be. He sat still, eyeing the boy suspiciously. The boy's taunting smile disappeared. He squatted down to see into the cage and swung his machine gun into position. "No kidding around. Get out of there. Fast."

McKusick crawled through the doorway into a steaming sun and was confronted by a pair of beige Gucci loafers. He looked up into the disapproving face of Jorge Estaban, who was eyeing him through the clear lower portion of his sunglasses. Estaban nodded toward the shade of a massive palm tree. "Why don't we sit over there."

They reached the shadows, and Estaban said, "Sit down. It will make him feel better."

McKusick glanced back at the boy, whose gun was still aimed vaguely in their direction, and sat cross-legged. They were in the yard behind the mayor's office, contained by a makeshift fence, barbed wire threaded through chicken wire. Beyond them was an open stretch of weeds where the forest had been cut back. Someone's horse was tethered there in the middle, grazing desultorily.

Estaban leaned down and, peering intently, took McKusick's chin in his hand.

McKusick shook free. "What are you doing?"

Estaban sat down. "Checking your face for bites. You look okay so far."

McKusick, undermined by lethargy and indifference, gave him a puzzled look.

"Chipo bugs," he said. "They live in the thatch. They bite you around the mouth and nose—the mucous membrane. The infection is latent, but after a period of years—complete breakdown of the nervous system. Very unpleasant."

McKusick touched his mouth, staring back at the hut. How long had he been kept there? He did not know.

"That was one of the risks I had to take," Estaban confided. "It was a consideration—but I thought you might rather take the chance than be unequivocally dead right away. I want you to know that I arranged for you to be detained here until Albriton and the girl were out of the country. There were other alternatives. Other suggestions, you see. The man has a rich hatred for you. I suppose I can see why. The blood tie is very strong. But I want to hear your side of it."

"Why?"

"I've made certain inquiries. The mayor has informed me of some of the local gossip. He said the child's mother was an Indian woman."

McKusick leaned down, linking his fingers behind his neck.

"I made some investigations at the embassy. Kathleen Albriton died in March 1977. Kathleen McKusick was born in December 1977, to Peter McKusick, an American citizen, and Isada Ochoco, a Colombian." Estaban seemed to be resting his case. There was silence, except for the leaves rustling overhead.

McKusick looked up, aware that some kind of

response was expected. "What difference does it make?" he asked.

Estaban was tapping a cigarette against the side of his lighter. "I'm an attorney with a powerful and prestigious firm. I have a reasonably strong stomach—one has to in my profession. But a man has been killed and a child has been taken away from her parents. You do not seem particularly deranged to me, by the way. I simply want to know why this has happened."

"I don't care to talk about it."

"Oh," he said, nodding. "I see."

Estaban took a long, thoughtful drag on his cigarette. He picked up a twig, tapped his shoe with it a couple of times, then threw it away. He looked beyond McKusick's hand to the backs of the dismal buildings of Arepas. "So how is the Red Line construction going?"

McKusick did not comprehend.

"The last time I was in Harvard Square it was a total mess. They had half the Yard dug up as well, which made for a very dusty tenth reunion." He paused for another puff. "I was class of seventy. Law School seventy-three. How about you?"

McKusick was silent.

"Boston is a very pleasant city," Estaban continued, "with excellent medical care, as you well know. I'm sure your daughter will improve. I'm also sure your despair is pointless."

After a moment he gestured toward the guard. "That boy who is watching us. For five dollars he will shoot you. For fifty—he will have to share it—he will set you free. Right now I plan to have lunch. Then I can get back on my plane and leave you here with him and the chipos, or I can take you with me. It's entirely up to you."

McKusick considered the offer, if that's what it was. "What do you want out of it?"

"Simply the truth."

McKusick let out a long sigh, then for a moment studied Estaban's face.

"How much biology did you have?"

48

IT WAS CHEAP CALIFORNIA wine, soaking into an extraordinarily expensive rug. Liz was on her hands and knees, trying to blot it up with a towel from the bathroom off the study. The wine, Mondavi Red, was hers; the rug, an Oushak brought back from a vacation in Istanbul, was Kluer's. Kluer had always said that quality was indestructible in rugs . . . in automobiles . . . in people. Perhaps her quality just didn't measure up. She was very definitely falling apart. Fraying at the ends. She had knocked over the wine jumping for the telephone. She had a call in to the American embassy. She had been on the phone with Mac's old roommate in California. He had promised to be in touch if he heard from him. But the caller was merely Ute Mayr, checking in. Liz would have liked to talk but for the need to stanch the flood of table wine and keep the line open. She wanted to talk to someone. She had to find something to do to

SPIRALS   289

fill the time. She dug at the fabric with the fluffy yellow towel, now blood red. The rug, which had probably seen as much wine over the years as Kluer's cellar, showed no trace.

She poured another glass and curled up on the couch, drawing the bathrobe over her knees. At least Bayard was gone. Thank God for that. One of the family planes had been summoned to Hanscom Field and whisked him off to Nassau. Most people went there to gamble and lie in the sun. Kluer went there to sign papers. If he had been in the house, with his stern presence, his self-centered preoccupation, she would have gone raving mad. She had been utterly livid when she first read about his scheme with Harvard, but the anger died and was replaced by a kind of satisfaction. It simply eased her guilt. She felt nothing for Kluer now but contempt.

She closed her eyes and tried to draw warmth from the brass floor lamp glowing at her shoulder. She loved this room. The teak and leather, the walls of books. It was seductively comfortable, but at such a price. Their desks faced each other—a perverse romantic notion left over from their first year together. Ever since then, she had tried to arrange her schedule to avoid him. He would sit rigid with concentration, oblivious to outside stimuli, flinging words onto paper like a demon with that machine of his—an IBM Correctible Selectric II, with interchangeable fonts for Russian, for German, for mathematical symbols.

It was frightening that any mind could order sentences and paragraphs so errorlessly, with so little hesitation. Her mind did not work that way. It was subject to doubt and fatigue. It was distractible. She did not envy him that mind of his, so deep but so narrow, so icy in its perfection. She could, however, have made good use of his typing speed. Her father had refused to let her learn for fear that she might wind up typing papers for boyfriends or a husband, and then settle for an office job. She had avoided that. Elizabeth Altmann from Pelham had succeeded beyond her father's wildest dreams.

The doorbell rang, and then again. She put down the wine glass and tightened the robe around her. For once she would be happy to captivate the police or the reporters with idle chatter. She did not want to be alone tonight. She would invite the Save-the-Whales canvassers in for a drink. She would even discuss religion with the Jehovah's Witnesses. She flipped on the porch light and opened the door.

He squinted at the light.

"Mac . . ." she whispered.

He was pale. His lip was distorted by a swollen cut.

"Can you help me?"

"Come in, come in."

She closed the door behind him and then took him in her arms.

He was trembling, nearly limp. "Where is she?" he asked.

"She's okay, Mac. I think she's okay. She's at Children's. The Albritons have her there." Pressing her head against his chest, she could feel his heart pounding. She rubbed his neck, his back.

His arms tightened around her, but at that moment she could have been his sister, a doctor, a priest. He needed to hold on to something or someone.

They were still standing, body pressed against body. "I'll help," she said.

"She's dying, Liz."

"Maybe not. They have Rycliffs and the whole staff working on it."

"No. I know it. She's going to die." They sat together on the couch, and he let his full weight fall across her.

"I'm so sorry for this. I'm so sorry for all of it." She brought his head down against her breast. "You need me. I need you, too." She squeezed him, nuzzling her face in his hair. His shoulders felt thin. His body was bruised, exhausted. She reached over and switched off the telephone. And as he massaged his face into her shoulder, her robe fell open. She wanted to give him all the tenderness she knew. She brought his face down again and he kissed her. She pulled the robe back further. She wanted to penetrate the barriers that had arisen between them over the years, to let the strengths and depths of understanding they had once shared flow back again. This was no time for coyness, seduction, romance. She began unbuttoning his shirt, stroking his chest, caressing his back.

"Don't do that," he said.

But she ignored him. He was still far away, lost somewhere on that other continent, but she would find him. She was commandeering his body to soothe it, but also to break down the most immediate obstacle—her fear of him. There was so much that she did not understand, but it would wait until morning. She sank her teeth into his shoulder and felt his arms tighten around her. He came to life in such a sudden surge that she could not tell if it was passion or rage. They grappled like wrestlers as he pushed back the robe and roamed her body with his hands, not so much caressing as searching, recapitulating. This was what he had wanted. This was life. Perpetuation. Long ago their two separate lives had combined within one cell, but that was impossible now. Her surgery was irreversible, a barrier erected to keep him out and to enrage him with frustration. He wrapped himself around her, covering her as if their skins would dissolve and they could merge by surface pressure. She was frightened, but only for a moment. He reached down and gripped her buttocks. He was huge, stiff, urgent. And then he was inside her, filling her, channeling every need into one driving force. His skin was on fire. His heart rate was maniacal. He kept throbbing, pulsing, pounding against her. Liz began to cry. This was not his way. He was not making love to her. He was trying to die.

Upstairs he found a razor. He could not afford to look deranged. He leaned over the gleaming sink, inhaling the steam, and focused closely on the reflection of his jaw. He could not bring himself to look into his eyes—there was simply too much there. He could face the sadness, and possibly the guilt, but he was desperately afraid of the crazed animal that might be staring back at him. He had gone too far with this. He knew how the world would look at it. But he took some comfort in his dread. As long as he was afraid of losing his mind, he must be sane.

He was soothing himself with warm water and fluffy towels in a room of sparkling tile and tasteful wallpaper. The day before, his bathroom had been a paint can crawling with spiders. Which was real? How could they both be accommodated within a span of hours? Had he really traveled through the air, through the night, from one continent to the other? Did Kitty really exist? If she did, could she ever cease to exist?

Wearing Kluer's necktie and Kluer's shearling coat, he made his way quietly downstairs and looked in on Kluer's wife. She was nestled like a cat on the soft Oriental rug, lying under the afghan she had covered him with a few hours before. She must have loved him to have endured his abuse. Thinking about it now, he felt empty. Perhaps there would be time again for tenderness. Perhaps she could retrieve him from the disorder his life had fallen into. He would need her if he was going to survive. He had always needed her. But first there was Kitty. Right now, she needed him.

The night air was fresh. The sky was clear and the stars were in sharp focus. It might have seemed a perfect night, but to Mac it was as cold and empty as interstellar space. He walked down the uneven brick sidewalk of Linnaean Street, stumbling in the darkness. Few lights were on in the houses and apartments, but occasionally he would hear music; occasionally someone typing. He imagined students tracking down footnotes as if it were a matter of life and death.

At the corner of Linnaean and Mass. Ave. he slipped into a taxi. "Longwood Avenue," he said. "Children's Hospital." And then he settled back in the seat and tried not to think.

McKusick nodded with confident indifference as he passed the security guard. He walked briskly through the lobby and into a waiting elevator. He got off at the sixth floor and walked down the silent corridor. From each room came the dim glow of a night light. Some revealed anxious parents sleeping in armchairs.

At the nursing station he fixed his eyes on the teen-ager sitting behind the desk.

"Chart, please. McKusick, Kathleen."

The girl was flustered. She glanced around for help, then quickly flipped through the visible file in front of her. Her fingers were pudgy. Baby fat. "Uh ... she's not on our floor. No McKusick at all."

"I suggest you double-check." His tone was overbearing. Threatening. "I remember distinctly Rycliffs' saying she was on six."

The girl picked up the phone and waited nervously. Mac took the opportunity to pocket a stethoscope that was on the counter.

The girl mumbled into the receiver, "This is Candy at six south. Do you have a Kathleen McKusick?" She waited, then smiled. "Thanks." She looked up at McKusick and nodded. "Four south. I knew it wasn't us. Four twenty-four south."

He gave a nod, then turned and walked back toward the elevators. He held his emotions in check. He had to remain the arrogant young physician, even for his own sake.

"Chart for McKusick, please." The stethoscope was poking up conspicuously from his pocket now, but still he sensed resistance from the woman at the desk. "I'm Kluer from Neurology. Rycliffs called me for a consult."

She was older. Not so easily intimidated. She eyed him for a moment. He waited. He had learned to stare down nurses as a medical student. It was part of the training. She slowly handed him the file. "Here you are, Doctor. Four twenty-four."

Now it was done. He had found his daughter. Four twenty-eight, four twenty-six. He followed the descending numbers with rising anticipation. For a moment, the thought of holding her again drove from his mind the grotesque reality he was going to face. He stopped at the door. What if they were with her? The room was dark except for a shaft of light coming from the bathroom. The only sound was her labored breathing. He took a deep breath and got back into character, then walked through the door. The chairs were empty. She was alone.

In the half-light, he followed the sound of respiration to her bedside. She began to cough—a wheezing, hacking, throaty cough that contorted her body. He came closer, and then recoiled. What he saw was a breathing corpse, withered, ghastly, and pale, with only the diminutive size to remind him of childhood. Tears streamed down his cheeks. This was not Kitty. This was not Kathleen. And this entire grotesque metamorphosis was his doing, no one else's. She was being taken away forever now by these accreting layers of age that were burying her alive. He looked at her and saw death itself, with decay impertinently preceding it.

He flipped on the lamp and scanned the hastily written entries in the chart. They were not even treating her. She was receiving medication around the clock—all of it narcotics. Still, some part of her must have felt the pain and fear and indignity of this. There must have been moments when she woke to partial consciousness and was horrified to feel the unaccustomed age in her body. She was alone, isolated, dying a slow, unnatural death. And when she died, the last thread would be broken. If he held any hope of a heaven or even hell, he knew he would die with her this time. But in his ontology, all that transcended the individual was love, and DNA, the urgent messenger that has fought back the entropy of the universe for four billion years.

Once again he could not accept her life arrested at this point, the promise unfulfilled, the story ended. If any faith could serve him it would have to be faith in his science, and in his skill. He had taken it this far—he could face it again. But not this.

He leaned over to kiss her head, holding his breath to block the smell.

He walked swiftly out of the room, down the corridor, and into the elevator. He knew it was madness. It was unthinkable. Yet what could be more insane and more perverse than letting a life you love slip away when there is any means, however desperate, to sustain it? Operating on instinct, he got off on three. Before him was a set of double doors that said NO ADMITTANCE— AUTHORIZED PERSONS ONLY. He had made the right choice. He pushed through the doors and found a darkened corridor. Silent. Sterile. Ice cold. Empty gurneys lined the walls, waiting until morning for the transfer of patients. The suites off either side were also dark. He stepped into the first doorway and found the light switch. With a flick of his finger the room gleamed with a blinding whiteness. Everything was in its place. The bloody sponges and soiled linens had all been taken away. The straps were neatly folded at the edges of the hydraulically adjustable tray. He went to the glass-doored cabinet that stood against the wall and picked up a set of instruments, still sealed in green cloth from the sterilizer. He found a half-liter specimen jar, also sterile, a packaged syringe, and a 50 cc injectible bottle of succinylcholine. He wrapped it all in a towel and wedged it under his arm.

The elevator doors enclosed him again like the seal of a vacuum chamber. He was no longer thinking, merely following a preprogrammed set of instructions. His senses were numbed. He had annealed himself like the polished floors and stark surfaces of this hospital.

He entered the corridor again, blocking out the cartoon characters frolicking across the walls. He walked swiftly to Room 424 and stepped inside. A shadowy figure hovered over the bed. McKusick was startled—but so was the nurse. She was not the angel of death.

"Just checking on her," she whispered. There

was a soothing intimacy in her voice. Her profession was comforting children.

"I'm her father," McKusick said. Caught off guard, he had resorted to honesty.

"A very sick little girl," she said.

Mac did not need to be told that. He was growing impatient. "Does she need anything else?" he asked.

"No. Just making rounds."

"I was going to try to get some sleep here. In the chair."

"I won't disturb you," she said, placing her hand on his. She edged past him toward the door, then closed it behind her.

Mac knelt down beside the bed and rested his head on Kitty's frail chest. His body ached, but no tears would come now. There was no release from the deadening grief he felt. Had it really come to this? The pain of losing her all over again? He reached down beside him and began to unwrap the package.

It was 3:15 A.M. when Mac emerged from the hospital. He was trembling as he walked through the automated doorway and began to run. He clutched a small package against his chest.

At the corner of Longwood an orange light flashed a warning unheeded at this hour. As he darted past the brightly lit entrance to the emergency room, a police cruiser slowed its progress toward Brookline Avenue. It pulled into the driveway of the Children's Inn to reverse direction.

McKusick slipped into the darkness of the loading dock alongside the Laboratory for Human Reproduction. He glanced back over his shoulder and saw the squad car flash by. What he did not see was the chain stretched across the driveway ahead of him. It caught him just above the knee and slammed him down on the asphalt paving. Cradling his package with both hands, he had nothing left to break the fall. He rolled on his shoulder, but his head still cracked against the ground. His thigh was ripped open. His forehead throbbed with pain. He struggled over the chain and scrambled to a kneeling position. The blood streamed down his forehead and into his eyes. He got up and started running again.

He was struggling to see the road, but there was too much blood. It was washing down with the rain water and mixing with Kathleen's. She was all but drowning in it, coughing it up. He could hardly see her face as he leaned into the hill, but he could feel her warmth.

"Sorry to be so melodramatic," she whispered.

"Shh. You're going to be fine."

"You look sort of dramatic yourself," she said, and then she was silent. The only sounds were the rain and his footsteps splashing up the roadway toward Stasson's. "Where'd you get all that blood? For effect, huh?"

"Hey, don't talk." He was panting. His lungs were going to burst.

"I love you, Mac."

He kept running, her warmth kept burning in his arms, and time contracted. He was dazed. If his mind had lost consciousness, his body had kept working. He had reached the house.

"Stasson! Stasson!" He heard himself yelling. He was climbing up the lawn. "Stasson!"

The man appeared in his underwear in the yellow light of the doorway. "Good God . . ."

Mac was on the porch. "We went off the road. Help us . . ."

"On the couch, Mac."

They worked together to lower her gently onto the cushions.

"Good God, man, she's soaked in blood."

"Stasson, help me! Don't just look at her, for God's sake. Don't just stand there!"

"She's dead, Mac."

"No, no, no. She's in shock. We need some blankets."

"She's dead."

"Don't say that, you asshole!" Mac gripped his shoulders and tried to push him away, but the Englishman's bulk was immovable.

"Mac, you've got to accept it, mate. She's gone."

"That's impossible. I'm a doctor! You're a fucking doctor! We've got all this shit out here. She can't die! We can't let her die!" He was kneeling down beside her, framing her face with his hands. "No way." The blood was clotted in her mouth, caked against her skin. Water dripping off his head trickled across her cheek and moistened the red stains. He fell across her, sobbing. Her hand fell loose and cracked down limp against the tiles.

Mac looked up at Stasson and muttered, "Save her." His own eyes were bloodshot now. The gash above his brow had left his face a bloody mask. "I want you to save her."

"Say, old man. We'll take care of her. I need a drink."

"I know what you know. I know about the kids. I know about Pia. I know. I know. And I want you to save her. I want you to keep her alive."

"Mac, Mac . . ."

"Do it, Stasson. I know you can."

"You don't want this."

"The hell I don't. Either you show me how or you're never leaving this fucking jungle."

Stasson's big rough hand explored the lines of his own face, as if finally assessing the damage done by time, and drink, and the equatorial sun.

"Save her."

He looked down at the crazed young man staring up at him, and then at the wasted young woman whose blood had failed her, transforming this room into a morgue. "There's a problem, Mac."

"I don't care."

"It's a serious problem."

"We'll work it out."

49

SHE WOKE UP COLD, remembering the heat of last night. It had been too long since she had felt that alive. She wanted that feeling again. She reached for McKusick, to snuggle against him, to comfort him, but he was gone. She sat up, the afghan clutched to her breast, and whispered his name. Then she checked herself. Kluer *was* gone, wasn't he? Mac really had been with her. That much she knew. She could still feel his weight.

Lights were on in the next room. "Mac?" she said again. Her clothes were still scattered around the floor and on the couch, but his were gone. Suddenly her anxieties returned. They should have talked more last night. She should have reasoned with him while she had him. Between Albriton and the courts and the media there was certain to be trouble. They were likely to be less than compassionate, and she was sure that Mac would not allow anyone to keep him from

Kitty. Sorting out their love affair would have to wait. She had to help Mac through.

She stood, gathering the blanket around her, and began picking up her clothes. Lying naked on the floor at dawn with an aching hip was not conducive to clear thinking. Kluer would find out soon enough, but not by returning to find his wife sprawled out on the rug.

She went upstairs and showered quickly. Things might get out of hand, and she needed to be there. He had been demonic last night. With that kind of rage burning inside him, control was out of the question. She would intercede for him. She dressed, drank a cup of coffee and a glass of grapefruit juice, and was ready to go. On the way out she thought to check her answering machine. The only message was from Ute. "Liz, you must destroy this fucking thing! I need to talk to you. It is all getting very strange. Call me." Whatever Ute's problems were, they could wait. She had to get to the hospital.

The one patrol car parked at the entrance made no great impression on her. It was a routine association—police, emergencies, hospitals. She walked directly to the main desk and said, "I've got to know what room Kitty McKusick is in. My name is Liz Altmann and I'm a close friend of Lawrence Rycliffs. I would hate to have to go to him for this simple information, but I will."

The woman glanced through her files. She seemed preoccupied.

"Are you a member of the family?"

"No, but I'm trying to reach the child's father. It's really very urgent."

The woman's spongy face drew into a thoughtful pucker. She glanced at her files again. "We have no one here by the name of McKusick."

"What do you mean? That's bullshit. She was here yesterday!"

The woman stuck to her ground. "I'm sorry. No one by that name. I'm afraid I can't help you."

"What the . . ."

The woman moved back from the counter and began speaking to a coworker.

Liz was dumfounded. She was furious. She was going to call Rycliffs and find out what the hell was going on in his hospital.

She was glaring ahead, not really focusing, until the television van pulled up and parked in the center of her field of vision. Through the plate glass she saw another police cruiser arriving, and an unmarked car pulling up alongside. Four men got out and came through the glass doors, two in uniform, two in suits.

The four men walked briskly toward the bank of elevators. Liz drifted over to where they stood, and waited with them. Fortunately the hallway was crowded. An elevator door opened and the men moved forward en masse. Liz lunged forward, but so much for chivalry. She was barely able to squeeze in before the doors rolled shut again.

"Hey, what's up, officer?" someone asked from the rear.

"Nothing. Just visiting a friend."

The car stopped at the fourth floor. "Excuse me," said the burly man in a suit. The four of them edged past her. She held back the closing door and slipped out, then immediately took a seat in the waiting area and picked up a magazine. The four men walked midway down the corridor, then paused. One of the uniformed officers stayed outside while the other three stepped in. Liz's stomach was churning. She wished she had eaten some nice bland breakfast instead of the hurried mixture of acids she had taken in. She had to prepare herself. She should have kept him through the night. Somehow, she should have made him stay until he was rested, until his mind had a chance to clear. Had she underestimated the demons she had felt inside him?

She could wait no longer. She had to have some sense of what was going on. She started down the long polished corridor, her heels resounding like hammers. She knew that any minute now someone was going to bounce her out on her ear. The uniformed policeman turned to watch her. The room he was guarding was 424. He did not appear to question her presence. He simply stared at her breasts with vacant eyes. She walked quickly past, affecting a sense of purpose, but by then she was approaching the nurse's station. A young woman was on the telephone. Liz stood nervously across the desk. The nurse saw her, put the receiver against her chest, and said, "Can I help you?"

Nothing subtle came to mind. Liz simply blurted out, "That's Kitty McKusick's room—four twenty-four—isn't it? Why are policemen in there?"

The nurse put the receiver back to her lips. "I'll have to put you on hold," she said. Then she eyed Liz tentatively, still holding the phone.

"We're not supposed to discuss that. And I don't believe you're supposed to be up here."

"Look, I don't want to create a problem for you, but I've got to know what happened. I'll leave, but just tell me what's going on."

"I can't. It's against hospital regulations. And I think you better go downstairs now." It was a tone meant for the mental cases, just before they call the attendants. Liz did not want anything like that.

"Okay. Okay," she said.

The nurse watched as Liz turned and headed back toward the elevators. Then she returned to the telephone.

The policeman seemed far less imposing now, compared to the cold determination of the nurse. He was eyeing her admiringly, and this time Liz returned his stare. Then his smile. She bounced a little as she walked.

"Hi," she said, glancing at his body, then back to his eyes.

His smile broadened considerably. "How are ya!" he said.

"What're you hiding in there?"

He rocked on his heels, grinning. "Evidence team."

"What happened?"

"Some guy killed his kid. Carved her up pretty good, too."

The blood drained from her face. The fall left a bad bruise on her right knee and an enormous lump on the right rear quadrant of her head.

*   *   *

When Liz opened her eyes she was looking into a familiar face that she could not quite identify. It was a nice face. A good-looking young man. Giacconi. The cop. Beside him was the stern young nurse from a few moments ago. The nurse was saying, "She'll be okay. I've got to get back to the floor."

Giacconi smiled down at Liz. He had brown eyes and smooth skin and a mouth like Al Pacino's. "How do you feel?" he asked her.

Now she remembered. She simply shook her head.

"In a minute, maybe we can talk some more about Peter McKusick," he said.

Her eyes began to redden. She was beginning to cry.

"You see, this is why I wish I could have gotten to him before. You get people under a lot of stress and they do strange things. The child's dead. There was no way to prevent that. But now McKusick's also in a hell of a mess."

"What did he do?"

"The medical examiner hasn't ruled on it yet, but it's pretty obvious he put her out of her misery. An injection of something. A muscle relaxant. I can understand that, you know? I have a couple of kids. I can imagine what it would be like to see them suffer. It was an act of love—but the courts still call it murder."

"That other policeman. He said something about cutting her up."

"Ah. That guy's a winner. And that's when you fainted, huh? It wasn't like that. I don't understand it. I can't even speculate on it, but it wasn't like that. The nurses found her on their rounds this morning. She was arranged peacefully, you know. The sheet was pulled up over her face. But there was a three-inch incision down here. In her abdomen. A surgical incision— opened, closed, and neatly sewed up."

"I don't understand."

"Neither do we."

"You mean Mac did that?"

He shrugged. "Maybe you can give us some idea why."

Liz simply stared.

"This whole case is bizarre as hell. I mean the little girl looks like she's eighty years old, and the doctors don't have a clue. Then there's his hiding her all those years, which sounds sort of borderline. Possessive. Protective. But I mean this really puts it over the top. Why does a man operate on his dying child?"

Two circuits aligned to give a vague glimmer of perception. Liz remembered Ute's message on the tape. She remembered the urgency in her voice. For a moment she drifted, but then Giacconi's earnest face brought her back. "To keep her alive," she muttered.

"But that doesn't make any sense."

"You're saying that he's crazy." She began to rise on her elbow, and the detective helped her the rest of the way up. "Why should what he does make sense?"

She reached the lobby and went directly for the bank of telephones.

"Ute, this is Liz. I got your message. What happened?"

A man's voice was loud in the background.

"A very strange thing, my dear. I thought maybe it was sabotage. The right-to-lifers, or even a rival. We have some madmen, you know. But then I found this jacket. I remembered it."

"What jacket?"

"Kluer's. The sheepskin with the fleece. I mean his name is on the label, for Christ's sake! It is his coat. So will you tell me what the hell is going on? Has your Dutchman lost his mind?"

"What did he do?"

"He ransacked my lab. In the middle of the night. He broke up the place. He took equipment. He took my entire store of human ova—now that is very strange."

Liz was silent, thinking. She remembered the razor and shaving cream where Mac had dressed upstairs. "Egg cells," she whispered.

"He was quite thorough. I haven't mentioned the coat to the police, but I may have to. Now will you tell me what this is all about?"

"I will. I will. But later."

50

THE LIGHTS WERE ON in the culture lab. Liz could hear him muttering to himself over the clinking of glassware and the low hum of the incubators. She stopped just inside the door and watched him. He was huddled over a Petri dish, his face set in grim concentration. In his right hand he held a Pasteur pipette penetrating the thin layer of paraffin oil that covered the V-sloped bottom of the dish. Beneath that paraffin membrane, immersed in a droplet of fetal calf serum, were two haploid oocytes, extracted from Kitty's barely formed ovaries. Into that tiny bubble of life he was adding a drop of polyethylene glycol to melt the cell membranes separating these two capsules of genetic instructions, to make them one.

"Mac?" she whispered.

He glanced up. The energy of obsession radiated from eyes bleary with exhaustion. He had not really slept for days. His surprise gave way to a look that was both loving and pained, both needing to see her and dreading it. "I've got to stay with this," he said.

"I heard about Kitty. I'm so sorry, Mac."

Tears welled up in his reddened eyes. He nodded his head in acknowledgment.

"We need to be together," she said, inching forward. "You need to rest. Come back to my house and let me take care of you. Okay?"

"Liz . . . I've got to work. We'll talk. I mean . . . you'll have to understand what I'm doing, but right now it's critical."

"Sweetheart, you're not thinking clearly. The police are looking for you, you know. They can probably find you about as easily as I could."

His jaw tightened as he looked at her. "Then you're going to have to help me. Even if you don't understand."

"I do understand, Mac. I know what you're trying to do. I know about Kitty. I know about the cells from Ute's lab."

"And you think I'm nuts. You've got that 'humor the patient' kind of calm in your voice." He was angry, nodding his head as if pumping up his own resolve. "I know what I'm doing this time, Liz. Stasson screwed it up because his technique was sloppy. But I am *precise!* You know that. I'm good, right? You make the big theoretical breakthroughs and I make them work out in the lab, right? I can correct the error in transcription. It's on the MHC. That's what I've been doing up here. That's what I was doing in fucking Colombia for three years! I found it. And I can correct it. It's all here in the protocol. All written out for you."

"Mac, honey . . ." She took a step forward, then held herself in check. "That's good, honey." It hurt to see him like this. She did not know how to talk to him, but she had to try. She took another step. "But she's gone, Mac. You can't remake a human being in the lab."

"You still don't understand, do you? You haven't figured it out." He threw up his hands in exasperation. "Liz, why do you think I kept her a secret from the Albritons? She was born almost a year after Kathleen was killed, right? Don't you see it? She wasn't Kathleen's child, Liz. She was Kathleen."

There were footsteps in the hall. A moment later, Michael Giacconi appeared in the doorway, followed by two uniformed policemen and a Harvard security officer. Giacconi came forward and was just at Liz's elbow before she finally turned around. She had been staring fixedly at McKusick. In a matter of heartbeats, her entire view of life had been fundamentally altered.

Giacconi nodded to her, then turned to Mac. "Dr. McKusick, I'm sorry about your little girl."

Mac stood silently. Waiting.

"We need to talk a little bit about it. We'd like you to come with us."

He shook his head. "I can't do that right now."

Giacconi glanced down, then fixed his eyes squarely on McKusick. "It's not an optional trip," he said.

There was nothing McKusick could do now. It was completely in her hands. He studied her face, and it seemed to him that the look of fear was gone. So much had passed between them. Surely it was enough.

She stepped forward. "Mac . . . I can wrap that up for you." She half-turned, glancing back uncertainly at this room full of policemen. "You don't have to worry. It's just a matter of following the protocol, right?"

Giacconi rose once on the balls of his feet and said, "I'd have to say the project's over, Dr. Altmann. Whatever you have in the dish there has to go down as evidence."

"It's just fibroblasts," Mac said. He shrugged and shook his head, but the gesture continued in a palsied rhythm. He was trying so hard to stay in control, to remain calm. These men were merely doing a job. He was in another realm entirely, traveling where no one had ever set foot before. "It's just part of our work," he said.

"Fine. The police lab can have a look and then return it."

Mac was leaning forward on the laboratory bench, one hand to each side of the Petri dish, sheltering its contents, two halves of the human complement at that very moment becoming one living soul.

"Liz," he said, "come closer." She hesitated, then made her way around the lab bench to stand by his side. "We have to flush the dish right now with medium to stop the PEG. But then we're going to need an appropriate container, right? Are you with me? The morula will have to be firmly attached."

His voice was faltering. It was insane to ask this of her, but he had abandoned rationality the moment Kathleen died. The last four years of his life had had nothing to do with reason. "Maybe Ute would help you," he said.

She owed him nothing, yet he knew that some part of her, whether the maternal or the scientific, would be tempted. She nodded, tears filling her eyes. He sounded so distant. He was talking to her as if through a closing door, as if his own life were somehow coming to an end.

They looked into each other's eyes, and they were lovers again.

"Kawecki. Wilson."

Giacconi barked out their names, and the two men began to move forward. Giacconi stood his ground in the center of the room, but to Mac it was as if an army were converging on him. There was no way of getting past these men. It was pointless to resist, yet he could not allow them to tamper with the life taking shape in the glass before him.

He stepped in back of Liz, then came around to her other side. Suddenly, he shoved her into the corner and leaned forward, gripping the massive Dewar flask at his side. He braced his foot against the wall and pulled. The lid fell open as the steel canister crashed to the floor in a shower of broken glass and a billowing cloud of vapor. One hundred liters of liquid nitrogen spilled across the floor, crackling and sputtering in contact with the warmer surface. The first policeman braved the cloud until his feet were engulfed in the supercooled liquid. For a moment he seemed to have vanished. Then a cry came from the densest center of the vapor, a loud piercing howl of agony and disbelief as his toes and the soles of his feet, frozen solid, broke

off with the force of his momentum. He fell
forward, his head emerging from the cloud, his
eyes staring up at Liz in dazed horror.

Mac was gone. He had disappeared through
the doorway to the adjoining lab. Liz hugged
the corner while the other men, climbing over
the counters, came to the aid of the policeman
writhing on the floor in front of her. But then
they heard Mac's footsteps in the hallway racing
away from them. The security guard stayed
behind. The others clambered back over the
counters and out the door.

McKusick was well ahead of them. He had
covered the long, echoing corridor and was racing down the stairs. He had no real hope of
breaking free, but he needed to give Liz time.
She could switch Petri dishes in an instant. The
cells were sealed off under their coating of
paraffin, nourished for the moment with serum.
If she would only hide them now, soon she
could have all the time in the world.

He hit the ground floor, and as he saw the
daylight filtering through by the main entrance
his heart gave a surge. Maybe he *could* escape.
He would have time to coax Liz more, to win
her over completely, to be sure of her. But then
he saw the uniforms. It was the Harvard police,
milling about in the foyer, their radio receivers
crackling with irrelevant information. He skidded to a halt, but not before they had seen him.

"Hey! Hey! You! Halt! Right there!"

He spun around and raced down the corridor toward the stairway with the emergency
exit. He heard their footsteps behind him, the
thudding of heavy black boots. He made a skid-

ding turn and threw open the fire door. There, half a flight below him, a pudgy young security guard leaned sulkily against the exit. Their eyes met in mutual astonishment, and Mac realized there was nowhere to go but back up. He leaped at the stairs, taking half a flight at a time. He knew he had five floors of possibilities. He had a rabbit warren of a hundred laboratories. If he could simply gain a clear lead, he could keep them searching this place for days.

The pudgy young guard had been slow to start, but now his fat thighs pumped for all they were worth as he hustled up the stairs after McKusick. He had thought he was out of the game, left behind to watch the door, and now he was on the scent. McKusick spun off on the second floor and raced down the hallway. He ran past an eye rinse and the emergency shower. He stopped, came back, and twisted the spigot, flooding the hall with water. The guard burst through the door from the stairwell.

"Stop!" he yelled. "You! You stop!" He was fumbling for the sidearm strapped below his gut.

McKusick turned into Cohen's developmental lab. He raced over to the glass cabinet on the wall and smashed it with his fist. He reached in, grabbed a jar of sodium crystals and a jar of ether, and raced back out the door. The guard was on him, but McKusick was running low. He dropped into a crouch and threw a body block that flattened the bigger man, then splashed through the shallow puddle and put it between them before the guard could get to his feet. Mac turned, and, like Merlin in a rage, threw down the jar of crystals, which shattered against the wet cement. A wall of flame leapt up, dividing the corridor. Through it, though, Mac could see Giacconi and his men racing toward him from the opposite end of the hall. He retreated, backing away. The flame was dying down. Just as the running men reached his failing barrier, he heaved the jar of ether. It flashed like an incendiary bomb, forcing the men to the floor and igniting the ceiling.

McKusick was back in the stairwell. He flew up to the fourth floor and ran down the block-long corridor once again. Up ahead, he saw a blue cylinder of carbon dioxide leaning on a wheeled cart. Behind him, the police were spilling out into the hall. He slid into the cylinder and dumped it to the floor. He began to kick at the valve, once, twice, again, but it held tight. The cops were halfway down the hall, and his frustration was building into rage. But then he saw the fire cabinet. He kicked it in and pulled out the ax, and with one sharp blow broke off the gasket and unleashed the bottled pressure. The tank shot down the corridor like a rocket, spinning and sputtering, still dragging the cart, scattering policemen like bowling pins.

He was left with only the corner stairway, the one set of stairs leading up to five, the only path to the roof. He raced up the steps. The fifth-floor doorway was not locked. As he burst through it he was met by the forlorn howls of caged dogs. The smell of detergent competed with the stench of feces. Off this hallway was the animal facility, and the attendants were wading in their hip boots, hosing down the cement floor. They had moved the animals into the hall—rack upon rack of mice held in plastic tubs, dismayed rabbits, yipping dogs, cats pacing and crying, and two carts of rhesus monkeys fretting wildly in their temporary cages. Mac slammed the door shut on the attendants, locking them in with their scrub brushes. Then he began shoving the animal carts against the door to the stairway. They were large enough, and the hallway was small enough, that he might be able to wedge them together to form a permanent barrier. The monkeys shrieked at him, baring their teeth and blood-red gums.

The police were shouting just beyond the door. Mac turned and ran as they began smashing into his barrier. He came to the door to the roof and threw his weight against it. Nothing happened. He tugged and pushed at the waist-high bar, but it was useless. The door was sealed.

He glanced back at the jam of cages filled with panicked animals. The carts were beginning to jostle with each wave of force hurled against the stairway door. Wheels twisted. The jam was coming unstuck.

Mac watched from the other end of the hallway. He was cornered now. Escape was out of the question, but he could still draw out the chase. He could still keep them away from Liz. There was one more doorway off this corridor. It led to the P4 laboratory, the maximum biological containment facility.

A cart of rabbit cages slipped backward, and the whole barricade gave way. The door was shoved back, and uniformed arms emerged to shove and poke at the wire enclosures. The

men pushed forward and the cages began to
tumble. Mice spilled out in white, scampering
waves. The dogs broke loose and ran madly
toward McKusick's end of the hallway. The
enraged monkeys were going berserk, leaping
from blue shoulder to blue shoulder, attacking
the men with their claws, sinking their teeth
into necks and faces. The men fought them off
with nightsticks. There was an explosion of
powder, and a huge rhesus male fell to the
floor, shot through the head.

Mac pulled back the outer door and stepped
into the air lock. He heard the cogs and rollers
of the inner door clamping down. As long as
one door was open, the other would refuse to
budge. He closed the outer seal, then stepped
into the small vaultlike chamber. The second
door opened easily now. He took off his shoe
and wedged it into the inner doorway, locking
the outer seal, closing himself off completely.

Outside there was chaos, an interspecies battle for control. Inside there was only the hum of
the negative-pressure fans. A flask shaker was
jostling a half-dozen beakers of nondescript liquid that could probably kill a horse, or every
horse on the planet. The frenzy going on outside was irrelevant to McKusick now. It was
utterly serene beyond the thick steel door. He
tried to rest for a moment. He was breathing
heavily, exhausted but feeling secure. Then he
glanced down quickly at the cuts on his hands
and arms. A tooth-extraction site had proved
fatal once under similar circumstances. For all
its order and gleaming cleanliness, this was one
of the most highly contaminated places on earth.

He did not know what work was in progress, but it had to involve an extreme biohazard or this lab would not have been used.

He became conscious even of his breathing, wondering just what it was he was filling his lungs with. He looked into the tall fermenter resting under the safety hood with its negative-pressure fans. *E. coli,* no doubt, growing rapidly under ideal conditions, creating more of itself, and, very likely, more transplanted tumor genes, with each cell division. But *E. coli* was strictly a bacterium of the gut. As long as he touched nothing to his lips he knew he would be fine. He would survive, and despite it all he did want to survive. He wanted to live to see Kitty once again. His trust in the genetic link was like a religious faith, but to share in this version of life after death he had to keep on living.

At first he heard the wrenching sound of metal bending metal. The seal was being broken. They were going at the outer door with crow-bars and cutting torches. He had put too much faith in the possibility of containment. Bacteria could penetrate certain barriers that would frus-trate a tank commander. Yet this facility was designed to be impregnable *only* for bacteria, and a second-rate burglar could make short work of it.

McKusick glanced around trying to prepare one last desperate effort. He was frightened. How was he going to confront these men after all this? He was trapped. He spun around in a rage of futility. He had run out of options. He had run out of weapons. He had even run out of time. He grabbed at the portable gas cylinder

next to the safety hood just as the first policeman burst into the room. McKusick spun around.
The cop was nervous and overeager, but he was
not out to kill. He fired low. The bullet shattered the glass walls of the fermenter, each in
turn, and a millisecond later traced a seemingly
innocuous path through McKusick's lower left
side.

51

It was a crisp sunny day in the hill country of central Texas. Lee Albriton stood silently, staring down at the freshly turned earth at his feet as the breeze covered his boots with dust. This was the month Kennedy had been shot. The same kind of day. It was November—deer season—and the weather alternated between bone-chilling drizzle, Indian summer, and just plain hot. He squinted into the sun, and his eyes followed the line of the low wrought-iron fence that separated this corner of the churchyard, itself bounded by a fence of piled stone and cedar. This was the family plot. His great-grandfather was buried here, as were three of that man's children. Lee and Nina's first child, too, the infant wisely left unnamed. And their second, whom they had named Kathleen. Now her child had been added, lying beside her under that pathetically small mound, camouflaged with sprays of flowers. They had found her only to lose her. Just when they thought they were beginning to handle the pain of Kathleen's death, all the emotions had been stirred up again, the wounds reopened. He would never understand. He could never forgive.

Marie and Dean, his two remaining children, would survive. They would have to. Somehow he would interpose himself between them and any harm. They would marry and have children of their own. And for a moment he tried to gain some comfort from the thought. The expanded circle of love. The expanded circle of anxiety.

52

"JUST WHAT THE DEVIL was he trying to do?" Kluer was stepping cautiously through the jumble of overturned equipment in Mac's lab.

This was his first opportunity to survey the damage firsthand. The entire building had been sealed off for three days while Wharton's detoxification crews flooded the fifth floor with disinfectant.

"He was trying to re-create her," Liz said. Her voice had a calm resonance.

"A lunatic," Kluer muttered. He was standing on bare concrete where the linoleum had been eaten away by liquid nitrogen.

"Kitty's death was very hard for him," Liz went on. "He couldn't accept it. Scientists are all guilty of a little hubris now and then. His was just a little more dramatic."

"The media are having a field day. That ward healer is sitting down at city hall gloating."

"He won't for long." She reached up to touch

Mac's lab coat hanging from a peg on the door. "This is the acid test. A P4 facility ransacked. A disaster in terms of containment. And so far nothing's spread beyond the initial victims."

"What's his prognosis?"

"Not good. The bacteria were very opportunistic. The bullet perforated his intestine. Perfect point of entry."

"And the policeman?"

"He seems to be responding to treatment."

"We'll watch and wait. Maybe you're right. Maybe it's good once and for all to test the worst case. Get it over with. But I want strict damage control with the press. A mercy killing is one thing. But the rest of it . . . Just how did he anticipate this condition of hers? This bizarre progeria? That's what this private research of his dealt with, no?"

There was a pin sticking in the lapel of the lab coat. It was red and black—a ladybug made of porcelain. She unfastened it and held it in her hand. "Maybe it was a coincidence," she said.

"Ridiculous. He must have induced it somehow. He and that witch doctor Stasson must have been responsible. But that's a closed chapter. We'll never know the answer to that one. What did the police lab make of the sample in the Petri dish?"

"Fibroblasts. From our lab."

"No trace of cells from the little girl?"

"Not a one."

"But he did make the incision. They were sure of that. He must have disposed of the egg cells. Or hidden them." Kluer glanced up at his wife. "I want them to stay hidden," he muttered.

"I'm sure they will," she said.

53

"I'M HIS FATHER-IN-LAW, you see."

The attendant sighed as if this was simply *too* much to endure. He put down his magazine and stroked the edge of his finely trimmed mustache. "Look," he said, "I can save you a *lot* of grief. The man's under the strictest kind of quarantine. I mean, really. You can't get anywhere near him. And heavy sedation. He's not even going to know you're there."

"I just want to see him once more. It would mean a lot to me."

"Okay. Okay." He stood and brushed down the front of his pleated white pants. "I can let you on the floor. You can take a look through the glass, if that's what you want."

"That's what I want."

The little man walked with his hands in his pockets, leading the way upstairs. The vinyl covering of the steps was cracked. The paint, discolored and peeling, was stained with water spots. It was a gruesome place, a nineteenth-century idea of a hospital. A place for the poor to die, to keep them off the streets. Located on a spit of land jutting out into the harbor, it reminded Albriton of the fortress in Galveston he'd played in as a kid. A fortress built for the Spanish-American War.

They walked down the corridor together, the attendant's crepe-soled shoes squishing as if they were full of sea water, Albriton's boots thudding solidly. Occasionally he glanced off the hallway through doorways revealing large rooms lined with hospital beds. These were the wards. The end point of the public welfare system.

The attendant waved his hand with a mock flourish. "Here we are," he said.

They were approaching a pair of glass double doors, set in a wall of glass curtained on the other side. "Wait here a sec." The man stepped through the doors. In a moment he reemerged and nodded toward his left. "Let's go this way."

Twenty feet ahead they saw the curtains being drawn back. A large black woman stood inside, making a nonchalant gesture toward the corner bed, the only bed occupied.

"That's him?" Albriton whispered.

His guide shrugged as if to say, "What did you expect?"

Peter McKusick lay propped on a pillow, his eyes closed. A stretch of thin green tubing curled out from the wall and over to his face, where it was taped so as to remain inside his right nostril. A bottle of clear liquid hung from an IV stand at his bedside, dripping into the tube inserted into the back of his wrist. His hair was closely cropped, his skin pallid. Except for the faint movement of breathing, he could have been dead already.

"What's the situation? What's going to happen?"

The attendant looked at him closely, sizing him up. "Well, if you'll forgive me for being blunt, this fellow has a carcinoma Marcus Welby couldn't cure."

"Cancer?"

"From head to toe."

"Is he in pain?"

"Nooo. High as a kite. Morphine by the hour. You or I should know such bliss."

"But he isn't going to recover."

The attendant made a confidential pucker, eyes closed, and shook his head from side to side.

Albriton stared ahead, as if memorizing every detail. "Good," he said. "Because if he does, I'm going to kill him."

54

LIZ ALTMANN WALKED with her husband back into his office. They were both tired and, if the term could apply to Kluer, emotionally drained. A single telephone call to the press had destroyed his plan to become czar of biotechnology at Harvard. He was unaccustomed to disappointment. He was even less accustomed to betrayal, but for the moment he was simply too exhausted to care. He would save for another day the question of who had made the call.

Liz squeezed his icy hand and then went over to the small refrigerator hidden within the paneling. Kluer took his usual seat on the couch. His age was showing. His face already had the pale gray look that he would wear to meet his maker. "What on earth are you doing?" he said.

She was walking toward him with a bottle and two glasses. She had a faint smile on her lips. Provocative, peaceful. A beatific glow.

"What do you have there?"

"Dom Perignon. I hid it away for us."

"Is McKusick's lunacy contagious?"

"Be a gentleman and open it, would you?"

With grunts and smacks of exasperation he began unwrapping the foil. "What, pray tell, are we celebrating?"

"That the worst is over. That the NCI contract went through. That we'll have our own corporation. Actually, I'm glad Harvard backed out. It'll be more fun as just ours."

"This is very encouraging, my dear. I would have sworn your interest in business applications was dwindling to nil."

"We have to look to the future, of course. Responsibilities. We haven't seen enough of each other lately, Bayard. It's time for us to relax more. To enjoy our time together. I worry about your health."

"You're being quite mysterious." He was straining with his thumbs against the cork, nudging his pulse rate upward.

"Well, there is a little something else," she said, smiling.

"Yes?" He allowed the cork to ease into his hand with a subdued, discreet pop.

"You know I've been seeing Ute these last few days."

"And?" He filled each glass evenly and set down the bottle.

"I wasn't sure. That's why I had to keep going back. But now it's certain. I'm going to have a baby."

For the first time in years, Bayard Kluer's impressive mental capacity was truly challenged. Long-forgotten circuits fired and misfired within that intellectual forehead, behind a face that remained blank and placid. He was stunned. Uncomprehending. A tremor of suspicion began to ripple from some moist corner of his gray matter, but the elegant control of his super-ego quashed the thought before it could be fully formulated. The scion of the East Antigua Company, the eminent scientist and power broker Bayard Kluer, was beyond disgrace or humiliation, especially within the boundaries of his own perception. His wife was an honorable woman.

"Why that's marvelous, my dear. I'm so surprised."

"You shouldn't be. It happens, you know. Even among biologists."

"Yes. Yes."

Then, each hand trembling slightly, they raised their glasses to toast the new life rising up within her.

Liz finished hers off in one gulp. Kluer merely touched his to his lip. "That's marvelous. Marvelous." Then he returned the glass to the table. "I have to make a call."

Kluer went over to the desk and began dialing. Liz poured herself another glass, and drained it too. She had a lot on her mind. She was still trying to get Mac out of that horrible place and into a private sanatorium. She had lawyers working on it quietly. She could not be so optimistic as to think that she could make it right, but she could at least make him comfortable.

She had followed his protocol religiously, at least to the limits of her faith. Polyethylene glycol to break down the cell membranes. The merger of two haploid gametes, each taken from the same individual. Insertion of the resulting cell into a mature but denucleated egg. Phytohemaglutinin to trigger cell division. And ultimately, a human being in exact replica, created in a glass dish. That much was what Mac had asked her to do, to follow through with it. He must have known all along that they could rely on Ute to implant this extraordinary embryo. But he had underestimated the temptation Liz would face once she knew of the method. Perhaps he had forgotten about his own genetic material, frozen away for all those years in her lab.

Liz had acted decisively and taken the leap. She was on the frontier again. Yet her own little improvisation still troubled her at times. Disposing of the cells in the Petri dish was not betrayal. It certainly was not jealousy—she loved Kitty McKusick. She simply loved Peter McKusick more. And besides, Mac's lab notes had not satisfied her doubts. How could he be so sure that his manipulation had corrected Kitty's genetic error? How could he be sure that it would not all happen again—three years of normal, healthy childhood, then disintegration? Stasson's cloning method still had the one flaw, and the risk of female offspring was simply too great. Liz had followed her heart, and her heart would have to answer for it.

She looked forward to sunny days and beaches and swan boats in the park, to helping shape a young and eager mind. She knew she would be a good mother. All it took was love—she knew she had that—and time; and for once she could think of nothing better to do with the rest of her life than care for her baby boy. Yes, it would be a boy. She knew that too. A baby boy who would grow tall and lean, who would have penetrating green eyes and brown hair growing in an unruly curl behind his ears. He would have an openness to life, and a wild curiosity. She would play with him, and love him, and teach him about the world—and probably about science. She would name him Peter.

About the Author

William Patrick is Editor for Science and Medicine at Harvard University Press.

SIGNET Titles by Stephen King You'll Want to Read

*Price slightly higher in Canada

Buy them at your local bookstore or use coupon on next page for ordering.

Thrilling Fiction from SIGNET

(0451)

- [ ] **ON WINGS OF EAGLES** by Ken Follett. (131517—$4.50)*
- [ ] **THE MAN FROM ST. PETERSBURG** by Ken Follett. (124383—$3.95)*
- [ ] **EYE OF THE NEEDLE** by Ken Follett. (124308—$3.95)*
- [ ] **TRIPLE** by Ken Follett. (127900—$3.95)*
- [ ] **THE KEY TO REBECCA** by Ken Follett. (127889—$3.95)*
- [ ] **EXOCET** by Jack Higgins. (130448—$3.95)†
- [ ] **DARK SIDE OF THE STREET** by Jack Higgins. (128613—$2.95)†
- [ ] **TOUCH THE DEVIL** by Jack Higgins. (124685—$3.95)†
- [ ] **THE TEARS OF AUTUMN** by Charles McCarry. (131282—$3.95)*
- [ ] **THE LAST SUPPER** by Charles McCarry. (128575—$3.50)*
- [ ] **FAMILY TRADE** by James Carroll. (123255—$3.95)*

*Prices slightly higher in Canada

†Not available in Canada